Chasing

Atatürk

R. W. Barwick

—

Sparakoff Press

To M and J, and our adventure

Chasing

Atatürk

The first fighter moved from his corner towards the center of the ring. The late morning sun mixed with the steam rising off his un-covered back to create the effect of his moving through space in slow motion. So dazzling was the sight that you could almost miss the second fighter, eyebrows arched, nostrils flared and dripping, stamping at the ground invitingly, mockingly.

They were feet apart now, and there was nothing else— the crowd (that numbered almost a hundred) disappeared, the music (chipper and inappropriate) silenced—only the two fighters, the blistering welt of the sun, and that second before action when the fabric of space seems to shake with the aftershock of future disruption.

The first strike was invisible, but the return of sound signaled it had taken place. The first fighter had miscalculated, struck too soon, been caught off guard, and sustained a heavy blow. Soon the pair were enmeshed in an unrecognizable multi-limbed blur with no head and propelled only by kinetic rage. The ever expanding dust cloud surrounding them glinted and twirled as it laughed and threatened to obscure the best views of the action.

Lane, bolt upright against the bleacher, grabbed Ibrahim's hand in the suspense of the moment. He held it tightly. Reyhan pretended not to notice.

It was horrific, pre-historic, and bordered on choreographed; and before even the fighters themselves had realized, it was over.

A final cry of anguish signaled the end. The five friends, near the top of the stands, had to wait for the dust to settle to see who had won. One figure standing, one helplessly prostrate, hump back heaving with each strained breath.

"So now I can say I've seen an honest-to-god camel fight," Colin said. The teasing hints of an Aegean breeze played with his long eyelashes as he slumped back into the uncomfortably hot bleacher. Lane noticed a large, framed photograph of Kemal Atatürk behind him on the highest part of the stands, watching, and perhaps silently coordinating everything going on in the tiny arena.

Matt had mentioned that before coming to Turkey he had fully expected to see camels in the streets of Istanbul, but had found none. He hadn't imagined he would ever see something so outrageous as two camels duking it out in a winner-takes-all ring match. And yet, there lay the loser, inconsolable, saddle blanket askew, in the middle of the oval.

But a camel fight is a confusing place to start anything.

L ane couldn't remember driving home from work.

　　She checked her pupils, felt her forehead, undid the top button on her blouse, and sighed. She was fine. She was also stone cold sober (not always the case these past few weeks). But still she couldn't remember—any of it.

　　Getting off work, starting the car, pulling into the driveway, locking the doors, putting her house key in its hole above the handle, pulling the screened door shut, taking off her shoes—nothing.

　　Yet there were her keys in the ash-tray-turned-key bowl, there was the screened door closed, and here were her tattered black heels in her left hand like always. The only difference was she was standing in total darkness. Flipping the wall switch, she thought that this must be the definition of impulse memory. How, after months and years of doing the same thing, over and over, a person becomes numb to the actual procedure. Starts to lose themselves.

　　She laughed at herself for philosophizing on a car ride and quickly remembered she was no longer in Religion 088; she was no longer in college, period. All the same, she didn't sleep very well that night.

—

Colin had never been able to multi-task.

He had a tendency for unprovoked moments of personal reflection and great tangents of thought. His ability to focus was only made worse if he happened to be drinking.

So it was now with dinner. Half a bottle deep into his favorite Argentinean merlot, and furiously at work mashing the potatoes by hand, he barely registered the front door swing open and missed completely the thin streams of smoke ushering from the corners of the oven.

Lane's gasp was the first indication anything had gone wrong. Meeting her at the entrance to the kitchen, holding out her glass, he was surprised by her less than ecstatic expression. In fairness, the bread was seconds away from being unsalvageable, but in the moment before he rushed to the stove, Colin thought he detected something more serious in her face.

Her auburn hair looked more out of place than usual. Or was it her eyes? True, they could both stand to cut down on the booze, but Lane's usually bright face and the skin on her bare arms had just a bit less color than normal. Then again, he could say the same for his own freckled cheeks and dark locks. Well over six feet, he could stand to put on a few pounds of healthy muscle. But such thoughts were dangerous, and might actually require motivation or even self-discipline. So he turned back to the bread and started to ask his roommate how she was doing.

Before he could even finish scraping the charred bits from the focaccia, however, Lane was herself again; spewing unrepeatable nicknames at her boss between large gulps of wine.

The house was a wreck. To be honest, it was a duplex, but the solid pre-war construction made if feel more like a proper house.

Crosby, Stills, and Nash played loudly and a bit too fast on the second hand record player. The front room was awash in spare jackets and shoes, and plunged into darkness to hide it all as usual. Both Lane and Colin's rooms being shut up due to lack of organization, the kitchen stood as the only clean or even lighted room in the entire house.

"Marrakesh Express" gave Lane the perfect excuse to pack another small bowl. Resolutely stationing herself on the love seat at the far end of the kitchen, she reached halfheartedly for the tiny leather bound box that they kept hidden in plain sight next to the table lamp.

"Why can't she just go ahead and die," was the question Lane had put to the peanut gallery this particular evening. "I hear her partner, Clara Fontaine, was a saint, and never intended to give up her half of the business, but there she was at Clara's death bed, like she always is, and—"

"—didn't even wait till the body was cold to snatch the shop away from her son…" Colin, without even looking up, finished Lane's story for her, knowing it better than she did.

"I know I talk about it a lot," Lane conceded, "but I'll be damned if that woman gives a shit about those antiques. She's in it for profit, plain and simple… well and the 'fame'" (she was referring her boss' appearance on last week's *Antiques Roadshow*, a coup for the shop).

Unspoken between them was the acknowledgement that this week marked one year of Lane's being personal assistant to Joanna Thornton, owner of what *she* would call "the best antiques store in the Southeast."

Joanna had run Essex House for the past fifteen years in the small university town of Middlesborough, North Carolina. She had survived on ruthless sales tactics and the persistent ghost of Clara's charm. She was cold, uncaring, and would sell her mother for the right price, but she was the only game in town, and everyone knew it.

Lane knew it too, those first few weeks after graduating from the University at Middlesborough, wondering not just what she would do with the rest of her life, but more to the point, where her next rent payment was coming from.

Staying in Middlesborough had never been her plan, per se. But since it seemed to be better than moving back home, she decided to use her love of Art History and take what seemed to be an interesting job at Essex.

Her parents, always supportive, thought the job sounded wonderful, but they would have loved it just as much if she had moved back to their far flung mountain town.

A year on, and she still couldn't figure out the exact moment when things went from 'interesting' to 'unbearable'. Probably, she thought, it was the moment the market went off a cliff and people stopped dropping thousands on two hundred year old bookcases.

"It's the weirdest thing," Lane said, a little smoke puffed from her nose, "Joanna has the best head for numbers, but she just can't quite grasp the recession. She keeps asking me why business is down so much. Can you believe that? The other day I told her that high-end antiques didn't exactly qualify as a 'necessity' and she gave me this blank look, like I was speaking Greek."

Colin, pre-occupied but still listening, stepped back to survey the stove top and said off handedly, "At least you're still working full time."

Lane was shocked, had he meant to say that out loud? And the same moment, Colin realized he hadn't.

Cooking was the only thing that transcended his mood when he got like this. That, and wine.

—

Ironic, Colin often thought to himself, that wine was the reason he had gone to work at Turnstead Plantation in the first place. And now it seemed to be his only escape.

Turnstead Plantation was an odd hodgepodge of faux antique buildings, tacky weddings, expensive soap displays, and overpriced food—with a rest home added on for good measure and built up in the middle of a civil war battle field several miles from Middlesborough. It was polished, embellished, homogeneous, and completely self-contained. It was a hit with the out-of-town, over-seventy crowd.

At "ye olde wine and cheese shop" Colin spent his time literally catering to the residents of Turnstead's parallel universe, the majority of whom were retired, bored senseless, and well-heeled. As such, they necessitated large quantities of alcohol, the sole source (within five miles) being the shop.

They came on foot, in cars, with the aid of walkers, and occasionally required Colin to come to them at the home. They bought whites, reds, roses, and even dessert wines; just as long as they could get them by the case.

It didn't take Colin long to realize that underneath Turnstead's crisp white exterior of fine country living, there was a frightening underworld where the average citizen was a gray-haired drunkard with a death wish and access to a golf cart.

Like Lane, Colin had been doomed from the end of college. Set loose on the world with a liberal arts degree, an interest in everything and a passion for nothing, his parents had packed him off for three months in Europe as a graduation gift. He thought it would help; clear his mind; teach him about himself and others; give him direction. He had returned more confused than ever. Lane had been there waiting.

Never more than passing friends in college, Lane and Colin's bond had formed about the same time everyone else was choosing their life paths senior year. They had smoked a few joints together clandestinely at lame parties. Both loved history and neither liked pretension.

One day they shared a bourbon and coffee before modern dance class, and the next thing they knew they were looking for post-graduation apartments.

It had been a convenient arrangement. They were close, but not too close. Like minded, but they had their own circles. The plan was simple, and even had a title: The Year of Me. Twelve months of pure self-satisfaction. They paid lip service to goals such as reading, writing, self-education, and travel. But thirteen months on, and the reality had been more like a cross between an art opening that got out of hand, and non-stop, year-long kegger.

It an odd thing: staying in a college town after school. They both noticed how quickly things can become stale when the place you live has a phone book that reads more like the University directory. It soon became clear their social scene had dwindled from a few thousand to a few dozen the minute they switched the tassels on their graduation caps.

Not that things hadn't been fun. But a hangover is bad enough, and between the two of them, they had one that would last well into the next decade.

"What are you saying?" The immediate effects of the booze prevented her from raising her voice, which often unnerved the secretive Colin.

Grudgingly, he turned to face her with a plaintive look.

"Don't worry, if you don't want to talk about it…" Lane had learned over the past year not to press for information; Colin usually revealed his thoughts, but it was always on his own time.

"No, it's fine, it's not like I can keep it secret anyway. They've cut hours at Turnstead."

"They've what? Wait, what does that mean for you?"

"That means I'm working half as much as I used to," Lanes ultimate question must have been evident because he continued, "It's not enough to live on."

"So… what are you gonna—"

"I'm not sure," he said, and just as quickly turned back to the stove and the small matter of dinner.

While Lane's normal reaction would have been to discuss the problem endlessly, she realized that with Colin there was nothing more to be said for the moment. Instead, she slid the still smoking bowl toward him as he plated and served the meal on the sturdy coffee table that served as the heart of the house.

"You want to come have coffee with me in the Oak Room soon? Joanna's at the Baltimore show all next week," she offered.

"I would," he managed between shovel-fulls of bacon-laden spinach, "But I'm taking my day off to go see my parents and pick up some more ingredients for Wine Monday."

Lane recognized the signs of his growing depression; the more complicated a recipe, the more he must be struggling. She knew that dinner with his parents wouldn't help matters. Still, it meant she usually got a grade-A meal, so she couldn't help herself from asking, "What's on tap for this week?"

"Don't worry about it, just know it's going to be fantastic," he smiled. "And don't forget the wine."

"No, I thought it would be better to have 'cheap beer Monday'" she smirked and made a mental note to get something fizzy. Despite Colin's news, or perhaps because of it, she knew that week they would need a celebration.

—

Wine Monday was a simple idea. Still young enough to be unconcerned by a Tuesday morning hangover at work, every

Monday night, they gathered around them a revolving cast of four or five people they still knew and six or seven bottles of previously untasted wine.

This Wine Monday was already shaping up to be one for the books. Lane had gone overboard at the larger, more well-stocked wine shop in town (Colin refused to give Turnstead any of its money back). Sneaking into the kitchen a little past six to grab a corkscrew, she thought she had spied truffle oil in Colin's grocery bag, but was quickly whisked back into the living room by the kitchen tool of the same name.

Outside the house, Matt Ortega stood in the blue half-light of Smith Avenue, listening to the thumping beat of the ELO song that emanated, along with a warm yellow glow, through the front screen door. A smile appeared on his face as he thought about all the Wine Mondays he had been to over the past year. Still lost in thought, he slightly flinched at Mara's uncharacteristically soft touch on his arm.

"Come on," she said imploringly, her eyes gesturing toward the house, "Let's not let this spoil everything."

He nodded his head slightly in agreement, his curly light brown hair tumbling forward with the motion. Steeling himself, he placed his bike helmet back on his head for effect and bounded into the living room unannounced.

Lane was in her room debating between identical black tops when she heard the front door. Without even venturing out, she knew by the time that it would be Matt and Mara, who always showed up right after the first glass, and seldom left until the last had been drained.

She ran into Colin in the hallway and both were completely unsurprised to find the couple already helping themselves to deviled eggs from Colin's Grandmother's 1960's platter.

Colin often thought about what an odd couple the two were: Matt, a thoughtful hipster and Mara, a strong willed over-achiever. Still both ostensibly in school, Matt and Mara maintained the tumultuousness of a college romance. They were never both completely happy at the same time it seemed, yet something about their interactions told Colin they liked it that way. 'Ostensibly' was how he always described their studies, since he seldom saw either of them do any actual work, and had just learned Matt was technically only a part-time student anyway. But they were a last, best link to a college life that existed just half a mile down the road, but felt to Lane and Colin to be worlds away.

Lane thought for a second that she detected something off about the two of them, but then realized it was probably just that they weren't fighting. Before she could give it a second thought, however, she remembered the crudités and raced to the refrigerator.

Matt, realizing the unease in the room, asked Mara to tell her latest anecdote about the school of public health, and soon the night was back on track.

Leo arrived just as the cheese plate was being set out, his long fingers grabbing a glob of brie before the dish had even hit the table. A student at Middlesborough Law, Colin had met him through an ex-boyfriend and had maintained contact long after he and the esquire parted ways. With him was a breathless and red faced John Parker Crane, Lane's date to her first (and only) rush function before she had decided sorority life wasn't for her. Like Leo, Parker was a souvenir from a different time in Lane's life. The two of them, Lane and Colin, had a habit of collecting the best from a situation and then moving on.

And, just as expected, half way through glass number two and right as dinner was coming out of the oven, Big D announced his presence in the front room by switching out Doobie Brothers on the record player for Bowie and strolling into the kitchen with a half-cocked smile and a lighted cigarette dangling from his unshaven upper lip.

"Get that fucking thing out of here!," Big D said mockingly to himself before Lane could even get the words out.

"You know that's what the damn bottle is for!" She yelled after him on the side stoop.

Of all the reasons to leave Middlesborough, Big D had to be one of the best, she thought. Of a nebulous age, and possessing an unquestionable intellect: if being a townie had been an aristocratic system, he would have been crowned king ages ago. Lane and Colin had known him for two years and were still uncertain about his real name or college major (that is assuming he had gone to school, which they did for some reason).

Colin's truffle potatoes were a hit. Between large bites Big D did his never-fail impression of the one time Leo dropped acid, his stringy reddish hair and clear blue eyes only adding to the intensity of the faked seizure.

Mara's loud voice was soon heard above the rest. Her dark eyes flashed maliciously as she tortured Matt with a rendition of his latest bike disaster—involving an 80 year-old man, a shopping cart, and a quart of milk. Not to be outdone, he removed his Elvis Costello glasses and brought up Mara's fender bender from last week; still funny no matter how many times he told it. Despite the story, which did require a certain dramatic flourish, Lane noticed how animated the usually low key Matt was that evening.

The festivities continued well into the evening: Leo trying, through an alcoholic haze, to explain the meaning of "tort reform"; Lane giving a play by play to John Parker of the chamber orchestra luncheon at the shop that day; Colin officiating a ridiculous game of "blind taste test" in which Mara displayed an uncanny nose for the difference between a seven and ten dollar bottle of wine.

Soon, however, the conversation drifted to the latest and most depressing economic forecasts.

"That's why I'm going into public health," Mara proclaimed, "I'll always have a job."

"I wouldn't be so sure about that," countered the mostly sober John Parker ('Crane' as he was known on Mondays), "North Carolina's budget shortfall is one of the worst in the country, unless you're a doctor, you really don't have job security anymore."

"Booooooooring," mocked Mara to a room full of laughter.

"So I guess that 100k I borrowed for law school was money down the drain," Leo's wry humor often had a way of cutting to the quick.

"Don't worry Leo," offered Colin, "I'm sure you'll be able to land a sugar mama to pay off that money for you." Leo's dating life in Middlesborough was constant fodder for jokes around the dinner table.

"I don't know," Matt offered in all seriousness, "Seems to me that even the rich are cutting back on non-essentials. Wouldn't that include gigolos?"

"Hey, I prefer 'companion'" he shot back.

"Y'all, this is for real," Mara was smiling and drunk, but still serious, "What are we gonna do when we get out of school?"

"Grad School," Crane and Matt said in unison.

"Big D, what about you? What do you even do now?" Lane loved screwing with Big D in front of people.

"I'm gonna keep on doin' what I do best—being a *survivor.*" Getting a straight answer out of Big D was like asking a five-year-old if he ate all the cookies.

"Speaking of," he continued, "This has been chill, but I gotta start laying the ground work with a sugar mama of my own."

"Don't you mean 'layin' the pipes'," Crane said as Mara hit his arm with a look of false disgust.

"Naw, man. This chick is a lady—I gotta win her over with *respect*," he said, "I'll let y'all know how it goes—peace dubs!" And he was out the door to a hipster party downtown.

The mood of the evening took a noticeable downturn with his exit. Recession and dwindling job prospects weren't really party friendly subjects. Lane, however, saved the day by remembering the Spanish Cava she had stashed in the bottom of the fridge.

"It's so hard to be sad while drinking something sparkling," she observed while passing out glasses, taking special note of Colin's forlorn face, "Matt, the bubbly's from Spain like you!" she said, trying to lighten the mood.

"Very funny," Matt replied, "I wish I was, or even my dad. Then I could bounce to Europe for as long as I wanted."

"Aren't your grandparents?" Mara asked.

"Chile. Thanks for paying attention," he joked while she made an apologetic face, "But who knows, I might be able find another way out…"

"Keep dreaming Ortega, we're all stuck in America," Leo said dryly. And then, turning toward the two hosts, "So what about the two of you?"

Lane froze and looked to Colin whose glance said immediately that he'd rather not talk about his situation.

"What do you mean," she said casually.

"Well, the two of you have stable jobs. Planning on holding on to them for a while? Or are you going to go to law school and start a firm with me like you know you should?"

"Leo, our law firm would go under in a month," Colin had rejoined the conversation to Lane's relief.

"Yeah, but we'd have a hell of a month!" Everyone laughed, but Matt didn't seem to want to let it go.

"But neither of you seem happy at your jobs—what's your next step?"

"Well, I don't know about Lane, but I'm going to have to leave Turnstead soon." Colin responded.

"And then what..." Matt trailed off.

"You tell me," he said with a smile and began cleaning up.

The wine kept coming. Leo, Crane, and Mara made a mass exit somewhere around midnight and Lane, Colin, and Matt continued drinking and talking well into the one o'clock hour. It was, like any other Wine Monday, a great success—until just before one thirty, when Matt revisited his earlier question.

"So what *is* your plan, anyway?"

Colin had been laughing so hard, it took him a second to realize Matt wasn't talking about Mara's mother anymore.

An uneasy pause set in as Lane and Colin looked at each other, back at Matt, and then around the table, as if the answer might exist in one of the half-eaten pieces of bread. Matt, though far from sober, continued his steady gaze. He knew it was the perfect moment to put his plan into action.

"Colin said it for me, I don't have one" Lane admitted.

Matt faked a shocked look, "You mean schlepping Joanna's shit all over the South and sucking up to all those rich old people isn't a long term career choice?"

"Wow, someone decided to get really honest, really fast" Lane wasn't hurt though. How could she be? It was all true.

"Turnstead cut my hours," Colin offered up.

"They did?" Matt turned to Lane for confirmation. She nodded. "When were you going to say something? What happened?" He didn't know what to think.

"Never? I don't know. It just happened this week, and yesterday I had this moment of 'Thank God'."

Lane, hearing this for the first time asked the obvious, "You did? I mean, I know you hated it, but why?"

"It was the funniest thing," he continued, "Mrs. Worthy came in for her usual white zinfandel yesterday, and as I was wrapping up the bottle, she commented on how nice it was that she could still come to the shop after she moved into the home next week. And that was it, I thought, 'If I stay here long enough for that woman to go from self-sufficient to dead, I might as well stay for life.' I guess I was kind of scared before now—I mean, now I have to actually do something with my life, right?" He grinned, but no one was laughing.

It seemed like the end of the evening, but just as Lane and Colin were turning their attention to the large pile of dirty dishes they were amazed to hear Matt's rarely authoritative voice pose one last question, "So then, what are you going to do about it?"

But before either of them could stammer a response, he continued, "Mara and I broke up."

They were both stunned. Matt and Mara had been together since their sophomore year, and despite their constant unease and occasional outbursts, no one had ever even tried to picture them apart.

"You what?" Lane had almost been struck sober by the statement.

"We broke up."

"But the two of you—tonight—you—" Colin attempted to argue but fell silent.

"I'd rather not talk about it honestly, but I thought it was the right thing. And after talking to the two of you, I'm sure of it."

Neither knew what to say.

"So, since I'm on a roll, I'm just gonna continue with what I came here to ask," Lane was literally on the edge of her seat. Colin, completely forsaking the dishes till morning, was in the middle of pouring the last of the New Zealand white into his glass. "What do the two of you think about moving abroad?"

"Do we think about it at all?" Colin looked to Lane for confirmation.

Seeing that a direct response was unlikely, Matt repositioned himself, put both his large feet onto the wine stained floor and started to explain, "I don't know if I told the two of you that my brother did it in Warsaw, and said he had the best time—and it's really not that hard—well not as hard as people say, but—well, ok, maybe a little harder for Americans, but you don't have to go to like, Saudi Arabia or anything, you just can't exactly do it in France—but there are tons of other places, great places, and I was just thinking—"

"How do we start?"

"How do you what?" Matt hadn't thought that far ahead in the conversation, but Lane, expedient as ever, had cut directly to the chase. "I want in, how do we do it?" Her firm gaze and steady glass told him that, even though definitely wine-fueled, she was serious.

"Oh, uh, I mean, wait a minute, lemme look up a website—where's your laptop?"

Lane retreated to the front room to search for an available computer somewhere beneath the debris. Meanwhile, Colin had grown silent and was taking long, contemplative sips from his wine glass.

"You're talking about just leaving?"

Stunned but quickly gaining confidence, Matt responded, "Well—yes, just leaving."

"And your plan, it's not very well thought out?"

"Well, I mean it has the bones and all and... well, ok, no. Right now it's just a thought."

"Like, you're not sure where we would go first, or even if that country would work out..."

"Well of course not, I mean I just came out with it, I never really thought—wait. Did you just say 'we'?"

"I might have."

"Does that mean you're in?"

"It depends. One last question: What are we even talking about doing?"

Matt laughed as he realized he hadn't actually said the words, "We're going to teach English." And with that, everything seemed to click in an odd way. Matt studied Colin's face for hesitation and then posed his question once more, "So are you doing this with us?"

"Let me see, I could stay here and find another crappy job at a place like Turnstead, slowly killing myself with booze until one day I got wasted and walked right into the ravine south of campus—or, I could follow the two of you half way across the world on a half-cocked scheme that could be the best or worst decision of my life…"

Lane almost tripped over herself as she re-entered the kitchen. "You know, I realized I had just signed up for something I didn't even know the details of. Did you even say what we'd be doing over there…?" But after opening the laptop and waiting for her ancient version of Windows to load, she finally looked up and realized something was happening.

"What did I miss while I was gone, boys…?"

Matt's face slowly turned upwards into a smile as he finally managed to pull his eyes off of Colin, standing silent in the corner. Looking Lane straight in the face he said with wine-soaked casualness, "We're going to teach English—and Colin's decided to come with us."

—

The next morning was beautiful. Summer's late September Southern death grip had finally loosened just enough to let slip through a short preview of autumn's coming attraction. It was a special time of every year. Indian Summer would return in two or three days. But for now the morning shown with a brilliant white stillness. Never pulsing like the days of spring; never rustling like fall; these days always stood transfixed; a part of no season.

Lane's eyes popped open as if she had fallen asleep at the wheel. She was in those first few seconds of consciousness, where her memory hadn't flooded back, and she still existed in a dream world. Soon though, she remembered everything, played the whole night back in fast motion, skipped to the end and pulled in a deep breath that she held as if underwater, for as long as she could. Was it all true?

Emerging from her room she discovered by the clock on the wall that it was much earlier than expected—not even nine. She smelled coffee. She heard nothing. On her way into the bathroom she noticed Colin's door ajar. He wasn't in his bed.

Cold water on the face, glass of ice, aspirin—it was a Tuesday morning ritual.

Fully medicated and prepared for an interesting breakfast conversation, she slowly padded her way into the kitchen, but there was still no sign of her roommate.

The unmistakable ratchet sound of a cheap lighter wafted in from the front stoop. Intrigued, Lane grabbed the nearest hoodie (perched on top of the cluttered desk that was the "business center") and made for the front door.

Tuesday mornings were always harsh, but the cool green air revived and invited her, like somewhere Moby was playing on hidden speakers. As her eyes adjusted to the pine shaded beauty of the front yard, she caught sight of Colin's tall frame, standing motionless and upright against the last of the morning mist. A lighted cigarette in his unengaged left hand was the only indication he was alive.

She said nothing. He turned to face her.

"Is it that big of a day?" Lane inclined her head towards the cigarette which had obviously come from their emergency pack in the freezer.

"I think it is." Colin flashed a small grin.

"Do we need to talk about this?" was the obvious question, so Lane asked it.

"What's there to talk about?" for the first time in their relationship Colin was the one ready to proceed without caution and Lane seemed to be posing all the relevant questions.

Colin sensed the role reversal, but decided to remain silent.

Lane slowly lifted the cigarette from his hand and took a drag. Eyebrows raised, she said, "Nothing that I can think of... I just want to know what we were going to tell our families."

Checking their email over breakfast, they both found two things: a welcome letter for an online English teaching course and an e-receipt for a one way ticket to Athens.

"We had a fabulous time at the beach last weekend…" Marla Yates trailed off into her coffee cup while leafing through the 'Life, etc.' section of the Raleigh News & Observer.

Robert Yates, absent mindedly over-stirring the contents of his cup while lost in the sports section, grunted in agreement.

"I've got something I need to talk with y'all about." Colin felt like he should be nervous, but years of strained relations with his parents had made their reactions to his life choices mostly muted.

"I'm thinking about moving abroad," he continued.

"Well that could be a positive experience," Marla failed to look up from the paper.

"No—sorry, what I meant to say was that I *am* moving abroad." Usually well spoken, he often became indecisive and unclear when he was with the two people who had raised him.

Robert ('Bob' to everyone else, but Robert to Colin) finally looked up, but waited for Marla to take the lead. She demurred. There was an uneasy silence. Colin spoke again.

"I'm sorry, I didn't fully explain everything. I've signed up for an English teaching course online and made arrangements to leave for Athens. Lane and Matt and I are planning to go there in a couple months. It's really not as shady as it sounds—it'll be an adventure. All the websites say that employment is almost guaranteed...." he drifted as he realized his parents were motionless across the table.

Finally, his father spoke, "Do you need money, son?"

Colin was quiet for a moment. It was the exact question he hadn't wanted to hear. If it had ben four years ago, he thought to himself, this conversations would've be very different. His parents would want to know everything about his decision. They would drive him crazy about the details of his plans. They would ask for every bit of information on Lane and Matt. Basically they would care.

An only child, Colin had been the product of years of hope and prayer (and more than a few doctor visits). Bob and Marla had loved him desperately, and, as the center of their universe, life was wonderful for him.

Then, he entered the second grade. Mannerisms began to show. Other students started making comments, or worse. It was somewhere around this time Colin noticed his parents, while concerned about his welfare, also started—slightly—pulling away. His father, first, and then, by the time he graduated high school and came out to them, his mother, also.

There were no big fights, no tearful interactions (Colin would have almost preferred some). There was just a slow, agonizing parting of ways. On paper they did everything required: paid for college, asked all the right questions, and even gave him guilt trips about coming home. But when he was with them—it was almost like they weren't even in the same room.

So here they were, the three of them, parents and child, but almost strangers; his father asking him if he needed money in the same tone someone would use with an acquaintance who couldn't pay the check at a restaurant.

"No, dad, I don't need money," Colin managed without betraying his unhappiness.

Marla Yates looked a bit bewildered, but finally offered what she thought to be the best response, "Well, what an exciting adventure. You will be sure and put me on your email list, won't you?"

"Of course, Mom," was all he could manage to get out before he excused himself and spent the rest of the night shut up in his high school bedroom.

—

Matt Ortega looked on as his sister, Marnie, cleared a path for him from the door of her room to the small sitting area in the bay window. Outside, the Charlotte skyline just peaked out from behind the tall oak trees.

Books were the main pollutant in her large space, but other debris included loose papers, magazines (Marnie loved celebrity news), and half-finished glasses of water.

Still in high school and already living like a professor, thought Matt.

Matt's Parents, Steven and Marie, The Professors Ortega, had given each of their three children very distinct genetic gifts. His older brother, James, had gotten, from both of them, extreme academic prowess. While living in Warsaw, he had completed the field research for his doctoral thesis and taught English. He spoke four languages and wrote regular political science articles for several journals.

Marnie and Matt often wondered how James did everything he did with a mixture of envy and apathy.

From Steven, Marnie had received the curse of complete disorganization. She could seldom find anything she needed in fewer than 20 minutes, but constantly insisted on having her own 'system'.

Matt had inherited Marie's tendency toward indecision; hence the five plus years of College.

All of the Ortega children, had, however, gotten their parents love of reading, introspective nature, and appetite for the unfamiliar. (Family dinners growing up had ranged from Thai curry night to Columbian fried ants, with long conversations well past bedtime.)

Sitting now, gauging Marnie's reaction, Matt thought about how out of character his decision was for him.

"So you're just getting on a plane?" She seemed almost concerned.

"I know, it's kind of shocking for me, too."

And then, accepting it, she shrugged and smiled, "Well it's about time you got out of Middlesborough. Are going to graduate?"

"I let you in on a secret, but you can't tell Mom and Dad. I've been able to graduate for a year, but I kept signing up for online classes. I can finish everything over email and get my degree in the mail."

"You bastard! That's genius!" she squealed.

Happy with her approval he continued, "How do you think Mom and Dad are going to take it?"

"Are you kidding?" she said, already rooting through another pile for some unnamed object, "They'll be thrilled. Don't tell them, but they've been worried you were going to go straight to grad school without seeing the world."

Matt thought about the statement, it sounded just like them, "So where are they anyway?"

Marnie made a face as if he should already know the answer to the question, "Mom's on campus and Dad's doing 'sabbatical research' in the basement," she used air quotes for the phrase.

"So he's smoking a joint and Mom's probably at the bar with her TAs," he said.

"Sounds about right, I would wait until dinner to tell them, but whatever you do don't mention Athens, you know how they feel about that city…"

"What do you mean?" Matt called to her, but she was already knee deep in papers inside her walk-in closet.

That night at dinner, Marie Ortega, per usual, dissolved into happy tears at the news. Steven, perpetually low-key, developed a grin that lasted the rest of the evening.

"I'm so happy you're not going to Athens either," Marie managed through dessert.

"Horrible place," Steven concurred.

"Mom, you two got mugged, it could happen in any city," Marnie observed with little emotion.

"It's more than that! Not a soul would help us. We slept on the street that night and were lucky to escape with our lives," Marie's flair for the dramatic was family legend.

"You did not sleep on the street," Matt corrected.

"Well of course we didn't, I was too afraid to sleep," was all she would offer.

"You know as a political scientist I hate to discount any country—but just look at their economy. That's all the proof anyone could need," The usually level headed Steven Ortega was always more than outspoken about Greece. Matt realized it was something he and Marie could share; a kind of anti-best-vacation-ever-story.

"I'm just happy you decided on Turkey," he continued. "It's really one of the most politically interesting places you could have picked."

It was white lie Matt decided he could correct once across an ocean.

—

"Laney!" Myra Cameron's voice rang out from the kitchen and reached Lane at her post by the large picture window at the front of the house.

"They're not here, yet, Mom!" Lane called back, her eyes never moving from the winding mountain road that lead up to their rambling, secluded log house.

She was trying to remember what life had been like as a teenager in rural Haywood County, but the memories seemed further away every time she came home.

Just then, a jab in her back let her know Charlotte was finished with her conference call in the office.

"You know, you can't run away forever"

Lane looked at her sister, taller than she was, perfect hair, polished looking even in casual clothes, "Who said I was running away?"

Charlotte gave her younger sibling an all knowing look and then decided to drop it, "When are you leaving, anyway?"

"Forty-five days," said Lane and returned her gaze to the window.

"And I suppose you think you're going to get a job on some Island and boat to work every morning?"

Lane was constantly surprised by Charlotte's ability to read people, but tried her best to play it cool, "No. I'll probably have to get a job in a city somewhere. That's where all the big schools are."

At the same moment, however, she was picturing herself, coffee in one hand, rudder in the other, piloting her way across the Aegean to an early morning class.

The guests, Lane's Parent's best friends, had just pulled up, and her father, Mitch, cut her day dream short by insisting she come to the door to greet them.

The day before, when Lane had laid out her plans for them, Mitch and Myra had taken the news well. They had learned long ago not to be surprised by any of her passing interests, but Myra's face did show her concern when Lane handed them a printed flight receipt.

Charlotte was the only one to voice an opinion.

"Where are you going to stay?"

Lane thought she was ready for any questions, but her sister's argumentative nature had always unnerved her.

"Um, oh, well we have an apartment already set up and—"

"So let's say you don't get a job," Charlotte continued without pausing.

"Charlotte..." Myra began to caution, but clearly wanted to know the answer herself.

"There are plenty of jobs," Lane managed to get out.

"I'm sure Laney's thought of everything," Mitch said over his paper. A loving father, his life advice to his adult daughters was limited to the subjects of long term savings, auto repair, and the stupidity of sudden-death overtime in football.

"I just want to make sure she *has*," Charlotte backed off, but Lane knew she hadn't heard the end of it.

Growing up, the two girls had been at each other's throats more often than not. Perhaps because of their similarities, Lane often thought; and then rolled her eyes at how ridiculous that sounded. Mitch and Myra, wonderfully warm and loving, had been at a loss. The minute both girls entered high school, it was as if they stopped being able to understand them.

Charlotte was bright, beautiful, and highly motivated—intent on achieving a high degree of success before the age of thirty. Lane was dreamy, smart, and interested in everything. Both girls were headed somewhere outside of their small mountain town.

Lane could always convince her parents one of her ideas was a good one, but when she dealt with Charlotte it was different; she had to fight, defend her choice, give examples—it was exhausting.

"Are you going to email me all the information?" Charlotte was now asking.

"Of course," Lane said. And then gave the question a second thought, "Wait, are you saying you think it's a good idea?"

Charlotte gave her a smug smile and cocked her head, "I won't go that far, but if you do manage to land a job, I'm not going to pass up a free place to stay in Greece."

Lane knew it was the best endorsement she would get and decided to do whatever necessary to make her adventure a success.

—

Six more weeks in Middlesborough. Two resignation letters. One last Wine Monday. And before they knew it, the three were on a plane bound for a city none of them had ever been to, and completely uncertain about when they would return.

The approach into Athens by plane was not the average decent pattern. In almost every city Lane had flown to (which weren't many), the plane seemed to hang in an endless bank of clouds, until, at the very last minute, it broke free from this natural blindfold and (given the right weather conditions) she got a quick glimpse of whichever place she was visiting before the plane's altitude dropped below viewing level.

As they approached Athens however, she knew she had arrived long before she even felt the airplane moving slowly downward. Endless ripples of mountains seemed to last forever, uninhabited and ageless below her until she noticed things slowly become greener. Hours ago, the white spotted North Faces of the high mountains had disappeared.

Buildings—Lane was sure of it, in tiny clusters below as the land evened out and opened up to the possibility of life. Then it happened; they crested the cap of a mountain so large (and flying so low) that she was amazed they didn't scrap against it. And there it was, the city of Athens, sprawling, smoking, baking (even in winter) in a bowl in the earth. And spilling, quite literally, into the Saronic Gulf.

They were suspended above the city for what seemed like forever; passengers on a hot air balloon, with no plan or particular reason for landing. Then they were out over open water, headed for Egypt it seemed like, until, finally they banked hard and swung back toward the white and gray quilt of the city. As they made their final approach, she though she saw—yes—there—the acropolis. She knew it had been there for millennia, but all the same it was nice to know it was exactly where it should be. The whole thing was a pop-up map for children, an interactive video game. Whatever it was, it couldn't be real. Like Santa Clause or Big Foot, Lane thought, you'd recognize it in a second, but never believe it to be real.

But just as Lane was becoming adjusted to the idea, it was out of sight, and they were dropping quickly toward the runway on a rocky patch of land, near a small, modern terminal, in a very different country.

Atlanta was all she could compare it too. The boys made fun of her, but the comparison wasn't completely wrong. Both cities had suffered ridiculous amounts of urban growth in horribly short time spans. Both cities represented the economic and political center powerhouse of their regions, holding sway over much of what the surrounding areas did. And, perhaps most importantly, both cities had recently hosted the Olympics. From the time you hit ground in either metropolis it was obvious that whatever the local language, or traditions, or even traffic patterns, things had, at least for a short time, been geared to a very international audience.

This was helpful to the three newly minted world travelers, as Greek is not a language very hospitable to first timers, and the only thing any of them wanted was a warm bed and a hot meal (in what order, they didn't care).

—

The "apartment" they had rented, sight unseen, over a sketchy website, luckily turned out to be not *too* different from the three grainy, digital photographs Lane kept of it in her travel planner. Near a metro line, but definitely light years away from the "center" of the Greek capital, the flat was a standard cinderblock number with slightly yellowed linoleum, a two burner gas stove, and wildly colored floral linens. The most attractive feature was definitely the price; even with the countries endemic economic problems the term "cheap Greek vacation" was a thing of the past. It did, however, have a small balcony in the back that overlooked a large unkempt ally way.

Cleaner than expected, the trio quickly realized that a "3+1" did not, in fact, mean each person got his or her own room. Somehow the odd number combination had indicated a two bedroom place, with a large living space (the "3") and a kitchen (presumably the "+1"). Too tired to argue and lacking the necessary verbs to do so, they decided the boys could share for now, and they would look for something more appropriate as soon as they all had jobs.

Lane took one last look at where they had ended up. Matt stood with all his weight on one foot, stirring tea bags in a small pot on top of one of the burners. His curly hair had become unruly since they had made their plans a few short weeks ago, and it now stood on end from long hours of airplane travel. Colin was fiddling unsuccessfully with the ceiling fan, he had gotten a buzz cut just before leaving; a kind of "new start" he had said. Lane was surprised how much more grown up he looked in the dim evening light. They were all too tired and excited to try and sleep, but started going through the motions anyway.

Exhausted and sticky from the gyro they had grabbed on the corner, Lane ran cool water over her face and took one last look at her travel worn eyes. She removed the band from her smooth hair, scrubbed her hands as best she could without soap, and barely managed to remove her coat before falling asleep, fully clothed, on top of her rickety bed for more than fourteen hours.

—

The next 10 days were a flurry of activity. Armed with pre-printed resumes, English Teaching Certificates from their online course, and tiny phrase books, Lane, Colin, and Matt took a divide-and-conquer approach. Their goal was to hit every language school and private institution in two weeks. It was fun at first, getting up early, chugging Greek coffee over the English language newspaper at the corner bakery. Going over that day's strategy, so as not to overlap, and then meeting back up for a celebratory dinner of cheap beer and store bought spanakopita.

Soon, though, things didn't seem so exciting.

Week three rolled around without any word from schools. Lane had gotten a positive email from one language center, but the offer fell through when they asked if she had European Union working papers. Nightly, Matt would remind her and Colin both not to worry. James had had the same problem in Poland, he said, and it had all worked out fine by week four.

Colin couldn't help pointing out, however, that James student visa and University grants had given him all the time he needed.

"What are you saying," Lane tried not to sound panicky.

"All I'm saying is that we're on a time limit," he smiled—but the words lingered.

Things went from bad to worse. Government debt still loomed. The street protests of the year before hadn't started again, but an entirely new set of government pay cuts were in the works. Lane expressed concern. Matt kept quiet. Colin didn't know what to think.

Thanksgiving came and went.

Money got tight, so they started to cook at home. Mediterranean dishes filled the kitchen as Colin worked his way through all the online Greek recipes he could find. Every night he would put on his own personal Food Network show for an audience of two. "Stuck in Greece with No Money" might have had a limited fan base, but the concept was genius.

The would-be teachers learned the local alphabet (no small task), took walks in public parks, and bought cheap bus tickets to the island of Piraeus.

And then it was week five. Matt called a house meeting and Lane and Colin both knew it would be a serious one—he had sprung for the expensive bottle of Italian wine.

"So where do we stand?" he had decided small talk was a luxury they didn't have.

Lane spelled things out clearly, as usual, "I've gotten three 'you need EU working papers', three 'we don't need you until February' and one three week job that starts next week, but is only part time. All-in-all I'd say it's the best any of us have gotten."

Matt continued, "And I've heard back from two schools that want me for February also, and one woman that I think is more interested in getting me into bed than learning English."

Colin smiled, "Seems like you could charge more for your lessons that way. Weren't you the one that said we shouldn't turn down anything that paid?" Matt's response was a tiny Greek coffee spoon hurled at Colin's head. To Lane's surprise, the two boys had become fast friends in the five weeks they'd been traveling partners.

"When the two of you are finished…" was her mockingly annoyed response, "I guess we just couldn't manage to outrun this damn recession. Matt, you seem to know the most here; what are our options? Is there anywhere that still wants to hire expensive foreign teachers in this economy?"

"Well first, I think recession is a euphemism at this point. The government is still in the worst shape it's been in in decades. They say Greece might even be taken off the Euro soon, in which case, we'd be—what's the word? Oh—fucked… so, I've been doing some research." The news was a bit shocking to Lane, who followed current events but had never stopped to think of how European monetary policy might completely co-opt her personal needs and desires.

"So have I." Said Colin, opening a small notebook with several folded print outs.

"Ok, what have you found out?" Matt continued with his smug tone.

"Lots of stuff, douche bag," Colin laughed, "The way I see it, we can do one of two things. First, focus on finding another

European country that will have us. From what I can tell, that means Hungary, the Czech Republic, or even Poland. I don't know about the two of you, but I'm not sure how much I want to move to Romania, even if they are in the European Union."

"I agree," Lane spoke up, "but I've been sending resumes to those countries, and the response hasn't been great."

Matt took a swig of wine and completed everyone else's thought, "So I think that brings us to a second option. We could leave tomorrow, take the train, and arrive in a major city with a place to stay, a guaranteed job, and someone to pick us up."

Lane looked to Colin who only nodded in response. She racked her brain.

"So what is it? Where is this fabulous city, *near here*, where we automatically have jobs and a place to stay?"

Colin involuntarily chuckled a little, while Matt continued his staring contest with Lane through his coke-bottle lenses. Lane's tiny nostrils flared with mounting anger, despite the fact that the corners of her mouth had turned up.

"Seriously y'all, this is too much, where *is* it?"

Matt finally cracked, "Istanbul. We're talking about Istanbul."

Lane stared blankly, her mouth still frozen into an involuntary smile. After a long pause, she grabbed her wine glass and slumped back into her chair with a sigh, "Fine, if the two of you can't be serious…"

Colin and Matt couldn't stand it any longer and burst into gales of laughter. Lane was uncertain what was going on, but refused to give them the upper hand.

"It's not a joke," Colin finally got out between laughing fits, "and don't worry, I thought it was a joke at first, too."

Lane's eyes widened from behind her glass. Reaching blindly for the bottle, she cut Colin with a questioning stare, "Wait. You're serious. Are you really talking about—Turkey?"

Matt answered for him, "Last time I checked, that's where Istanbul is."

Lane rolled her eyes. "You can't be serious. What about all the 'I don't want to move somewhere sketchy' talk. Honestly, I would have been less surprised if you had suggested Cairo."

"It's serious. Honestly, I have my doubts about former soviet states like Belarus, but Turkey's been reformed for almost a century, and this job is the best offer we've gotten from anywhere. And who knows, it could be an adventure." Lane could see Matt had actually given the whole proposal some thought. She turned to Colin in a last attempt at deciding if the whole thing was a hoax. He met her gaze, though, and the way his mouth didn't quiver told her he wasn't joking.

"I know none of us have ever been there, but I emailed some teachers from the school, and they said it was great. And the best part is, we don't have to worry about work permits, EnglishSpace takes care of everything." Colin sounded like a spokesperson which in turn made Lane laugh.

She steadied herself long enough to respond, "EnglishSpace? Is that a real company? It sounds like a joke about a Language school. Like the place someone would go to teach English in a movie. Admit it, you made it up."

Matt produced a half-cocked smile, "It's all true, and yes, it's a ridiculous name, but it's where my vote is. Hell, if we hate it, the worst that happens is—we leave."

"Why are you so keen on this," she responded, "You almost sound like a commercial."

"OK, I'll be honest," Matt half grimaced, "It's where my parents think we are already—but don't think that's the only reason—"

"Oh, great! So we're moving to a country based on a fib you told your parents?"

"No, no! Listen, this is a real opportunity, not to mention it would help me with my little geographical problem…"

This had to be a prank. Contrary to her normal procedure of making a decision and examining it later, she slowed her breath, took another sip of wine, and, summoning all of her twenty-three years, tried to respond as an adult would.

"Well, this is a lot to take in. I'll be honest, I don't think I would have considered moving to Turkey a few months ago, but then again, I'm not sure I would have ever pictured myself sitting in a Greek kitchen either." Finishing the wine, Lane pursed her lips and continued, "I'm going to have to think about this. It's a big decision, and frankly moving to Turkey isn't the direction I ever saw my life going in… It's just, well it's a big decision. It's going to take some thought, and research, and serious consideration." She was repeating herself. "Yes," she said, one last time, as she headed off to bed in a haze, "it's a big decision…"

—

The knock on the door hadn't woken her up. Rather, it was the fall from the top berth that jolted Lane from her no-so-peaceful slumber. The train had stopped abruptly—the fourth time that night. Only this time, instead of a brash boarder guard asking her questions in Greek and then broken English, she was herded out of the train in a single file line with ten other passengers. She was constantly surprised how leisure travel in the Mediterranean could quickly turn into something more reminiscent of *Schindler's List* than *Roman Holiday*. Hitting the frigid night air with nothing more than her Middlesborough tee-shirt on, she had the horrible feeling that an altercation was about to take place on a stretch of deserted train track somewhere between Thessaloniki and Istanbul—and that she might not survive.

Instead she found herself packed into a small un-heated building staring at a rather large man behind a desk. It was well past mid-night and the faces of the various travelers around her showed it. Her two companions were not with her in this particular tobacco stained room. Probably an intimidation tactic, she thought. After several uncomfortably cold and silent minutes, the man behind the desk roughly took her passport and examined it theatrically. He removed from a small pad what looked like a large postal stamp and placed it onto a blank page. Over top of the stamp he wrote something illegible and then glared up at her. She later realized he was trying to be nice, but his voice had still come off as harsh.

"Welcome to Turkey," he said, "Twenty American Dollars, Please."

—

Three years earlier at Middlesborough, in a class called "Revolution", Lane had noticed that in most democracies around the world, the founding of the republic is a similar story. There's a plot, a cast of characters, a triumphant resolution.

While that basic story held true in Turkey, also, she and the boys quickly realized one major difference. Instead of *several* founding fathers (and mothers) who shared the glory of establishing a new government, only one person seemed to receive credit for the modern Turkish state. His likeness was as ubiquitous as statues of The Virgin in Greece. His name, Atatürk, was everywhere from monuments to shopping malls.

And it was his literally chiseled face, larger than life and bathed in gold leaf, which greeted Lane, Colin, and Matt as they disembarked at Serkeci Train Station.

After finding two men with horribly stereotypical mustaches and a sign reading "Math Ortega" the three crammed into the back of a tiny four door compact, still not completely sure if they were being transported to accommodations or taken on a ride from which they might not return.

They were soon flying through the streets of the unfamiliar city, silent except for the occasional gasp whenever the driver would pop a curve. Hot, yellow colored air from the bowels of street vending stands merged into tiny clouds of condensation that hung and were dispersed with violence by the mad stream of traffic. People were everywhere. At the station it had been mostly travelers like themselves, but racing down a four lane road, dangerously close to a tram, Lane noticed large clusters of locals huddled together against the wind, near the red, street-facing heat lamps of fast food restaurants.

Colin pointed animatedly from his perch in the center of the back seat towards something. Following his hand, Lane and Matt saw the crowd clear the cross walk and caught sight of something wonderful. Stretching out almost miles before them was choppy, white-topped water. The highway looked as if it would run straight ahead into the small ocean, but just as they approached the driver executed a hard left and they were zipping down the shore line. Finally they could see the city, two giant mounds of earth, separated by football fields of ocean, and rising from the water like uneven breasts, completely covered in camisoles of gray and dirt colored buildings. In the center, where a necklace would hang lifeless between two actual breasts, a massive, taught, suspension bridge formed a straight line across the horizon. Lane thought that if the bridge had not been there, the two land masses would surely have floated away from one another, as two boats in a rendezvous require a strong tether.

"It's the Golden Horn," Matt was saying.

"Which?" Colin responded.

"The water we're crossing right now."

They were turning right at top speed onto a long, low bridge that Lane thought she had seen people walking along the underside of. Before them, the left breast heaved with life as they approach. It was surrounded by water on three sides, and as all of their eyes traveled upwards they noticed its peak, which was crowned with an imposing medieval tower.

The man in the passenger seat finally spoke. Indicating the land mass before them he said, simply, "Pera!" And then, with just as much fanfare, he pointed in the opposite direction, behind their heads, and causally offered, "Sultanahmet."

All three backseat passengers twirled their heads as quickly as possible given the space constraints.

"Oh my god," Lane spoke for all of them.

Just as they were racing towards one large city "breast", another was retreating behind them. Much older looking and with a smattering of ivy covered ruins, its peak was capped not by one fat tower, but four skinny ones, encircling a giant dome of dirty beige set on large, un-windowed walls the rutty color of clay rich soil.

The city they were approaching was glittering and man-made. The one they were leaving behind had a mystery to it, as if, long ago, a race of giants had inhabited that place, and a toddler of unfathomable size had one day built a mud castle, using large fist-fulls of wet and dripping, brick colored mud.

Scaling the face of the approaching city, the tiny car began to wheeze and start. Lane was sure that at any moment the whole endeavor would end with the vehicle and its five unlucky passengers careening backwards, at top speed, into the Golden Horn. Soon, though, they had crested the worst of the hill and were approaching what seemed to be a clearing in the dense parade of buildings.

Finally Matt found the words to speak, "I'm sorry, Sir," he addressed the more vocal front seat passenger, not wanting to distract the already hurried driver, "but, where are we?"

Without turning around the man moved his shoulders slightly and then pointed forward again, "Pera." Not wanting to seem ungrateful, Matt accepted the repeated answer.

Just then the car slowed abruptly for traffic. They were in a clearing now, a large cobblestone square surrounded by a circular traffic pattern and fenced in by several multi-story buildings. Amazed, the three stared up at the glass-clad high rises. Matt noticed one of the buildings topped with a giant screen flashing what was obviously a cell phone commercial. Lane looked up to find a brightly lighted flower market and hordes of people moving in concentric circles around a large monument. None of them could express it; it was definitely not what they had expected.

"Taksim" the man said, turning slightly this time. But before any of them could respond, they had cut down a side street and were once again terrorizing pedestrians and rounding corners that didn't seem meant for automobiles. It was a roller coaster ride, and as such was over before the participants had even gotten used to it.

Jerked forward by a stop that seemed more accidental than on purpose, Lane, Colin and Matt didn't know what would come next, but knew they should probably exit the vehicle while they had the chance. The driver lighted a cigarette and began to fiddle with the radio while his mustachioed friend was already on the street unloading the sparse luggage from the trunk. Too excited from the ride to think of any pertinent questions, the car and its two occupants had disappeared before the three could protest. Suddenly they found themselves alone, bags at their feet, on a slightly depressing back street covered in slimy cobblestones and dark, barred windows.

Lane searched the boys' faces. Was this it, would they have to fend for themselves now, bags in hand, in a city where they didn't speak the language and held no currency?

Colin's face contorted into a squint as if he were about to say something but then caught himself. Matt started to rummage for the tiny moleskine notebook in which he recorded his entire life. After flipping through several pages, and then checking numbers posted irregularly on the nearby buildings he returned to his position in the middle of the street, looking unworried as usual.

"This seems to be it," he said by way of explanation.

Lane didn't know what to do, but did know that she had to use the bathroom and couldn't stand there much longer. (The train hadn't had what could be called a proper toilet, but rather an interesting hole in the floor she hoped she'd never have to use again.) But just as she was about to run off in search of a McDonald's that may or may not exist, they heard a latch click. Turning towards the sound, all three were intrigued but frightened to see the large, rusted metal door of the building behind them slowly opening itself as if in some horror movie. The entire structure was something out of a film: late 19th century classical façade rising, story after story into a gray sky. Not a single light in any window. Pockmarked and covered in a hundred years of grime, it would not have surprised any of the friends to find out it was abandoned. But instead of a homeless squatter, the massive door finally revealed a small, plump woman, with a large nose, light brown skin, and an electric green headscarf.

Rapid fire Turkish followed as the woman produced three keys (without key chains) and began making large swo0ping motions with her hands by way of herding the visitors inside.

Once off the street, things became no less odd. No one else seemed to be inside the building to translate, so for the next half hour all four participated in an interesting game of charades. The result was that each new teacher got one of the keys in the woman's hand which in turn unlocked one of the tiny rooms on one of the multiple floors off the grand and worn marble staircase that served as the spine of the building. After bags had been deposited into rooms and towels distributed the woman continued to speak loudly in Turkish as she descended the stairs for a last time, the volume of her speech remaining constant until cut off completedly by the slam of a door somewhere below.

Huddled in Lane's room, the three finally felt they could speak.

"This is too funny," said Colin, peering out the window for any sign of life.

"I don't know whether to be thankful or run away," Matt was smiling, but the whole thing had been an ordeal.

"I know one thing," Lane had decided somewhere on the bridge to just start taking things as they came, "I need to take a long, hot, shower. Then maybe I'll be able to think about my next move." With mock annoyance she pushed both the boys out of her tiny room, telling them she'd meet them in an hour, closed the door, drew in a breath, and turned to survey the situation.

—

Colin rubbed his eyes and rose quickly, remembering he was supposed to meet Lane and Matt ages ago. Throwing on a black fleece, he left his room in a hurry and was interested to find the hallway just as silent as before his nap. The last of the evening light filtered through the streaked window and onto the hardwood floors, playing tricks with his eyes.

Feeling his way up the dark stairwell he searched in vain for the light switch the short woman had shown him earlier. Finally reaching the landing of the sixth (and final) floor, he saw a pair of double doors with a strip of warm yellow light at the bottom. Hesitantly he turned the knob and pushed the left side open.

A rush of warm air greeted him followed by a burst of laugher from somewhere near the far wall. He heard American top 40 music coming from computer speakers. The smell of frying chicken hit his nose. He noticed his friends were two of several people in the large room.

"Oh, here he is now! The train ride was so horrible I think we all just passed out when we got here," Lane moved away from the tall, black haired boy she was standing next to and came to escort Colin across the room.

"What's all this?" Colin smiled excitedly and Lane widened her eyes in agreement. "Is everyone here…?"

"Teachers with EnglishSpace," Lane smiled broadly.

"Looks like we're not the only one's here," Matt was sitting on a tall stool in front of a paper strewn bar. It seemed to divide the room into 'living space' (worn couches, a table, a TV) and 'kitchen' (four gas burners, dirty pots and pan piling up in a large, industrial sink, a half size refrigerator).

"This is Marissa," Lane indicated a lean 30ish woman with deep purple tinted hair.

"Yeah, nice to meet you," an Australian with what looked like hand-knitted clothes, she gave a vague smile before returning to some kind of work on her computer at the table.

"This is Marshall," Colin shook hands with the fey looking British boy hunched on the couch.

"And this is Rocko." They had reached the black haired man Lane had been standing next to. "He's going to take us to get something to eat."

Colin suddenly remembered how hungry he was and how the smell of cooking food wasn't helping. Involuntarily looking toward the source of the smell, he realized there was one more person he hadn't met since coming upstairs. He left Rocko and Lane and ambled over to where Matt seemed to be engaged in deep conversation a petite girl behind the counter.

"Colin, come 'mere," Matt motioned even though he was standing right next to him, "Meet Rey, or—uh, I should say…"

"Reyhan, but seriously call me Rey, even my mother does." The girl wiped her hand on her dark jeans and greeted Colin. It was odd, the words came out with a definite American accent (Midwestern even), and she looked Russian more than anything. But he had seen names like Reyhan in the past twenty four hours, and it was definitely Turkish.

"I was just talking to Rey about how long she's been here, seems she's almost as new as we are."

"It's been two weeks, but I've been to Istanbul before on family trips." Reyhan seemed to know the questions the boys were formulating in their heads.

"So you're...?" Colin searched for a polite way to express something he was unsure of. He failed, but the girl seemed used to it.

"First generation American, my mother's Turkish, and my dad is from Bulgaria."

"I think you're the only person we've met here that actually speaks two languages—well I guess I mean thre—with the Bulgarian." Colin suddenly realized Matt was flustered and tripping over himself.

Rey laughed knowingly; she had definitely been through this type of question and answer session before. She was wearing small black glasses that made her already translucent skin look even lighter. Her dark hair was pulled into a causal college-study-group bun. She placed both hands on the counter comfortably and just then Matt noticed her only feature that was any different from most of the girls he knew back home: her nose. Long and with a slight angle, it was graceful and reminded him of a drawing he had seen of a Roman woman in some museum. He thought he might have seen it before, on a couple of women in Athens, shopping in high-end stores and lunching beneath the Acropolis.

Finally prying Matt away from his new friend, the three followed Rocko down the stairs and out into the thick darkness of the twisting back streets of the city. Just as she was about to raise a question, Lane noticed Rocko dart forward and disappear around a corner. She eyed Matt and Colin and then plunged ahead in Rocko's path.

It was a shift from night into day. A rush of sounds, smells and lights hit them in the face and came at them from all sides. Where just a minute before they had been the only four people on the street, they were now in a crowd of hundreds. Involuntarily, all three except for Rocko moved backward toward the nearest shop window.

"This is the Istiklal," Rocko offered as he moved deftly forward through a seething crowd of pedetrians.

Lane was beside herself. For the first time in weeks she felt like she was really traveling. It was fascinating and lively, but definitely nothing like what she had pictured. In her mind, Istanbul was a place filled with roaming animals, spice markets, and if she was honest about her preconceptions, people in flowy tunics and pants. But what she saw now was none of those things. She spotted a MAC Cosmetic store, there were shoe shops everywhere, and she could just make out further down, the familiar green glow of a Starbucks sign. The people were more diverse than she had ever seen in her life; travelers with blond dreadlocks; Middle Eastern clerics with long, white garments and skull caps; girls with raven hair and impossibly high heels. There were women with headscarves, but perhaps more interestingly there were more without. She noticed a small clutch of teenagers, white and brown skinned and disgruntled looking, all of them wearing limited edition converse sneakers.

Still trying to adjust to their surrounds, the three almost missed Rocko dart forward again into the small, wood framed door of a restaurant.

Inside they found themselves in yet another world. The noise from the street was still audible, but was quickly overtaken by the high, thin strains of gypsy music. Rugs covered the wall, but ironically there were none on the floors. Wood paneling filled in the gaps and from the rustic looking rafters large metal farm tools gathered dust. Next to the door, sitting on a few worn pillows, a woman in a white apron and headscarf sat splay legged in front of a large table inches off the ground. She was patting out giant disks of what looked like bread dough. It was like something out of a picture book until Matt realized she was sitting directly in front of the street-facing window; little children's faces pressed up against the glass as if she were some kind of bread-making diorama.

The whole place, in fact, was a show. Less like something you stumble upon in a small Turkish village and more like something found in the "Turkish Village" section at Disney world.

They were directed to a low table with a hard bench on one side and two rickety looking stools on the other. With Rocko's help, they ordered several small and simple meat dishes, some of the bread the diorama woman had made, and washed it all down with bottled water—just to be on the safe side, Lane thought.

—

Like everything else in Istanbul so far, the next morning was a shock. Instead of waking naturally, Lane was roused from her bed in the pitch dark of five a.m. to what, at first, sounded like a cry for help. Eyes wide, standing in the middle of the tiny rug on her floor, it took her a full minute to realize that what she was hearing was not a murder in progress, but rather the Islamic call to prayer. One man's sad and straining voice pierced the darkness, sounding practiced but still uncertain. She sat down on the edge of the bed and waited for the a cappella to stop. After several minutes the song died away, and Lane fell back into uneasy rest.

Exactly two hours later another song woke her. This time it was morning, bright and cold, that greeted her as she opened her eyes. Opening the curtains to shock herself into consciousness, she came face to face with a large pair of bronze eyes and a familiar name. The court yard of Atatürk middle school lay just feet across an ally way from her second story window, and just as soon as she had noticed the children lined up outside the building she also realized she was only wearing a small pair of boxers and a ragged tank top.

Quickly re-closing the large, dusty drapes, she could hear the song reaching its climax. It was ominous and grand and sung by a recorded chorus of a hundred voices. It had an official quality to it, like something out of Soviet Russia. Lane would soon come to know it as the Turkish National Anthem. Every morning, from the school's loud speakers, it woke every one of the teachers in EnglishSpace's temporary housing. A fact probably celebrated by the house's keeper, the large woman that had shown the three to their rooms and then disappeared.

Fatma was the only name the other teachers had given her; no last name it seemed. They knew very little about her. She was devout, got up every morning before dawn, had a husband only one person had ever seen, mostly kept to herself, and didn't speak a word of English. One thing was certain, however—she didn't need words to convey her judgment and constant displeasure with everyone living in *her* house.

It was Fatma who startled Lane with a heavy handed knock on the glass pane of her door just after the anthem had finished and the bell for first period had rung. Opening the door slightly, she was surprised to see the small woman, broom in one hand, looking inquiringly into her face. She produced a bulky cordless phone and shoved it into Lane's hand. She disappeared before any objections could be raised.

Lane put the receiver to her ear, "Hello?"

"Hello, Lane," The voice hadn't actually said her name, but something closer to the word 'lawn', "This is Fatih at English Space, how are you." It wasn't a question.

Lane vaguely remembered Matt speaking to this man in Athens to set everything up. Why he had chosen to call her, she wasn't sure, "Oh, I'm good, how are you?"

"Thank you very much," said Fatih, "Now, we would like to see you for *brunch* here at EnglishSpace, will you be coming?"

The fact that Fatih had said brunch made Lane chuckle. His tone hadn't suggested a deep understanding of the concept, "Yes, should we all three come now?"

"Yes, come now, thank you and see you soon." The other end clicked. Lane wondered what to do next. After dressing quickly and running cold water over her face, she climbed to the top floor where she luckily found Marissa and the two boys eating boiled eggs.

"Yeah, right, I'm just heading over there now," Marissa told the three after Lane had related her strange phone call, "You can come with, if ya' like." Still bewildered from all the events of the past twenty four hours, they donned their thick winter coats and emerged into an unseasonably warm morning.

—

Completely out of place, Lane thought, shocked by the imposing building they found themselves standing in front of. After an interesting ten minute bus ride back through Taksim square and North on an unfamiliar highway, Marissa had lead them down yet another set of winding cobble stone streets until they had come to a small square. All the buildings were relatively small, none larger than two stories. All looked slightly derelict and at least a hundred years old—all except for the EnglishSpace administrative building.

Sandwiched between a bar and an abandoned apartment building, the façade rose six stories, an unbroken plane of tinted glass. The entrance way was the only indication it was a place of business as opposed to a massive solar panel. Sets of double doors capped by an awning the color of a traffic cone. "EnglishSpace Orange" Marissa called it.

It was this special brand of orange that greeted them again once they entered. Not just as an accent to every beige wall, but covering nearly every surface that was not flooring. Books, ruck sacks, pens, office chairs, and even computer monitors; all dipped, it seemed, in the same huge vat of industrial orange, and then emblazoned with striking white block letters shouting "EnglishSpace."

Matt pointed out to the other two the entrance way. Directly applied to the floor were large sticky letters in the offending color:

"Bu Iste Inglizce Aralik"

And below them, the translation

"This Space is EnglishSpace"

Lane started to wonder aloud at the slogan but before she could, they were all herded into a small room where a table was laid with coffee cups, Nescafe, and cookies: brunch.

Despite protests, the three new teachers would be shipped off to different branches of the EnglishSpace "family". Matt lucked out by being placed in a classroom facing the Bosphorus. Colin was horrified to learn he would have to make a forty five minute commute every day to somewhere south of Sultanahmet, and Lane found herself teaching at EnglishSpace's flagship school, just off Taksim.

Three books, a class outline, and a set of markers was all they had received from Fatih's assistant. That and the English version of their contracts. Holding the EnglishSpace orange pen, Lane paused. She looked at the length of employment, written in capitol letter: ELEVEN MONTHS. She wondered what she was doing; she had only been in Turkey twenty four hours and she was about to commit to a full year.

Lane thought for a minute about what was in front of her. Then she thought about Essex Antiques, Middlesborough, and the life she had left not too long ago. Their Wine Monday conversation was still ringing in her ears. She tried hard to think of a reason not to sign. All that came to mind was Colin's face the day he had quit. All she could hear in her head was news reports of the worsening recession. She looked for guidance towards the wall where a small flag hung behind a desk. On it was the star and crescent of the Turkish republic, and the overlaid image of a commanding Atatürk. Something in his eyes told her to take the leap.

So, with a deep breath, she clicked the white tip on the pen, scribbled her mark next to the "X" and dated the copy. Her first class started the following Monday.

Three days later Lane found herself in the lobby of a large, crumbling building directly off the Istiklal. As she climbed the stairs of the EnglishSpace main branch, she noticed lighted orange signs with the company logo and catchphrase plastered on each stair step, creating the affect that she was moving up in line for an Epcot-style roller coaster.

Lane was strangely comforted by the sight of Marissa's wildly untamed hair as she entered the teacher's room. At the far end of the space bright morning sun streamed in from a pair of French windows that stood slightly ajar.

"G'morning," Marissa cooed from behind a desk on the opposite wall. Lane realized no one else was present.

"Good morning… are we the only ones?" She checked her watch, which told her it was, in fact, thirty minutes before class.

"Yeah, I only came in early to use the internet," Marissa seemed to miss the point of the question.

"And everyone else is…"

"Oh, right. They should trickle in sometime before the first bell," this time she didn't bother looking up from the ancient desktop computer.

"Good to know," Lane said to herself, and set about claiming her workspace at one of the carrels along the wall.

She quickly realized she had nothing to do, having planned the first week's worth of classes in a panic state the night before. So she began leafing through the worn reference materials kept in a tiny bookcase next to a set of lockers.

Just then, the sound of books dropping sent her spinning around to face a tall, disheveled man lumbering towards her.

"Bok!" screamed the unkempt stranger as he awkwardly squatted to pick up teaching materials. His coarse black hair and heavy beard made him appear middle aged, but as he rose, Lane noticed his eyes were those of a man about her age.

"Oh, heeeey," he said in too-familiar tone, "I'm Noah. I heard we were getting fresh meat—how are you?"

Lane tried not to laugh at the strange greeting and the fact that Noah's ill-fitting pants fell inches above his ankles.

"Hi, yes, I'm Lane," she made a motion to help with his books, but he had already thrown them into a waiting carol and offered his hand.

Who *is* this strange person she thought as she smiled back at him, "What was that you just yelled?" She asked.

Noah smiled widely, "Oh, it means *shit*."

Lane looked to Marissa for confirmation, but she was still staring at the computer screen, apparently avoiding conversations; or oblivious; Lane wasn't sure which.

"First day and what not?" The odd boy was asking her.

"Yeah, it's been interesting so far…" was all she could think to say.

"Yeah, just wait until class," he said, and before she could ask what he meant, he had jetted out of the room presumably in search of something. Lane turned again to Marissa, but before catching her eye several more teachers began to file into the tiny space.

The next few hours were a flurry. Lane's students, mostly college aged, were all surprisingly and unsurprisingly typical 20 year-olds: eye brow rings, skinny jeans, brightly colored Nike Airs. Lane's image of a room full of headscarf wearing women was again proven wrong. The traditional girls she did have made a point of wearing the latest jeans (as tight as possible) and carrying shiny designer (and knock-off) bags.

Between classes she took smoke breaks with her students and the other teachers (non-smokers were the exception). She met Thom, a kind middle aged man who wore a tie and greeted her excitedly as a fellow southerner. There was Marcus, a thirty year old with something to prove who spent the entire break hitting on much younger Turkish girls. Marissa introduced her to Noah again who, in turn pointed out Marie (an early forties Brit), Paul (a late thirties Kiwi), and Solomon, a dark skinned balding Canadian man.

After class, she caught Noah in the corner of the teacher's room while he was filling out papers.

"So how did it go today?" He said without looking up.

"Oh, great, my students are…" Lane wasn't sure how to place them.

"—Teenagers," Noah offered.

"Exactly," she conceded, "So…"

"So?" He looked up at her while packing his ink stained messenger bag.

"So does anyone else work here?" She wasn't sure what she was digging for.

Noah's eyes searched her and then something looked like it clicked, "Oh… You mean does anyone else our age work here?"

"That's exactly what I mean," she was relieved.

"Well, yes, but only a couple. I'll introduce you to them. Really most of the people our age work at other branches. Aren't your friends working for EnglishSpace, too?"

"Yeah, they are, but I wasn't sure how many branches there were."

Noah smiled broadly again as he began exiting, "More than I could name right now. Tell you what, come out tonight at I'll tell you all about it," he called over his shoulder. He was gone before she could ask where 'out' was.

Later that evening in her dusty cell at the teacher Lojment (the word she had learned for lodging or, based on the teacher residence, it probably should have meant halfway house), Lane debated whether or not she wanted to go out with a bunch of people she had literally just met. While thinking, she ambled down the stairwell to the floor shared by Matt and Colin. The crack under both doors was dark, and no one responded to her light knocking, so she headed up to the top floor 'lounge' area. They were nowhere to be found. Marissa, however, greeted her with unusual enthusiasm.

"Hey love, what are you up to?"

Lane was surprised but happy with her tone, and even more surprised to see the usually casual woman done up in heels and a slightly scandalous top, "Not much, I was looking for Colin and Matt but I—have you seen them?"

"Sorry, love. I *did* see Reyhan, but that was hours ago…"

Lane wondered why Marissa thought she would care what Reyhan was doing, "Oh well," she smiled and started to leave.

"Hold on, hold on, what are you doing tonight?"

Lane shrugged, noting the large glass of red wine in Marissa's hand "I guess nothing, which is fine."

"It most certainly is not!"

Lane's surprise turned to intrigue, why did Marissa care so much? "It's not?" she asked cautiously.

"Of course it's not! You're coming out with us. It is New Year's after all."

Lane was blind-sided. Had she really been so preoccupied that she had forgotten the date? Marissa seemed to take her silence as acceptance, because she quickly grabbed the half-empty wine bottle and whisked her by the arm down to her room, "Ok, let's see what you've got to wear!"

Standing in front of the rusted metal locker that served as her closet, Lane began to ruminate on why her friends had left her to her own devices. But as Marissa started throwing skirts at her while simultaneously pouring her wine, Lane decided the best course of action was to accept the invitation in front of her—after all, she thought, sitting in her room would only give her more time to get depressed.

"There's just one problem," Lane called to Marissa while changing behind the open door of the locker, "I think I have plans with Noah."

"Mate, it's the same party. There really aren't that many of us…"

Emerging in a thick fall skirt that was still too light for the frigid New Year's air (it was confusing how quickly the temperature seemed to change), she was pleased by Marissa's fervent applause. Still, as they exited the building, she couldn't help feel a twinge of sadness as she passed the boys' floor.

—

EnglishSpace was not a mom and pop operation. The central office turned out to be only the tip of an orange colored iceberg. Ten different locations in Istanbul alone; seven on the European side, three on the Asian, two specified "testing and resource centers", and innumerable kiosks in every mall and public square in the city. The Starbucks of English language schools, as Noah put it.

Marissa gave her the lay out on the way to the bar, and once inside, Noah continued the debriefing.

The empire didn't stop with EnglishSpace. Its holding company was a much larger and less visible organization.

Within the first week, Lane had heard reports that the all-powerful "Taş Group" owned, among other things, an insurance company, various travel agencies, and (most disturbingly to her) the second most read English Language newspaper in Turkey; a seriously hilarious publication they were encouraged to use in class.

Lane listened intently in the back booth of a loud bar tucked into a sketchy alleyway downtown.

Noah leaned in close as he explained the ins and outs of the nebulous organization they worked for. The music was a strange mix of Turkish pop and Turkish traditional which emanated alternately from several loud speakers scattered around the small, wooden space.

The people in their group were the odd mix of EnglishSpace teachers, mysterious non-EnglishSpace foreigners, and what seemed like Turkish EnglishSpace students.

"Has anyone seen Matt and Colin?" she asked Noah after a few beers.

He looked unconcerned and answered casually, "They were here earlier, but must have gone to Taksim for the light show."

"Do we want to go there?" She asked.

"God no! Have you ever been to Times Square? It's even worse," Marissa shouted across the table as she handed them both shots.

Lane was a bit disappointed, but decided that being with her present company was better than wandering the streets of Istanbul alone on a holiday night. Not wanting to seem ungrateful she quickly downed the small glass of milky looking, licorice flavored liquor.

"Great!" She yelled over the music, "Uzo?"

"No!" Noah screamed back, "Raki!"

—

Undaunted, Colin continued searching for the correct bus (having just gotten off two incorrect ones). If getting to his new job was this hard, he thought, how bad would the job itself be?

He was cold, and still unnerved at having not seen Lane for the past couple of days. (He, Matt and Reyhan had searched all New Year's for her, but seemed to always just miss her.)

One hour and five Turkish Lira later, he hopped off in the middle of nowhere. Rows of cinder-block housing stretched unbroken to the Marmara Sea like giant frozen waves. On the bus ride away from town, he had passed through the ancient Byzantine walls of Theodosius. "Great," he thought to himself, "I'm in a 1,500 year old suburb."

He was surprised how happy he was to see the bright, day-glo orange of the EnglishSpace logo above his school. At least he hadn't ended up miles from where he was supposed to be without any language skills or sense of direction.

Wedged between two identical townhouses, the Bakirköy EnglishSpace branch looked as if someone had stuck a multistory shopping center in the middle of a residential neighborhood not zoned for it—a thought he soon found out was very close to the truth.

As he opened the large, modern, glass door emblazoned with the school's brand, he heard a shrill cry behind him. Turning, expecting to see a robbery in action, he was instead greeted with a strange sight: a long row of chickens walking resolutely down the very urban sidewalk.

"Are you going in or out?" A voice shook him back to reality, and he turned around once more to find a tall girl with a defined bob about his age, standing in the half-open doorway.

"Uh, in—definitely in," he managed, and the tall girl laughed loudly; slick, raven black hair swishing back and forth with the motion of her head.

"You look like you could use coffee," she said in an Australian accent. Or was it New Zealand?

"Um, thanks, but I should really get to class."

"Oh, don't worry about that, no one ever shows up on time. C'mon, we're just gonna pop 'round the corner," she didn't leave him much option as she had already begun walking away while speaking.

"Um, ok," Colin hurried to catch up, and then wondered why he was following a complete stranger at top speed, but instead of asking her name he simply said, "Are we going for Turkish coffee?"

The strange girl laughed loudly again without turning around and replied, "Not unless you want your fortune told. There's a Starbucks just up the way."

Now he was seriously confused, "You mean all the way out here, in the middle of nowhere?"

But the girl marched on, twisting and turning down side streets until she had led him out onto a large boulevard.

Colin noticed the buildings open up into a flat, surprisingly modern public square. At the far end a giant, polished, maroon and tinted glass structure loomed over the other buildings.

"What is it?" he said in an almost reverential tone.

Laughing uncontrollably now, the girl stopped, turned to him and simply said, "I know they have malls in The States."

Half an hour later in the plush seating area of a fairly new Starbucks, Bethany, as she called herself, had filled him in on almost everything. Above her, a discreet, framed portrait of Atatürk reminded Colin that they may be inside a very American franchise, but they were still in Mustafa Kemal's country.

"Oh, and one more thing, if you ever need to do a number two, come here to the mall," Bethany ended her tutorial.

Barely containing himself at her use of "number two" Colin felt comfortable enough to ask, "Dirty bathrooms at the school?"

"No," she said casually, "I just imagine you wouldn't be used to Turkish toilets yet."

Still wondering at her response, Colin asked one final question on their walk back, "Is your name really Bethany?"

"How did you know?" She smiled slightly.

"The way you ordered coffee, and something else, I'm not sure what."

She wrinkled her nose slightly, which emphasized her freckles, and then, just as quickly, developed a slightly serious look, "It's Bilgin, actually, but don't mention it to the students, education from a native speaker is worth four times as much, and you'll find out how picky they can be."

"But you *are* a native speaker, aren't you?"

"Of course, but perception is everything."

"So you changed your name for your class?"

"Well technically EnglishSpace did, but it was just easier to have all the teachers use the same name, so eventually it just, kind of became who I am here," she laughed again loudly as she rushed off to class and left Colin to think about what kind of an organization he had signed up with.

—

Bilgin/Bethany quickly proved to be invaluable. Colin's Los Angeles-sized commute meant he spent the entirety of five days a week in the odd, parallel city that was Bakırköy, so an instant, Turkish-speaking friend was almost too good to be true.

Within the first week, Bethany had successfully introduced him to almost every corner of the teaming edge-city: shopping centers, best buffet lunch, streets to avoid, Burger King, Sephora (for free perfume samples), train station, residential districts, the houses of the super-rich and super-poor (often on the same block), street vendors, historic sites, government buildings—it was all too much. Colin struggled to understand how a self-contained megalopolis could exist so far from the center of the city.

"It's called a borough," Bethany observed in a rye tone, "Haven't you been to Brooklyn?"

And she was right, everything that existed north of the Golden Horn seemed to have its equivalent in the far south.

"Is there a whole world like this on the Asian side?" Colin asked awestruck over lunch one day.

"No, over there everyone rides camels and weaves rugs for a living… I'm joking," she quickly added when Colin looked like he believed her, "It's like this in a lot of places," Bethany responded, "You could live your whole life in Istanbul and almost never hit Taksim—if you didn't want to."

And apparently she didn't, Colin noticed. Every night for the next two weeks, he begged her to come out uptown with the rest of the teachers, and every night she politely declined, citing a lack of money.

Staying in Bakirköy for drinks that Friday, Colin finally wrestled the truth from her.

"My family's just moved back from Australia, and there's really no work to speak of. Both my parents have had to take low paying jobs."

"And you?" he inquired politely.

"And I'm making a decent living… all of which goes to pay for my little sister's schooling."

"Aren't there public schools?" he asked before thinking about it.

"Of course, but have you ever seen the inside of a school for juvenile offenders…?" She laughed loudly, and, despite wanting to know more, Colin laughed with her.

—

Colin soon realized most of the other teachers at the branch were going to keep to themselves. Sitting quietly inside the crusty teacher's room in the back of the building, he would wait patiently for one of them to introduce themselves, but after a few days he figured out the introductions weren't coming. His southern sensibilities were slightly offended, and his standoffish nature kept him from introducing himself like Lane or Matt would have.

Finally, Bethany let him in on the secret. Leading him up an impossibly narrow set of stairs on the fifth floor during a break, she reassured him once they neared the dark, top landing.

"Don't worry, you're going to love it," she smiled, "By the way, do you smoke?"

But before he could answer she had turned, opened a rusty half-door and plunged ahead into a blinding rectangle of daylight. Emerging from the Alice in Wonderland rabbit hole and shielding his eyes against the light, he was struck to see the majority of the teachers lounging on tiny stools on a large roof deck; huddled against the bitter wind; all of them puffing away like tiny, rooftop chimneys.

"So this is where everyone disappears to…" he drifted off realizing Bethany was across the roof gesturing to him. Wrapping his coat collar against his neck he joined her and three other teachers by the railing.

"So?" She nudged him.

Colin ignored his fellow instructors and turned completely around, captivated by the scene laid out before him. Crumbling apartment blocks, piled one on top of the other in a motionless race toward the sea, cold and smoking in the winter air. For miles in each direction all he could see were ochre and rust and taupe colored rectangles in every size and shape. On the horizon, the gray Marmara Sea stretched to infinity, holding in its grasp a large clutch of giant Russian tanker ships.

Along the coast line, which stretched in a gargantuan curve into a misty vanishing point, he saw several, large domed roofs, the size of city blocks and seemingly supported by soaring, cone-topped spires. It was as if this mosque-line was holding the entire city back from falling immediately into the water.

Far to the North he saw a familiar (albeit foreign-looking) site. It was the point at which the three major water ways of the city came together in a peaceful union. The break in the land where Europe stopped and Asia started.

"This is…" Colin started.

"A good reason to smoke?" The voice was a new one that had come from behind him. Turning, he saw a ruddy looking face and a close-cropped, white beard that belonged to a man as tall as he was. The gentleman was older, mid-fifties, Colin thought; kind face and professional dress.

"Hi, I'm Garrison," The man said, "I'd shake your hand, but," he raised the cigarette in his right hand while exhaling.

"Ha, don't worry about it," Colin said.

"And this is Mary," said Bethany, "and Adelaide."

Colin waved awkwardly to the two thirty-something women to indicate a greeting.

"Sigara Istioymusin?" Bethany held out a thin, white cylinder.

"I assume that means would I like one?" Colin said, "I really shouldn't—wait, is that a Winston?"

"Yeah it's about all you can get around here that isn't too expensive," Mary said.

"You know I think I will have one."

"What's so special about Winstons?" Bethany asked, intrigued.

Smiling, Colin realized it would be easier than he thought to find friends in this new city, "Let me tell you a bit about North Carolina…"

—

Reyhan Bereket bit her tongue as she watched Matt ramble on helplessly in Turkish to the waiter. After he had finished, she coolly ordered her ice cream in slowly spoken English, to which the man said a grateful thank you and retreated to the kitchen.

"How did you know he—" Matt was stunned.

"This is Mado, all the waiters speak English," Reyhan said of the upscale ice cream parlor they had gone to after Matt's first day of work.

"But you could have ordered in perfect Turkish," he was still a bit confused.

"Well perfect is on overstatement," she said casually, "and sometimes it's nice to just be an American, you know?"

Matt wasn't sure he quite understood, but he liked the way she had said it. "Are all the places around here like this?" he asked.

"Have you not been to Beşiktaş, yet?" She asked, continued quickly with, "Duh, of course you haven't. Ok, here's how it is."

Reyhan's thin nose and graceful eyes mesmerized Matt as she explained to him the upscale location of their school's branch in relation to the rest of the city. He was amazed at how she managed to remain slightly mysterious even when saying the word 'duh'. Finally she asked if he had any questions. He shook his head.

She laughed slowly, her smile broadening, "So what did I say?"

"North: rich. South: not rich. Asian side: mystery," he smiled back.

"Something like that," she said as she widened her eyes and dove into her ridiculously large sundae.

———

"I think it's assumed at this point, don't you?" Reyhan's sarcasm was undercut by a pitch perfect Turkish accent that she could slip into at will. She was referring to her and Matt's after-work cocktail, which had happened every day for the past week.

"I guess you're right," Matt laughed at himself.

"So where are we going?" The question, seemingly innocuous, came from the back of the teacher's room and made both of them cringe slightly. "I heard the W hotel has a *sweet* bar, and all the waitresses speak English," the voice continued.

"Um, that's a little expensive, Mitchell," Reyhan's response was amazingly civil.

"C'mon, I told ya' to call me Mitch," The boy's playful attitude was lost on them.

Matt searched Reyhan for an out, but she failed to come up with a response quickly enough. So, grudgingly, he suggested they all three go walking in the hopes of stumbling on a bar. Mitchell bounded ahead of them, leading the way in a country he had spent even less time in than Matt had.

Mitchell Haber was perhaps the only thing Matt found unsavory about his new workplace. Tall, and wide jawed, the late twenty-something could almost have passed for attractive until he started speaking, and speaking, and speaking.

Mitch was rich. And the more he let people know it, the less Matt believed him.

"I'm kind of loaded," he had said to Matt within the first five minutes of their meeting.

"You're drunk already?" Matt had joked, but Mitch didn't catch it.

Every day, Mitch would make everyone in the teacher's room uncomfortable with grossly over-acted and poorly told stories involving hardcore drugs, sexual escapades, money, or some combination of the three. Matt had almost found it so ridiculous that it was funny—but then Mitch decided Matt was his new best friend.

"M & M making the spot hot!" Mitch yelled as they entered the small tavern they found near the base of the Bosphorus Bridge. The two elderly patrons in the back cast disapproving stares toward the front door. Cringing, Matt turned to Reyhan, who executed a perfect deadpan stare behind Mitch's back.

Two hours and three vodkas later, Mitch was in rare form, speaking with such emphasis he didn't even realize neither Matt nor Reyhan had spoken for the past 20 minutes.

"Man, I am such a *duuuuumb assss*," he said suddenly, his Chicago accent drawing out every last note.

Reyhan was shaken awake, "Ha, why's that, Mitch," her civility had long since dropped and her words were pure acid, but Mitch didn't notice.

"Holy shit, you guys are, like, *on a date*."

Matt stuttered, not sure how to respond to such a ridiculous statement from such a drunken man, and then he heard Reyhan speak up.

"Dammit, you caught us Mitch, we *are* on a date." Matt didn't know what to think, so he kept quiet.

"Holy shit," Mitch said again even more loudly, "I have such a nose for these things! Well, listen, fuck me, I do *not* want to be in you guyses way... I mean *fuck me.*" Despite his protest he didn't move from his chair.

Taking a quick que from Reyhan, Matt leapt from his seat and uttered the only thing he could think of, "Don't worry about it dude, I mean happens to the best of us—"

"Right it does brother! Right it does…" Mitch said as they exited the tavern to the delight of the regular customers, "I mean *fuck me,* you two have a good time, and just *tell me* next time," he said and began making a semi lewd gesture while winking at Matt.

Biting his tongue so as not to burst into laughter Matt followed Reyhan quickly away from the still grinning Mitchell. Once safely down a back street and out of ear shot, the two let loose in howls.

"What the fuck the just happened to us," Reyhan looked genuinely bewildered.

"I don't know," Matt responded, "But all I can say is *fuck me!"*

Reyhan set off on a new bout of laugher that lasted for several minutes.

After a while, still smiling, Matt casually mentioned, "Quick thinking back there, that was good cover story."

Reyhan seemed a little caught off guard, "Oh that—yeah, I mean, that's the only thing guys like Mitch respond too, isn't it? Girls and sex."

"Ha, I guess you're right," Matt said searching for any hint of seriousness in her voice.

"You know, if it really works that well, we might have to pretend to be dating for the rest of the year," she laughed loudly and brushed his arm with her hand.

"That would hilarious," Matt said trying to laugh back, but soon they both fell into an easy silence that lasted for hours as they strolled north, tracing the edge of the Bosphorus until their feet gave out and they were forced to catch a cab home.

—

The first ten days at work were a struggle for Lane.

The job itself was the easy part. What happened after work, however, was far more daunting.

She quickly discovered the pointlessness of her native language outside the class room (and sometimes inside the classroom). Perhaps in Rome, or even Athens, she thought, her feeble attempts at sign language would have been met with a helpful face and a little bit of English, but in Istanbul, there was only one language, and at the moment she didn't speak it.

The words themselves were deceptive, constructed using the Latin alphabet, at first glance they looked like cake compared to Greek. But letters can have multiple meanings from country to country, and Lane soon found herself in a world of odd extra symbols and Arabic inflection. It was like a bad dream: the signs on the street looked readable, but up close they were a complete mystery.

Lane got off one evening exhausted from a four hour stretch trying to converse with beginner level students. Mentally unable to pull out her phrase book and try ordering at a fast food joint, she decided the grocery store was the best option.

The grocery store was god's gift to foreigners, she often thought. In a grocery store, she could make her selection without interruption, move through the line silently, read the total on the electronic display and pay without uttering a word.

She was not so lucky this night. Grabbing her items and moving through the line, everything was going well, until the gruff man behind the register posed a question. Lane had no idea what he had said, but at least she knew it was a question. Giving him the Turkish word for "please", followed by a "yes" and a scared look, she became petrified when he continued to question her. He grabbed the offending item (a bag of potatoes) and shoved it in her face. She was at a loss. Patrons were becoming annoyed, but all she could do was stand there, struggling intensely to mime the phrase, "I don't even want the potatoes, they're for my friend."

Finally the woman behind her moved and let pass a tall, clean cut man in a pinstripe suit.

"I'm sorry," the man said, "but he wants you to go back and weigh the potatoes."

Lane must have looked more desperate than she thought, because after a second, the older gentleman asked loudly, "Do you speak English?"

She stammered, "Oh, yes—ah… Thank you, I just got here and, oh—ah, thanks."

Completing her transaction as quickly as possible, she stuffed her purchases into her overlarge teacher bag and almost tripped over herself getting out of the store. Once on the street she noticed she had left her large bottles of mineral water, but refused to go back for them.

She had an immediate instinct to retreat behind the large metal doors of the teacher house but just as quickly realized all that waited for her was a solitary dinner and Turkish television. Turning in the opposite direction, she walked as if in a trance across Taksim Square and down a cobblestone side street she had never taken before. Her teacher bag swung with the weight of the hard-won potatoes as she descended the steep incline of the street.

The bright neon of Taksim lighted her way for a few blocks and then generally died away; the more subdued yellow of the occasional street lamp taking its place. She noted how quickly the buildings had turned from icy glass covered high rises to shadowy and crumbling turn of the century façades. Soon even these faded as the neighborhood transitioned into the sagging and dusty clapboards of the one and two story mid-century buildings that made up the bulk of the city.

Lane had seen these buildings before, stretching like sad matchboxes into the horizon from her vantage point on one of the bridges or the roof of some Beyolgu restaurant. But she had never been this close to them before; their worn, peeling paint chipping under her fingers as she ran her hand along them; their normally pastel colors turned to a monochrome of sepia by the streetlamps.

It wasn't long before she had no idea where was. She realized she must have been walking for at least half an hour. She thought she should be panicked, but the incident at the grocery store and an intense pang of hunger were all she could think about.

Rounding a corner in what she thought was the right direction, she came to a narrow street lighted only by the green-tinged blue sign of a tiny restaurant.

It was the kind of place she normally wouldn't think twice about. No more than fifteen feet wide, she could see from the street a single lightbulb dangling from the ceiling and the back wall covered in large, faded photographs of prepared dishes. It was a greasy spoon; and not the kind of hidden gem greasy spoon the New York Times would rave about but a real, dirty, uninteresting place where the customers were all local and the food was just food.

Something she couldn't put a finger on forced her across the deserted street and into the door with a slight jingle from the tiny bell above it.

A man looked up, after a pause, from behind a small refrigerated case. Lane was surprised to see him smile. She approached the counter slowly, discarding her heavy bag in a chair at one of the two tables. The man remained mercifully silent.

She looked at the large food posters and noticed one with a spinach pastry that looked like spanakopita. The word "börek" was printed on it in large, yellowed letters. Lane absentmindedly repeated the word to the man and he immediately produced a large square of brown and green.

Sitting and eating in silence she studied the oily surface of the flowered table coverings, the cracked marble top of a plant stand in the corner, and the looming but benevolent smile of a fez-wearing Atatürk in a small picture behind the counter.

Finishing and returning her plate, she pulled a creased map from the bottom of her bag and could only muster the strength to ask, "Taksim?"

The man nodded, and without a word grabbed a small ball point pen from the counter and traced a black line from their current location back to the center of town.

"Teşekkurler," Lane managed in one try. She wanted to say so much more and realized her eyes must have said it for her.

"Teşekkurler," returned the man, his eyes telling her he understood. She hit the street again feeling more peaceful than she had all day.

Back at the Lojment she climbed the icy marble staircase to the sixth floor kitchen. The room was empty. As she stashed the potatoes under the sink she remember it was Colin who had asked her for them. Where was he?

The day before, she and the boys had all bought cheap, pay-as-you-go phones she lovingly referred to as "fisher price mobiles" because of their kid-friendly, bright blue plastic shells. After rearranging all of her food inside of the refrigerator she checked hers for messages while descending the stairs to her room: there were none. She read her emails in bed after brushing her teeth: no word. She stopped herself from sending plaintive text messages to her two friends but went to bed more concerned than she wanted to admit. Matt and Colin had every right to do what they wanted, she told herself. Even so, it was hours before she fell asleep.

On a frigid morning two weeks later Lane awoke late for class. Never completely warm, her room that morning was even colder than usual; she could distinctly see the hot stream of her breath against the morning light. Racing down the treacherous stairs of the teacher house, she didn't even think about her choice of footwear, but was soon horrified to find herself standing in a half foot of lightly packed snow, still white despite the less than clean alleyway in which the teacher house was located.

She stopped and sighed; never once in all her packing for Greece or plans for Turkey had she thought about winter wear. Istanbul doesn't exactly scream snow shoes, but standing shin deep in a small drift of white powder she had to question her assumptions.

No time to think, she began cutting a narrow path down the middle of the backstreet.

Her usual route to the large Taksim branch took her though several small side streets, onto the wide pedestrian Istiklal shopping avenue and across the square itself. On the best of days it was an obstacle course, first avoiding cars that seemed to prowl the small alleys looking for victims, next shoving her way through an endless throng of ambling shoppers, and finally darting across the four lanes of high speed traffic in the square. On that day, however, things took a different course.

Bursting onto the Istiklal with a good deal of speed, she had given up worrying about her soaked shoes. The usually gray avenue had been bathed in an icy primer, and very few of the usual shoppers had braved the weather. The worn façades of the buildings on either side usually conjured images of a faded empire with their European accents. But against the canvas of snow, and shaded by the red glow of neon lamps, they looked theatrical, like a carefully crafted stage set in which decay was something to be celebrated rather than hidden.

Taking her time in Taksim square, she noticed the entrance to the Marmara Hotel, one of the tallest buildings in the city. Giant SUVs formed a long steaming black line in front of the revolving doors while patrons wrapped in enormous furs buzzed around the valet stand and past an icy bust of Atatürk. It was a Turkey she hadn't seen before: simplified, understated, luxurious. Lane thought she could be in New York or Paris except for the large snowcapped domes of mosques peeking out from behind glass covered buildings like giant full moons.

Ducking down a side street towards school, she stopped briefly at the entrance to the multistory building. Since Taksim was one of the highest points in the city, most of the streets off of it inclined down towards either urban valleys or bodies of water. The street EnglishSpace was on fell sharply downward toward the Bosphorus and opened up into a view of the straight and the Asian side in the distance. Mesmerized, Lane watched as flock of gulls shot down the street and, reaching the bottom, rocketed upward through a small cloud and out over the water. They disappeared towards the Asian side, which, white and smoking, resembled a dream city.

—

That evening Lane met Colin and Matt at a restaurant in Tünel, a small square at the end of the Istiklal where you could either walk down an endless flight of stairs towards the water, or take the easy way out and hop on the funicular train.

Climbing a narrow staircase inside the eatery, she was surprised to find the two boys with Reyhan from the teacher house.

"Hey Lane!" Matt greeted her with more than his usual enthusiasm, "I brought Reyhan, but you don't have to talk to her, she's just here to translate."

"Shut up!" Reyhan gave Matt a playful punch. Lane was a bit shocked and looked to Colin, who was nose deep in an Eye Witness Istanbul.

"So I take it things are going well at the Bosphorus school?" Lane smiled.

"Oh just great," Reyhan answered before Matt could open his mouth, "I feel like I've already met so many people and my students are just great. Did Matt tell you that we're sharing an activity class? Oh my god, Matt, tell her what that middle aged student said today!"

It was a lot to take in. Lane hadn't had time to really get to know anyone in the house, and even if she did, most of them seemed to be in their own world. She hadn't even really talked to anyone at her school, but kept telling herself that she just needed to give it another week.

"First I want to hear about Lane's day. Did you get to work ok this morning?" Matt asked.

"Yeah, it was ok—quiet. And then I passed a view of the Bosphorus, and I was late, but I still had to stop it was so—"

"Oh, sweet, the food." Colin threw his book down and started moving glasses to accommodate the plates. Lane started to continue, but the boys were already involved in another conversation with Reyhan about the proper way to ask for ketchup.

After dinner, Reyhan ordered Turkish coffee for everyone, which came piping hot in four slightly mismatched Persian flowered cups. She instructed the other three to add as much sugar as possible and warned that it wasn't like the espresso they were used to. Lane, never afraid of strong coffee, passed on the sugar and started to drink the thick black liquid straight. The top foam was okay, she thought, but as she got further into the cup an unintentional frown started to form on her brow. Colin and Matt sat entranced, listening to Reyhan explain how her Aunt could read the grounds to tell your fortune. Lane was confused; were the rest of them drinking the same beverage? The dark coffee sat on her tongue while she tried to make up her mind to swallow. The strong scents of coffee and chocolate filled her nose, but in her mouth things took a bad turn. She tried to think of nice ways to describe it—leather? Tobacco? But mostly she just wanted to call it what it was—burnt and gritty. And hadn't they served them the same thing in Athens and called it Greek coffee? She looked to the other three for confirmation but only saw delight on their faces as they dipped tiny cookies into the tire-flavored syrup.

"So what are you up to this weekend Reyhan?" Colin asked casually.

"Oh, actually I'm taking Matt over to the Asian side, I can't believe he's been here a month and not been yet!"

Lane was surprised at the tone this girl was using, so familiar, like they had known each other for years. She decided to jump in before things got out of hand.

"Colin, I was actually going to ask you if you had plans, I'd really love to go see that palace on the Bosphorous."

"Oh, sounds like fun, Lane, but I actually have plans of my own, my class is taking me out in Sultanahmet for drinks, which

should be fun since half of them don't seem to approve of booze."
Everyone laughed except Lane.

"Oh, that's cool, good to get to know your students,
right?" she awkwardly responded. She looked back toward Matt,
fully expecting him to invite her along on his trip with Reyhan, but
soon realized the invitation wasn't coming.

Spilling back onto the Istiklal, the foursome broke apart
near the teacher house to run errands. Lane tried to put her finger
on what had been weird about dinner, but quickly forgot about it
when she realized her feet were soaked and on the verge of
hypothermia.

—

The magic of a white Istanbul faded almost as quickly as the snow.
Soon the metropolis was just another big city with large, black and
yellow mountains of shoveled ice lining the streets and a lot of
pissed off residents.

Lane tried to take it all in stride, thinking that such Nordic
weather had to be an anomaly and would soon break. But the cold
continued for weeks, and, being from the South, she was sure
conditions couldn't be much worse in an actually cold city like
Moscow or Helsinki.

Lane wondered if things might be better if she had
someone to share them with. Two months ago she had been
wearing a short sleeve shirt and sitting under an orange tree with
her two companions on the terrace of an Athenian tavern. Now her
days were a struggle to navigate the harsh streets and shops of an
unfamiliar city. She would return each night to her increasingly tiny
room at the teacher house only to find the few people she *did* know
were nowhere to be found.

Matt and Reyhan were spending more and more time
together. One day they were on the Asian side, the next they were

exploring one of the Ottoman fortresses that anchored the northern end of the Bosphorus. The first few times, Lane had waited for an invitation, but quickly realized the pair were becoming more than friends. Whenever she did see them, they were too wrapped up in inside jokes from their school or new Turkish sayings to realize she had been spending most of her time alone.

Colin had been MIA for days, always hanging out with students, he said. She could never catch him for longer than a meal, and even then he seemed evasive and quiet about his days. She couldn't understand. In Middlesborough they had talked about everything and always had time for each other. Now every time she saw him he absentmindedly asked about Matt, assuming she had been with him.

Lane found herself alone for the first time in her life. Not alone in the way she had been in her single dorm room in College, and not even alone the way she had been that week she did the Baltimore show for Essex Antiques without Joanna. But really alone: in a single room, in a foreign country, unsure if she could even find an acquaintance to have coffee with.

She thought of all the books she had read about lone travelers. In a memoir you only get the good stuff, she thought: meeting cool strangers at a museum, closing down a bar with the owner, even an interesting robbery. No one ever talked about what happened most of the time you were by yourself in a foreign place: eating alone at a crowded restaurant, the wasted hours in your room, not going out late at night as a single woman in a large, unfamiliar city.

It was a reality check unlike anything she had experienced before. Where were the life changing cultural experiences, the interesting international friends, the hole-in-wall eateries with food she had never and would never get again?

She was seriously on the verge of self-pity. And then—she stopped herself.

Direct as always, she was more interested in a solution than a problem. So Lane started to make plans. If she couldn't be with the people she had come with, she'd find new people. If her friends, a hipster and a gay man, could make a life in this strange country, she was certainly up to the task. She went to sleep early that night, full of ideas.

—

A muscular, tattooed torso danced with robot precision on the right sidebar of Colin's browser. *Am I doing this?* He thought half-heartedly as he hit the 'complete profile' button at the bottom of the page. *'One in five relationships now start online'*, he quoted a Match.com commercial he had seen a few months back. *But does that include Turkey?*

The weight of his tiny room at the Lojment had become oppressive in the past week. Cozy at first, it now seemed akin to a comfortable version of a Turkish jail cell. He was feeling claustrophobic, he told himself. He was feeling anxious, he reminded himself. He was feeling sexually frustrated, he finally conceded to himself.

Two weeks earlier, Bethany, sensing his less than happy mood during a rooftop cigarette break, pressed him for details.

"It's nothing really, probably just the Winter, you know?"

"You're frowny face, mate—that's not just the Winter."

Bethany's hokey observations were always strikingly accurate. Colin didn't know how to respond.

"Tell you what," she continued, "What's say we go out?"

"You're kind, but really—it's hard enough for me to make it back to the Lojment at night, let alone go out in Bakirköy."

"Silly billy, I'm not talking about here, I mean a proper night out. Taksim, bars, drinking… maybe a special club I know about. You've got Fridays off, same as me, right?"

Colin was dubious, "You've never come out with me before. And what do you mean by 'special club'?"

"Maybe a place where you could find something you're looking for," she winked and poked him awkwardly in the ribs, "And don't worry, my parents are away visiting friends, so it'd be nice to go up town for a change. I can crash in your room, right? Not like I have anything to worry about," again, she jabbed at his midsection, on the verge of a loud laugh.

Colin wanted to be incensed, but was starting to laugh himself, "Hey, stop that. We've never talked about that…"

"Did we have to, love," Bethany continued winking. "Yeah, find you something to put on your plate…"

"Ok, I get it," Colin grinned as he swatted at her multiple, light punches.

"Something to wet your whistle…" she purred.

"Ok, ok!" his eyes widened in gratitude.

"And bring your damn friends; I meet depressingly few people our age down here."

Colin's happy smile faded.

"What's wrong, love," Bethany asked.

"Um, nothing, you know, they really are all busy most of the time."

"Too busy to go out on the town?"

"Yeah, well Matt's on the verge of having a girlfriend, I'm pretty sure. And Lane's never liked gay clubs. Hell, I've never liked gay clubs. I think she has her own thing going with her co-workers anyway."

"That's a shame," Bethany seemed to believe him, "But you must have them come out soon—gay club or not. I'm a rare sight north of the Golden Horn."

He smiled as she left the room, and then wondered why he had been so quick to uninvite his friends. *It's not something they'd be interested in,* he told himself, and just as suddenly began to wonder what he'd gotten himself into.

—

"Well hey, stranger!" Lane instantly regretted her awkward greeting, and then questioned her regret more than what she had said, "What's new?"

Colin's face displayed what looked like displeasure, but Lane rationalized it as a trick of the poorly lighted Lojment hallway. It was the first time they had even been slightly alone in two weeks. It was early evening, and, having no plans, Lane was heading to the shower and wearing her Middlesborough athletic shorts. Colin, however, was freshly shaven, fully clothed, and smelled of his rarely worn Ralph Lauren cologne (a holdover from college).

"Hey," Colin responded distractedly, "Not a lot," he had failed in his mission of getting out of the Lojment unseen.

"You look nice," Lane tried to act casual as she nodded toward Colin's dress shirt, as if the past month of sparse communication and awkward interactions hadn't happened.

"Thanks… no big, my students are going out downtown, and I don't get to dress up that much anymore."

She believed him, but still didn't know what to say. If it had been just a month ago, she would have told him jestingly to fuck himself, and then asked if she could come along. No, she thought, he would have asked me to come along before I had the chance to.

So Lane waited, but in a couple of seconds, it was clear he was headed out without her, and didn't care to even explain it. She did the only thing she could do.

"Well, I'm beat," she lied, "Have fun out, and find us a good bar to frequent! I haven't seen anything nearly cool enough since we got here."

"Ha, they'll probably take me to some low key Tea house, but I'll scope out the scene," he said as he almost slid down the incredibly slick marble staircase.

Lane returned to her tiny cell/room with its harsh overhead light and absentmindedly turned on the TV (even though all the channels were in Turkish) just to have some noise. *What just happened?* She thought helplessly.

—

Once outside the Lojment, Colin recoiled at the bitter night air, and, sucking in a deep breath, flipped the collar of his pea coat against the slight wind. *I'm hiding.* He had finally said it, and just as quickly decided it wasn't true. *I'm not hiding.* He thought defiantly. *I know she wouldn't judge me for going to a gay club, but if I asked her to come, she wouldn't want to, and then I'd feel stupid. She was about to go to bed anyway.* He thought, but still couldn't shake the feeling that something had been off.

As he approached the club, he tried to put the whole scene behind him. *She's fine, I'm the one who's trying find a man in less than accepting country. And I'm sure Matt and Reyhan are more than willing to hang out if she wants to.*

The thumping of the street was undeniable at that point. Colin quickly forgot whatever it was he had been concerned about. Bethany, decked out in sequins and tight black pants, jumped up and down in front of large, copper-colored doors. Leaping into his arms she squealed:

"How much fun is this, yeah?"

He realized that, a) it was the first time he had been out in a long while, and b) he was completely sober.

"I haven't pre-gamed at all," he said in total astonishment.

Bethany, though generally home bound, was definitely streetwise, "Is that the American term for drinking before you go out?"

"Yes," he smiled.

"Well we'll just have to get you something fast!" her shoulders moved to the beat of the pulsing music as she flung the door open and pulled him into the smoking light shower on the other side.

Once inside, Colin could barely think.

The scene was distracting; he had been here several times before, just never in this country. The half-naked bodies were right where they usually were. The beat of the music was comfortingly familiar. The atmosphere was decidedly European. Faux-hawks and body glitter transported him to a time he didn't even realize he remembered. The year 2000, perhaps?

Overwhelmed by the need to forget, Colin loosened the third button on his pressed Land's End shirt, and started to move with the rhythm. Bethany, by virtue of her thin frame, had already made it to the bar and back. She handed him a tall, cylindrical glass full of the milky colored liquid he had become familiar with over the past few weeks.

"Thanks!" he shouted as he downed the licorice concoction with less hesitation than ever before.

The night wore on, and Colin began to, through his drunken euphoria, realize that regardless of who showed interest in him, this night was exactly what he needed.

He and Bethany danced in the unapologetic way he had only danced a few times in his life. She, screaming at the top of her lungs, drowned out by the crowd, and no doubt trying to forget a set of problems all her own.

The music said 'put your hands up', and they did, as high as they could go and as long as possible.

Colin went home alone, but feeling better than he had in a long while.

A week later, Colin realized, through the haze of a happy memory, what had really happened that night.

He and Bethany had become true friends—but that was it. The men in the Turkish gay club *looked* the same as the ones he had seen in the clubs in Raleigh—but something about them felt different. Desperation was all he could really remember. A group of close to a thousand gay men, and instead of excitement or even sexual satisfaction, all Colin could remember was an overwhelming—need.

"What was weird about that?" he had asked Bethany.

"What'd'ya mean, mate?" she returned, "I had the time of my life. Sorry you didn't find a bloke, yeah."

"Yeah, you're right. No, no worries." He mimicked her easy, down-under drawl.

Holding a cigarette he didn't really want and caught in an odd, cold, backwind on top of the EnglishSpace building, Colin looked south into a mist-shrouded expanse and decided he would have to take matters into his own hands.

So here he was, in a darkened room at the Lojment, his face illuminated by the cold light of his computer screen. He could just see the slight wisp of his own breath as it approached the heat of the laptop.

This is my best option, he told himself as he clicked through the first row of pictures on the gay dating site Garrison had recommended to Bethany. *I'm certainly never going to meet a guy at a club*.

And just as he had finished the thought, a high pitched tone sounded—he had a new message.

———

Lane eyed Colin from the door way of her new apartment as he sat, mesmerized, in front of his computer screen.

"What's happening over there?" she inquired casually.

Colin quickly slammed his laptop closed and tried to act nonchalant.

"Lesson planning," he lied, and then tried to change the subject, "You know, it should really be the two of us moving in together."

Lane finished his thought, "You're right, the two of them are going to end up spending every night together anyway."

She watched as Matt followed Reyhan up the steep stairwell to what would be the boys' new flat. It might have been a little presumptuous of Lane and Colin, but still, Matt never once took his eyes off the bright eyed Turkish/Bulgarian/American girl in front of him.

Lane had to admit it—their new living arrangements were almost fated.

Just five days before, all four of them had been living in the Lojment, desperate to find an outside apartment, and unsure of how it would work when they did.

"What are we going to do?" Colin had asked Lane, in reference to their looming housing issue, on the one occasion they had been alone together that month.

"I don't know," she sighed, looking helplessly around the depressing 'living room' of the Lojment, "I've been on the internet, but everything's in Turkish... obviously, I guess. I don't know how we're going to find a place."

"So does that mean you want to live with me still?" Colin's eyes were searching, and Lane, though shocked and happy, tried to respond with dignity.

"Um, of course," she faked annoyance, "like it or not, boo, we're in this together."

He was genuinely relieved. Then a concerned look came over his face, "What the hell are we gonna do about Matt and Reyhan?

But Reyhan swooped in—rescuing them all and banishing any awkwardness.

"Ok, I've found two places, and I'm so sorry if this was presumptuous of me," she directed the statement to Lane for some reason, while the four of them sat at a Taksim-adjacent watering-hole, discussing their options over acma pastries and Efes beer one day, "but I've set up a time for us to see them."

Lane, Matt and Colin were silent; all equally astonished; Matt even more than the others. He and Reyhan had never discussed living arrangements, and both knew enough to realize their nebulous relationship was far from the move-in stage.

"Hey, Rey, can we talk about this in private?" He motioned toward the door, unsure of how he would proceed once they got there.

She smiled broadly as if she hadn't heard him; her cowl-neck sweater moved rhythmically with her motions as she continued, "So I realize it's a bit awkward with the fact that I just met the three of you, and I'm sure you want to live together but I think I've found a solution—that is, if you'll have me! What if... the boys live together, and Lane, you and I are roomies!"

Lane had to admit Reyhan's excitement was infectious, but the idea seemed unplanned at best, and intrusive at worst, "Um, I don't know, I haven't really talked with anyone about what I want to do yet..."

"Yeah, I don't know if Lane would want to live that far away from us..." Colin was un-characteristically vocal.

"That's the beauty!" Reyhan squealed, giving them all a sense of concern mixed with intrigue, "The two apartments are in the *same building*, just two stories apart!"

"Seriously?" Colin couldn't contain himself anymore.

"Yes, I mean, of course you guys have to see them first, and I'm not trying to force you into anything but the landlord is the cutest Turkish girl, and we got along soooo well…"

"Wow, It's a lot to take in," Matt had spoken for all of them.

But just as soon, they all felt the same way Reyhan did. Walking through the two identical apartments, they were dumbfounded. Both were up-to-date, cheaply priced, and just a couple minutes from the metro.

"How did you…" Lane started to ask.

"Um, Craigslist, duh," was all Reyhan had to say. Lane could only shake her head in amazement.

"And what's the name of this low-key neighborhood you've brought us to?" Colin asked while staring out the window at a small group of well-dressed men on the corner.

"Welcome to Nişantişi," Reyhan spread her arms in an exaggerated fashion, as if welcoming them into the Garden of Eden. Lane was the only one that realized she wasn't kidding.

—

The next day they met Damla, their would-be duel-landlord, for coffee a few blocks from the apartment building. Colin could barely pay attention to where his feet were going as they strolled down a street that seemed definitely out of place.

Lane, completely giving up on cool detachment, continually pointed out grand, turn-of-the-century buildings, and chic clothing stores to the others.

Matt eyed Reyhan with astonishment, to which she gave only a knowing smile.

Damla was everything Reyhan said she would be, and more. She spoke basically perfect English with a slight Canadian accent—something she had picked up while at McGill, she said. As she handed over the keys (two sets for the boys and two for the girls) she gave them a sly look and then said knowingly, "The super's wife can be a real problem, especially if she thinks there's anything less than kosher going on. If she gives you any problems, just call me—and whatever you do, don't let her make you feel self-conscious. Turkish guilt can be a real bitch."

Reyhan laughed loudly, giving the others permission to do the same.

Walking back down the Nişantişi high street, Rey pointed out a gilt-covered neo-classical dream building, "Nişantişi Camii" She said.

"So it's the local mosque?" Matt had understood the word that had bypassed Colin and Lane.

"It's a little bit more than that. It's kind of like the who's who of Istanbul society. If you're anyone important, you have your funeral there."

Without missing a beat, Colin chimed in, "So it's the posh mosque?"

Reyhan squealed again, as she had been doing all afternoon, "I think we're going to have the time of our lives here!"

Lane hung back. She agreed that it all seemed too good to be true, and that they couldn't help but have a good time. Still, she noticed the others had moved ahead of her quickly and didn't look back until they reached the metro.

—

After all the bags had been unpacked, the beds set up and living room furniture moved around, the four said goodbye to the Lojment.

"Good riddance," Matt offered as they walked out the door for the last time, a thick cloud of hundred year-old-dust trailing behind them.

"Come on, you guys, didn't we have fun there?" Reyhan's optimistic nature always won out.

"No," Colin and Lane said in unison, and continued laughing all the way to the new bar they had found just a block away.

—

Lane was beginning to feel like she had missed an important meeting along the way. Like teaching, the first week in the new apartments seemed to go well for everyone but her.

She was happy for the temporary flurry of activity that the apartments had brought, but as the dust started to settle, she noticed her friends were gone or tied up even more than they had been before.

As expected, Reyhan spent most of her time upstairs in the boys' apartment; never quite sleeping over, but never quite catching Lane during waking hours either. Lane was sure that her presence in his apartment would drive Colin to spend more time downstairs with her, but realized after a week that he was nowhere to be found—in either flat.

"I haven't really seen him…" Reyhan trailed off as she stared unhappily at the clothes hanging in her wardrobe.

Lane realized, standing in the door way to Rey's room, how ridiculous it was that she was asking a semi-stranger where her best friend was. She remembered her promise to herself to make the most of Turkey, whatever the circumstances.

Reyhan, still deep inside her closet, asked if Lane wanted to come to dinner that night, but emerging, blouse in hand, she found the door way empty.

—

"Hey buddy," Matt said in a mock parental voice to Colin as he entered the tiny eat-in kitchen of their new apartment, "What cha got goin' there?" he raised his voice in the same teacher-questioning-student tone, indicating Colin's open laptop.

Colin cleared his throat and instinctively reached to close the computer, something he had done many times over the past few days, "Um, nothing… just screwing around online. What's new with you?"

Matt casually slipped into the chair opposite his roommate. He wasn't going to let Colin off the hook that easily. He sat silently for a minute, narrowing his eyes on the thin boy with the dark hair he had known for years, but only really gotten to know in the past few months.

"You're going online for sex aren't you?"

Colin's cream colored skin instantly flushed pink and then deep burgundy. His eyes searched the ground for an escape.

Matt realized he had struck a nerve, "Oh shit, I'm sorry, I didn't mean to embarrass you. I was just taking a guess—"

"—No, it's good," Colin said unexpectedly.

"It's—it's what?"

Colin had regained composure and was looking Matt straight in the eyes, "It's fine, I need to be honest about what I'm doing, otherwise I might as well still be in the closet."

Matt smiled, "So I was right…"

Colin rolled his eyes in admission, "Yes, yes, I'm trying to find a guy online—that's what this damn country has brought me to."

Matt, still smiling said sincerely, "Well, I think it's good. I wasn't quite sure how you were going to find anyone at EnglishSpace. I mean that Garrison character seems a little old for you…"

"Thanks for your concern," Colin laughed, "We'll see if anything comes of it, but whatever happens, it's gotta be better than going to the clubs—or *the* club."

Matt looked a bit surprised, "Oh, you've been? Did you and Lane go?"

Colin grew serious again, "God no, she's never been one for gay clubs—I mean, neither have I really. Speaking of, don't mention any of this to her would you? I'm not sure how she would feel about it—she's always talking shit about how dangerous this kind of thing is…"

"No worries dude, I don't really see her that much anyway," Matt ambled over to the half-sized refrigerator and grabbed a can of Efes beer.

"You don't?" Colin asked, while motioning Matt to hand him one of the large blue and white cans.

"Not really, I mean, I try to invite her to dinner with me and Reyhan, but she's never really around… we kind of thought she was with you."

Colin started to speak, stopped, and then started again, "That's funny. I thought she was with the two of you most of the time. I went down to see her the other day and she was gone then, too. We should all really check our cell phones more I guess…" He trailed off and then, his eyes brightening, spoke again, "You just said *we,*" he laughed.

Matt was now the one turning all shades of crimson, "What are you talking about dude?"

"Dude, you just said 'we'—meaning you and Rey,"

Colin would have thought Matt looked angry if he didn't know him any better, "Um, whatever, it's just a pronoun."

Colin was as close to giddy as he ever got, "Just a pronoun my ass, you've got something going on."

"Alright man, seriously, nothing's happened, we're just friends…"

"Matt, you know you want something to happen and so does she."

"She does?" Matt asked before he could catch himself.

"Of course she does," Colin said as he re-opened his laptop, "It's obvious. I'm actually kind of surprised it hasn't happened yet."

Matt, speaking freely at that point had to concede, "You know, I've kind of been wondering the same thing myself."

—

That night Reyhan came upstairs as usual and Colin quickly disappeared into his tiny room in the back of the apartment. She barely knocked anymore, which made Matt even more sure about the question he was about to ask her. Standing, barefoot (no one in proper society wore shoes in doors she constantly reminded him) in the half light of the entry way, he was struck by how large her dark eyes were.

"So I've been thinking…" he said as she flopped down on the worn, faux-antique love seat in the front room.

"Yeah…" she smiled coyly.

"We should go out sometime," he said, suddenly developing a slight knot in his throat.

Reyhan's expression wasn't exactly what Matt had expected. Instead of delight, her face registered more a look of shock.

"What are you talking about, silly—we go out all the time," she turned the TV on in an obvious attempt to cut off the conversation.

"I know," Matt continued undaunted, "But we should *go out* go out sometime, you know?"

Reyhan, realizing the conversation was quickly turning into the one she had feared for weeks, turned the volume down on the TV, and calmly turned toward Matt, "Matt, I understand what you mean. And you know I want that, too…"

"Do you?" Matt did not know that.

"Yes," she said with reserve, "but I have to be honest with you, I'm not trying to fall into anything serious…"

Matt let himself slide into the seat next to hers, picking up a throw pillow and shielding himself with it. He ventured a question, "So where does that leave us?"

Reyhan, almost sadly, said, "That leaves us watching TV…" and just as Matt had given up and turned his attention to a Turkish commercial she added softly, smiling, "and yes, we should go out sometime…"

—

Lane had never been the praying type, but she figured 'when in (new) Rome' and made a quick appeal to Allah himself. She was about to die, and she felt strangely calm about the whole thing.

But just as she had made her peace with the local deity, the clunking metal contraption she was in came to an abrupt and life changing halt.

Marissa pushed her out of the sliding door as the vehicle lurched forward and out of sight.

"What the fuck was that?" Lane's eyes were still bugged out from the fifteen minute ride.

Marissa didn't seem to register the seriousness in her voice, "Oh that's just the dolmuş, yeah? Fastest way to get around." Fast, perhaps, but at what cost? Lane wondered.

The 'dolmuş' itself looked strangely like a mini-van taxi, even painted the same color yellow she had seen in most cities. But the similarities stopped there. Instead of catching it, you waited at an assigned stop, paid a pre-determined fee, and the dolmuş followed a specific route. Kind of like a shuttle.

Within the first five minutes, however, Lane noticed none of these rules were very strict. After paying her fee, she saw that all the other passengers received change except for her. A minor annoyance she was willing to overlook for a shorter ride. Then they were off, and she realized the driver wasn't just living off the money from predetermined riders. He needed as many fares as possible; and the best was to get more fares was to drive faster and take on more people. Soon she found herself flying (literally for a second) down the hill from Taksim towards the Golden Horn. Instead of the maximum six passengers, she counted eight, two of which they had picked up on back streets, and one of which (an overweight grandmother) had forced Lane onto "the bitch seat." Not an actual seat, but a stool, identical to the one she had sat on at a restaurant earlier that day, which the driver kept up front for just such an occasion.

Lane tried to picture the dolmuş system in New York: terrified West Village residents sitting on unsecured stools as the van popped up on two wheels rounding a corner onto Broadway. She couldn't help but laugh a little, despite having just seen her whole life flash before her eyes.

Marissa nudged her in the arm and the shock from the ride finally wore off. She looked around. Where was she?

"Sultanahmet." Marissa answered her unasked question.

Lane had been far too busy watching the driver of her mobile coffin to see much going on outside the window, but somewhere the dolmuş must have crashed and killed everyone inside, because she couldn't believe the square she was standing in was anywhere on the same planet with Taksim, let alone in the same city.

Instead of the tightly packed high-rises of uptown, Sultanahmet seemed to consist of low slung two story buildings surrounding large open areas. For the first time in weeks, Lane saw green spaces and even small clusters of trees. Brightly patterned rugs hung against the wind as makeshift walls for open air markets.

Just then Marissa called to her and she turned, still transfixed. Before her rose two large domes, both propped up by a tumbling jacket of smaller rotundas. They were like two competing cities built on twin mountains.

To the left, Hagia Sophia, the dome from which all others in the city emanated (even though it had started life as a church). To the right—and a thousand years younger—Sultanahmet Mosque, displaying all the attributes of youth with its gorgeous, gaudy ornaments and six minarets (it may not be as old as Hagia Sophia, but it had two more minarets!).

So far Istanbul had been a city of new things: new food, a new language, even new traffic patterns. The things in front of her now, though, were completely different. Lane thought about how it always took something old to really make an impression on her. Was it a symptom of being from America, where man made things were rarely very ancient? Or was it something that affected everyone?

She turned to thank Marissa for inviting her, but realized her absent minded Australian co-worker was already ten yards ahead of her.

They toured Sultanahmet Mosque (and decided its nickname of "Blue Mosque" was misgiven; the predominate colors being purple and gray). Lane finally saw proof of what she had come to Turkey expecting, stone walls covered in the wistful Perso-Arabic script of the Ottomans. Giant circular chandeliers hung dangerously low to the thick carpeted floor, casting dim shadows on geometric textile flowers.

They walked the back streets of the old town and haggled with leather mongers. Turn of the century wooden Ottoman apartment houses punctuated streets lined with everything from

Ancient Greek cornerstones to 1960's tile covered convenience stores. Lane was amazed. Could this be the same city she lived in?

Then they crossed the Hippodrome and passed right by the Egyptian obelisk that still stood where Theodosius, the last unified Roman emperor, had placed it. Lane was amazed at how new it looked, as if cut yesterday, despite being seventeen centuries older than its worn pedestal.

She followed Marissa through the theme park turnstile in front of the Hagia Sophia and stood beneath its dark and gold speckled dome. A quietness surrounded her as she craned her neck with the glittering arch of thousand year old mosaics. Despite several clusters of tourists, she was sure she could hear a pin drop. The carved marble columns oozed stillness and commanded the respect of 1,500 years.

This is it, Lane thought, this makes everything worth it. As much as she could be sad about nights alone and awkward moments in grocery stores, it all seemed silly in the face of such permanence. The spot where she was had been there long before she arrived, and would stand long after she had gone.

She finally felt like she had traveled half way across the world—and all it took was crossing a bridge. Closing her eyes and opening her nostrils, she slowly took into her sinuses two millennia of history.

"Kinda makes ya think, yeah?" Marissa said comically, propped up against a Greek urn that predated even the church itself. But she was right, it did.

—

Lane's new mission was simple: discover as much of Istanbul as she possibly could, and accept every invitation she received.

Her thin brows arched, however, when Dorukaan, a high-schooler from her morning class, invited her out for tea, but she remembered her promise to herself and accepted his kind offer.

When they arrived at the tiny tea house after school, Lane realized the invitation had been from the entire class. She looked with surprise as every single student in her Level Two sat wide eyed waiting for her to take her seat.

The past two months at EnglishSpace had been very different from what she had expected.

Lane's idea of herself as a teacher was romantic to say the least. The first few weeks she had risen early every morning, donned fashionable navy skirts and crisp blouses and always made sure to have pens handy. She was going to be the Anna Leonowens of English teaching; winning over her students with charm, perseverance, and even a musical number if possible.

The reality, however, was something more akin to Teach for America; students unexcited about what English had to offer them, and even more unexcited about giving up their early mornings and weekends.

Lane did the math, and a semester of courses at EnglishSpace amounted to a small fortune in the eyes of the average Turkish family. As with most luxury, however, there is always someone around to take it for granted, and Lane became familiar with a new subsection of Turkish society; the disaffected upper middle class youth of Istanbul.

Daily she would open the day-glo orange text book, turn to a new section and hope for the best. Most of the time what she got in return was a lot of blank stares and quiet cell phone texting. Marissa had tried to tell her early on to just follow the material and fill the last hour with games, but she trudged on for weeks before finally submitting to the all-powerful Hangman board.

Looking now at the bright and interested faces of her students among the plush carpets and pillows of the tea house,

Lane could hardly believe they were the same glazed-eyed college kids she saw five times a week.

"You are welcome." Dorukaan, the youngest in the class, seemed to be the most eager to learn, but was still unable to master casual salutations.

"Oh, thank you... or—uh, teeee sheck you lar!" Lane had just that past week downloaded mp3s of all the basic Turkish phrases.

"Please, please, only English." Aysha, a small headscarf-clad girl said.

She was amazed, were these usually unmoved students really here to learn? Lane positioned herself on a comfortable divan near the window, still unsure of what to think.

"We are wanting to know where you are from," Aysha said directly. They hadn't gotten to the chapter on small talk yet.

"Oh, uh, well I'm from America."

"Yes, yes, but... where America?" Dorukaan passed her a small plate of cookies.

Lane was about to answer when the tea arrived. Chay, the students called it, tasted like strong Lipton to her, but came hot and sugary in hour glass shaped glasses not much bigger than thimbles. Lane drank and listened to all the questions being hurled at her from every side, answering as many as possible.

Over two hours later and well into her sixth chay, she was finally allowed to leave. Back on the cold street, she was amazed at what had happened. They had talked non-stop, fought each other over who got to ask the next question, and could barely wait for her to answer to ask more—and none of it was about language.

They began by asking her about herself. Easy enough until the questioning became intense: Are you married? Do you have a boyfriend? And her personal favorite: Do you want a children?

After she said she was single, no fewer than three of the boys offered their brothers as fine husbands.

Soon they were asking about her religion, her plans to stay in Turkey, and an entire line of questions about life in America.

They told her stories about cousins that had moved abroad or plans to move themselves.

"My sister is in Toronto," said Aysha.

The goth girl, whose name she could never remember, opened up for the first time about her love for California, and how she "will go to Los Angeles to work and travel."

Lane asked what she needed to go and the group fell silent. Finally, Dorukaan told her the visa was very expensive and took months to come through, if it ever did.

Mostly, however, they told her stories about Turkey. Grand narratives (given the language constraints) in which Turkey always featured as the untouchable protagonist. Turkey as political linchpin; Turkey as empire; Turkey as more of an idea than a place. It all reminded her of some of the 24 hour news channels back home.

Just as she was about to make her exit she closely studied all of her students sitting around her—ripped jeans, death metal tee-shirts, headscarves, Louis Vuitton purses, and even Abercrombie sweatshirts—talking about the greatness of a country so many of them were trying to leave.

She laughed to herself, but still couldn't shake an odd feeling she had gotten from one of the questions. Early on in the evening, Sercan, a tall, quite soccer player with clothes that weren't as nice as everyone else's, had put down his glass, looked her straight in the eyes and said, "Why did you come to Turkey? You can go anywhere."

She had given some kind of response about finding a job there and wanting to see Istanbul, but if she had been honest, she would have said she didn't know. Lane thought about it for hours until she finally realized what was bothering her. She *could* go anywhere—and Sercan couldn't.

After tea, Lane decided to return to the small restaurant she had found that night after the grocery store. She had written the name of it down, but quickly realized it wasn't the kind of place she could find on google.

Asking around among her students she discovered a neighborhood name: Tarlabaşi, and a direction: Southwest.

Heading off again through Taksim and down the side street she remembered. She watched again as the gleaming glass and steel walls and stately stone architecture of the city center faded into worn and motley lowrise buildings the further she descended the steep sidewalk.

She took as straight a line as possible, only turning when a dead end forced her to. Once the street leveled out at the bottom of the hill, Lane suddenly noticed in the daylight everything she had missed before. Cracked cinderblock walls and chain-link fencing seemed to prop up the spaces in-between the sad wooden homes on every corner. The Ottoman homes in her own neighborhood were large and freshly painted behemoths, reminding her of the Painted Ladies in San Francisco. But here, the same shades of pastel were so chipped and spotted with rust and mold, they only seemed to underscore how small the structures were.

A plastic ball bounced from an open doorway and into the street, chased by a small, dark haired boy. Lane suddenly noticed something very different from the last time she had been here: there were people everywhere.

She peered into the greasy window of a coffee house and saw the old men, too big for their tiny stools, playing backgammon in a thick cloud of cigarette smoke. Screaming children in winter coats raced dangerously down the steep incline of a side street. The smell of kebap meats roasting on giant upright spits caught her nose; deliciously unhygienic.

She rounded a corner she thought she recognized and was almost pushed back by a press of people moving down an oddly narrow shopping street. There was noise everywhere. Toddlers in torn sweaters and muddy khakis moved stealthily under the legs of adults shouting after one another. Men called out from shop windows advertising everything imaginable. Women in headscarves the same faded colors of pastel crowded around baby strollers and chatted loudly over the bouquets of flowers and bags of dirt covered vegetables.

Lane noticed a side street where plastic tarps had been hung from the roofs of buildings, creating an open air market. She ducked through, trying to avoid the swirling groups of shoppers. The bright sun radiated through the tarps, creating an ambient glow of green, blue and yellow. The chilly winter air was unable to penetrate the tight space, and the heat of the tightly packed crowd warmed her. The smell of cooking onions floated on the air as she moved past each makeshift stall, trying to remain as invisible as possible.

This place was very foreign from the ones she normally moved through. The Istikalal was full of people also, but they looked so different from the people she saw here: waxy floral shopping bags, faded jean jackets, black orthopedic shoes worn as slippers with the backs folded down or cut out. Children sat on sidewalks with tiny displays of brightly colored pencils and small rubber erasers, calling out their price.

Lane suddenly felt very out of place, and in a way, like she was intruding. She thought how odd it was that she could live two miles from a place like this and never know it existed.

Just as she was about to turn and leave, a small, elderly woman brushed her arm slightly. As Lane turned, she saw the woman was standing behind a tiny card table laid with metallic belts and rhinestone flip flops.

The woman said something Lane didn't understand over the crowd but she realized it was probably a price. She noticed a pair of cotton candy blue sandals and decided she needed them. She handed over a ten lira bill and was shocked when the woman placed nine lira and twenty-five cents back in her hand with the shoes. Lane started to protest and give her more, but realized it was useless. Instead she used her feeble Turkish to indicate she wanted a pair in every color, handing back as much of the cash as the woman would let her.

As Lane climbed the hill back towards Taksim and her spacious apartment over an expensive leather goods store, a cold wind cut across her neck and she had the feeling she was emerging from some kind of time machine. But as she looked down inside of her bag to see the rainbow of her new shoe collection, she smiled and started to feel warm again.

Seven
Proper Nouns

"Love is, but Turkey isn't."

"No, no, Turkey is, but love isn't,"

Gülara's face grew sad, and Matt knew he'd have to handle the situation delicately.

He still managed a fumble, "Because Turkey is real and love isn't." He regretted it the minute he said it.

"What?!" The girl almost shrieked, and the rest of the class soon chimed in with similar protests.

"Love is... love is *more* real than Turkey," Gülara returned without question.

Matt wasn't sure how to continue, "Yes, I understand, but Turkey is specific, and love is... is general?" he was so unsure he phrased the answer as a question. His crowded afternoon class didn't buy it. Looking up at the clock, he was relieved to see time was almost up.

"Let's go a bit early today... and we'll cover proper nouns tomorrow."

The class needed no further prompting and Gülara gave him a horribly nasty look as she exited the room.

—

Sometime in the past month, a strange thing had happened to Matthew Ortega. One night recently, in the confined comfort of his single bed, he had looked over to see the pale skin and long, dark eye lashes of a girl he barely knew. It was only the second night Reyhan had slept over. He thought about Mara and how long they had been together. He thought about how different this was. He thought, finally, as he lay next to her in the almost harshly bright moonlight that he might have—without knowing it—fallen in love.

The next evening Matt and Reyhan went together to a party held by their Bosphorus branch co-workers. Amy, a loud New Zealander, had extended an invitation for them both to come to the apartment she shared with three other teachers in the Cihangir neighborhood.

"Shouldn't we invite Lane and Colin?" Reyhan had dutifully asked.

"Good luck finding Colin, he's been going…" Matt knew where he'd been going for the past month but didn't want to say anything, "He's been going out with students a lot lately."

"God, kill me, if I wanted chay and stilted conversation, I'd go see my relatives," Reyhan quipped. They both laughed.

"Where's Lane?"

"You know, I've tried to call her cell several times, but no answer. Guess she's out of credit," Reyhan said, referring to the fact that none of them had yet gotten used to their pay-as-you-go phones.

"That sucks," Matt said, "I feel like I haven't seen her in forever," but before he could continue the thought, they reached the door of the Amy's apartment building.

Matt looked up in surprise. The area they had been walking through seemed nice: cafes, small bakeries, even a couple of chic restaurants, but as they descended the hill (Istanbul, like

Rome, was a city of hills), Matt had failed to notice things take a turn. They now stood in the middle of a street half paved with decaying asphalt that was slowly revealing its under layer of sturdy and ancient cobblestone. The buildings (that at one point were probably stately neo-classical homes or beautiful, wooden Ottoman villas) had all been torn down, save a couple derelict structures. In their place, tall, austere, soviet-inspired apartment buildings lined the street, punctuated by vacant lots strewn with bricks, and, randomly, children's toys. The whole scene was almost depressing, except for the oddly cheery colors of the buildings: sea foam green; bright salmon pink; mauve.

Just then, Amy buzzed them up (there was no speaker on the intercom so the inhabitants of the apartment just had to assume that all guests were friendly). Climbing the crumbling staircase, Matt wondered at what the inside of the apartment would look like.

At the top of the fourth flight Amy waited for them outside of her large, industrial gauge metal door. She was a slight, young girl, not even above college age Matt guessed. On this particular night, she had thrown off her regular black teacher clothes for an ensemble of tie-dye and skinny jeans. Leading them into a large central room Matt instantly noticed the refinished wooden floors and fresh paint. But the modern upgrades seemed to stop with the walls and floors.

The large door opened into a room that seemed cramped for a central living space. There was a couch, and even a coffee table—but that was the extent of the furniture. Matt and Reyhan looked around the small room at hordes of English teachers sitting cross-legged in a large, uneven circle. Everyone greeted them in unison, and Matt realized that further introductions weren't coming when Amy immediately offered them a drink. He accepted and followed her to the kitchen, leaving Reyhan to fight for a patch of floor on which to perch. As he walked out, she realized what it was that was so depressing about the scene—the only light seemed to come from one large, bare light bulb in the center of the ceiling.

In the kitchen, Matt was surprised to see ill-fitting modern appliances and a smattering of inconsistent cooking supplies. A large, faded calendar hung over the sink, sporting twelve very similar photographs of Atatürk. As Amy graciously fixed an 'Istanblue' vodka tonic for him and Reyhan, he notice a smattering of mis-matched spoons and several bags of loose-leaf chay.

Returning to the main room, he was greeted by Reyhan's hilariously plaintive eyes.

"Um, can we have a tour?" he asked Amy.

"Oh, sure!" The girl quickly responded, but qualified with, "You won't be that impressed, it's pretty much this room and then all the others shoot off of it."

As Amy led him from room to room, Matt noticed an odd trend—every room seemed to contain even less furniture than the main one; specifically, a single mattress on the floor and one large wardrobe.

"Where did y'all get your… mattresses?" Matt asked realizing how ridiculous the question sounded.

"You wouldn't even believe it! They were originally like, fifty lira, and we got them damaged for 30!" Amy was obviously ecstatic, but as Matt plopped down on her small sleeping pad he was disconcerted to feel his pelvic bones touch the floor.

"Firm!" he offered.

Out in the main room Reyhan had done her level best to keep the party going, Matt found her officiating a drinking game with military precision.

"No, no, NO," she yelled as he entered the space, "you weren't even close! Drink!"

He smiled and quickly took part in her show, sitting on the bare floor next to Leslie, a middle aged woman from Idaho, and Mitch, who continued to literally rib him throughout the night.

Around one, Reyhan deftly managed to get them both out of the drunken scene that had unfolded.

"If Mitchell poked me in the ribs one more time…" Matt said in a haze.

"I know! And what was with all of them sleeping on hard mattresses on the floor?" Reyhan observed.

"Oh my god, you noticed that?!"

"Um, duh! It was like being in a Boy Scout cabin!"

Matt, overcome with emotion, grabbed Reyhan's gesturing hand, and swiftly put his other arm against the small of her back. Pulling her close, he closed his eyes and leaned in for an epic kiss at the gates of Galatersaray High School—the stern face of a Bronze Atatürk watching over them from a nearby placard. And then, he felt her pull away.

Brow furrowed, he recoiled and opened his eyes, "Um…" he said in a questioning tone.

"I'm sorry," Reyhan immediately offered, "I'm just—I'm sorry. I don't know why…"

Matt assumed the best, as always, "Um, sure, don't worry about it." He slipped his hand into hers, which she held tightly. They walked that way the entire distance to metro, but the next morning, when Matt woke up, he couldn't get the moment out of his mind.

—

30 days, 25 messages, 12 replies, 5 'dates', and two hook-ups. Colin tried to look on the bright side, but having come to the end of his virtual rope, he thought the whole situation was pretty sad for a city of 17 some odd million.

"If this were New York or San Fran I would already have found a husband," he muttered to himself in an uncharacteristic tone. The glow of his computer screen lighting his tiny room, as it had done almost every evening for the past month.

The dates had been forgettable, except for the one that had ended five minutes into coffee when a slightly older Turkish man had asked him, in broken but still comprehensible English, if he, like most American boys, liked wearing women's underwear, and would he please do it that evening?

The hook-ups were okay. One was, perhaps predictably, a British ex-pat. Dinner, drinks, sex, and they parted ways. Colin didn't particularly like the boy, but was still unnerved at the finality of the situation. It was odd to admit, but he had secretly thought he was a catch for any gay, English speaking expat in Istanbul; the population being so small. It turned out they weren't all just looking for people like themselves. He was embarrassed at how narrow his scope had been.

He soon moved on. A constant barrage of messages began appearing in his Manhunt inbox from a Turk about his age. *This is it*, he thought, *I guess I'm going to finally hook-up with a local—like in some cheesy travel memoir.* And he did.

He and Can (pronounced John, he quickly found out) met, in true Istanbul fashion, at the mall. As he sat in an overstuffed chair at a large Starbucks opposite and arcade, Colin couldn't help but smile to himself at the American-ness of it all. He barely had time to taste his macchiato before he noticed a boy that looked like the pictures he had seen online—only shorter.

Can made his way over to the tiny table and large pair of chairs. Colin was a bit surprised, the boy looked a good five inches shorter than he did in his photographs, which meant that Colin stood at least half a foot above him.

"So good to meet you," Can beamed as he plopped down suddenly into the available chair.

"You too…" Colin returned.

Dark and black haired, Can's bright eyes were almost a shade of light gray, which intrigued Colin. They ended up chatting for a couple of hours, the boy never once let the conversation slip into Turkish, despite Colin's best efforts to at least ask questions in his new language.

Two more coffee dates, and before Colin knew it, they were making out regularly.

And then, the other shoe dropped. Noticing that Can had never slept over, Colin invited him to one evening. The boy reluctantly agreed, and showed up at his and Matt's apartment with an odd bag of clothes and bottle of raki.

After the requisite small talk with Matt, Can and Colin retreated to his room behind the kitchen. Things went well. Better than well, Colin initially thought. He wasn't sure if he was just sex starved, or if it had really been that good. Then, as they were lying there, locked in an embrace, and kissing deeply like teenagers, Can suddenly pulled away with startling force.

Colin looked up with astonishment, the dim light of his one lamp combining oddly with the dusk to create odd shadows around the room.

"What's up?" he said with concern.

"The Muezzin," Can whispered in a reverent tone.

"They what? Oh." Colin heard the faint strains of the evening call to prayer and breathed a sigh of relief, "Yeah, sorry, there's a mosque—I mean cammi, across the street, sorry it's so loud," and he dreamily reached out for the back of Can's neck. He was stunned again as he felt Can pull away a second time, with even more force.

"What the—"

"It's the Muezzin, please don't," Can whispered again.

Colin was dumbstruck. Here he was, in bed with a man, having one of the best times he had had in recent memory, about to embark on a rather long night of passion, and he was being told to cool it? For—what exactly?

"Are you serious?" he propped himself up on one arm and stared into the half light at the motionless figure of Can next to him.

And then, just as he didn't think things could get much weirder Can, in an almost accusatory tone, let out a loud 'shhhhhhhhhhh!'

Colin was enraged. He was enraged and he wasn't even sure why, which made him more enraged. He was enraged and he didn't even know how to handle it, which made him livid. Before he knew it, he was off the bed and ranting in a low tone; an attempt to keep Matt from hearing what was quickly becoming a very odd conversation.

"You're telling me that we in the middle of spending the night together—what could have been a great night, *by the way*—and you want us to cool it during the call to prayer?! You want to take a break from our having *sex* to listen and reflect?!" Colin heard the words coming out of his mouth and was shocked, but for some reason he didn't know how to stop. Just then he was cut off.

"Shhhhhhhh," Can responded even more loudly.

"Oh *fuck* no," Colin whispered at the top of his lungs, "absolutely not," and before he could even suggest it, he realized Can was off the bed himself and tugging his pants on as fast has his tiny frame would allow.

Matt, though deep in conversation with Rey in the front room, couldn't help but slowly amble toward the kitchen as Colin watched Can make a hasty exit.

"Is everything—" but Matt's question was stopped by Colin's pleading, upturned hand. He returned to his room.

And here he was a week later, still mad at Can; mad at himself for being culturally insensitive; mad at Can for making him mad at himself; but mostly just mad. His eyes still glued to the computer screen, wondering if he would ever be able to find something halfway normal in this city. He closed the laptop and went to bed, but the phrase "no new messages" haunted him.

—

The next day at work, Colin couldn't shake the feeling that he was in for a long period of abstinence and solitude. Bethany was gone, and as he sat alone in the downstairs teacher's room, counting the moments before his dolmuş arrived, he was arrested by a deep sense of having made the wrong choice in coming to Turkey. He tried to put the thought out of his mind, and as he rose to go, still fighting a sense of unease, he was met at the door by Handan, the cheerful Turkish branch manager.

"Oh good, Colin, I caught you," she had pronounced his name 'colon', but her sparkling, dark eyes and effusive nature made him instantly forgive her, "I have something I want to discuss with you," she said in technically precise English.

"Ok, what's up?"

Handan smiled at his American casualness, "I have a proposal for you," she continued in enunciated speech, "We have been asked to provide a teacher for private lessons for an executive in another part of the city."

She paused so he thought it was his turn to speak, "And you'd like to me do it?"

She was delighted he put the pieces together for her, "Oh yes—only if you want, of course, but I think you would very much enjoy this opportunity."

"Um," Colin didn't know what to think, but Handan's cheerful face and constant support had him answering before he knew it, "Yeah... I think—Yes, I'd like to do that."

"Oh wonderful!" He was happy he had made her happy, but immediately apprehensive.

"I will give you the address now if you have time, the lessons will start tomorrow if that is ok?" She had phrased the entire multi-clause sentence as a question.

Colin was caught off guard but had no choice but to agree, "Um, no that's fine…"

On the bumpy dolmuş home that evening he stared at the tiny slip of paper Handan had placed in his hands. It contained an address, a simple set of directions with bullet points, and a name: Metin Oldulogo.

———

The soft pulsing tones of hyper-modern ambient music caught Colin and carried him from the sleek revolving door to the even sleeker front desk of the lobby.

"Metin Oldulogo, lütfen," he said to the receptionist in his best Turkish accent. Looking around he was suddenly very aware of his un-tucked shirt, mud splashed shoes, and shabby teacher bag. Just as he was noticing the vast expanse of the lobby, a voice pulled him back to earth in a perfect British accent.

"Mr. Yates?" said the receptionist coolly, "Mr. Oldulugo has instructed you to the 20th floor, where he will meet you."

Colin thought the shock of hearing her voice must have been evident on his face, but he managed a simple, English, 'thank you' and made his way towards the elevator bank, following the graceful arc of her arm.

As he entered the nearest available elevator he read the visitor badge the receptionist had handed him. "Trump Towers, Istanbul." *How did I ever end up here?* He thought.

Exiting the plush elevator Colin was greeted by a large, dark wood reception desk, and yet another sleek looking Turkish girl, this time in all black.

"Are you Mr. Yates?" She said in a less convincing, but still impressive British accent.

"Um, yes," Colin returned in a low tone, to which the girl nodded and pressed an invisible button.

"Mr. Oldulugo will be with you in a moment."

Colin's first thought, despite everything around him, was *why does this guy even need my help? His receptionist speaks better English than my boss...*

Soon a door opened at the far end of a hallway off reception. Simultaneously, the receptionist motioned to Colin, "Second door on the left," was all she said, and indicated to her right with the same graceful arm motion employed by the girl downstairs.

Colin moved slowly through the dimly lighted hallway, surprised to hear the recorded sound of trickling water somehow coming from inside the inlaid wooden walls. Light emanated from a single open door in the corridor and Colin apprehensively moved toward it.

You've been in nice office buildings before, he thought oddly, *why is this one so overwhelming?*

Perhaps it was the unknown, he thought, as he turned sharply and entered the half open door to his left.

Blinding light assailed him from floor to ceiling windows. At first, he could only make out shapes, one of which was moving toward him with alarming speed.

"Mr. Yates!" A gruff, yet excited voice greeted him.

"Um, yes," Colin responded. Just then the room came into focus, "And you must be Mr. Oldulugo..." he said, and then trailed off as a large, taut hand almost encased his own. He looked up. He had been expecting... He wasn't sure what he had been expecting—but whatever stood in front of him certainly wasn't it. Mr. Oldulugo was tall; taller even than himself. He was dark haired, like both of the receptionists. But mostly, Mr. Oldulugo was... very attractive. Colin's attempt at covering up his own awkwardness only made him act more awkward.

"Please, please," Mr. Oldulugo said, "sit," and he indicated a sumptuously upholstered chair across from a low, divan-style sofa against the wall.

Colin obeyed immediately and then wondered why he had done so. Busying himself with arranging his teacher materials, he purposely avoided eye contact with his new student, but because of where his eyes were he witnessed the commanding way he lifted his expensive trouser legs and sat, comfortably leaning forward, the fingers of both hands lightly touching each other. Colin was afraid to look up and felt more out of place with every passing second. And then, as if a lightning bolt had struck, he dropped his pen on the coffee table, told himself to get it together, and straightened his back; trying, in one motion, to throw off the awkwardness of the current situation and the past three months.

He looked Mr. Oldulugo straight in the eyes—it was worse than he had thought—the man was smiling broadly.

"So!" the man said, and Colin went limp. *Of all the possibilities, why did they have to set me up with someone so fucking handsome!* He screamed internally, trying his best to keep a slight, but not too slight, smile on his lips.

"So I've got some exercises here that will help me determine your language needs and I thought, if we had time we could try some worksheets together, but that all depends on—" Colin was rambling and worse still, he was using a low tone that would have been hard for a native English speaker to understand. He was surprised and happy to hear the man interrupt.

"No, no, no!" Colin allowed himself to look up again and was perturbed to see Mr. Oldulugo still smiling, "I want to hear about you!"

Colin didn't know what to say, had he heard the man correctly?

"—Yes! Let's talk for a bit. After all, I am a business man, and if we are not compatible, then it will be hard for us to be business partners, correct?"

Colin knew this man had used the word correctly, but the way Mr. Oldulugo had said 'compatible' gave him a hot flash. When had he turned into a hormone-crazed teenager?

"Um, of course..." he said without understanding.

"So..." The man looked at him imploringly, but Colin wasn't sure what was expected.

"Yes?" he said.

"So! I'll start," The man decided, "My name is Metin Oldulugo. I am 29 years old. I work for Tutlus corporation, here in Istanbul. I live in Dort Levent. I have two brothers and a sister— this is the type of thing I am talking about."

Colin realized the man was instructing him on small talk, and became even more self-conscious, "Um, of course," he said and then paused again awkwardly, the words not quite coming out of his mouth.

"You are Colin Yates... You work for EnglishSpace..." He made slight hand motion as if to help Colin along on his journey toward coherence.

Finally, Colin's brain clicked into place and he was able to form a real, full sentence, "Of course, I'm so sorry! I'm Colin Yates, but of course you already know that!" He was slightly hysterical, "I work for EnglishSpace, and you know that, too!" He breathed deeply, "Um, let's see—oh! I live in Nişantişi, I am from America. I have no brothers or sisters..." he trailed off and looked to Mr. Oldulugo for confirmation.

"Very good!" The man offered, "And Nişantişi—very fancy. But no brothers or sisters, how sad?"

"Oh, it's really much better than you think," Colin answered honestly and was suddenly aware that he was conversing like a human again. He pushed his hand through his thick, short hair, which had just grown back to a normal length, absentmindedly adjusted the collar on his shirt and managed to maintain eye contact with the handsome stranger for a full thirty seconds.

The two men covered almost everything there is to cover in a first meeting: family, job, education, travel, likes, dislikes. Given the fact that everyone he had met so far in his new country had asked him whether he was married or had a girlfriend, he was happy that Mr. Oldulogu seemed unconcerned—or perhaps had too much professionalism to ask that about a stranger, he thought fleetingly. They talked on, covering Istanbul, Colin's impressions of Turkey, even touching on politics—and then, suddenly, Mr. Oldulogu abruptly stood.

"Oh, I'm sorry," Colin instinctively said, "I must have been rambling… We can do some exercises if you like…"

"No, no," The man smiled broadly again in the way that made Colin highly self-conscious, "I think our time is up…"

"Is it?" Colin had no idea what time it was.

"Yes, and I'm afraid it is I that has kept you too long."

Colin checked his watch casually and was embarrassed to see they had gone thirty minutes over the amount of time he was supposed to be there, "Oh shit, I'm—oh, I'm sorry for cursing, I just—"

"No, no, no problem!" Mr. Oldulogu said in a way that made Colin believe he really didn't mind, "It has been a wonderful experience!"

"Well Mr. Oldulogu," Colin said, rising, "I guess I'll see you next week, if that's ok?"

The man beamed in the oddest way, "Of course, of course, everything is fine—wonderful, I mean… I will see you next week," and then he nearly hit the coffee table making his way to the door before Colin in order to open it for him, "And, please, Mr. Yates, call me Metin—I insist!" he said before Colin could protest.

"Um, well, yes, um, sure! Please, you call me Colin, this isn't formal really," Colin had all but regained his composure, but as he slid down the side of Istanbul Towers, watching the skyline grow and fly up to meet him, he couldn't mistake the ridiculous thought that at the very end, Metin had been the one who seemed nervous.

—

The extreme cold weather had finally given way to a more expected Mediterranean winter and in celebration Lane spent every night that week out of the apartment, certain that sitting around wouldn't make her friends suddenly appear.

Middle aged, gay Thom from EnglishSpace-Taksim took her to a jazz club where the songs were all in English and the introductions all in Turkish. Marissa took her out for cheap beer with her advanced class.

For three nights in a row she found herself sloshing through the open gutters of the fish market that leads to the primary bar street, blinded by the wet reflection of hundred watt bulbs on that day's briny leftovers.

Tiny tables lined a three foot wide stretch of cobblestones that seemed to contain every bar in the city. In most towns she had been in, bars existed out in the open, on main streets, with big signs and overpriced martinis. In Istanbul, Lane found most of them to be hidden away, on back streets, and all packed in to the same two blocks. It was like a red light district, where the sex on sale was a watery pilsner that came by the half liter.

"This is Efes." Marissa said, referring to the pale golden liquid in the stein, "get to know it, get to love it." The brew barely registered as alcohol in the mouth, but Lane quickly understood what Marissa meant, since she couldn't find any other beer on the menu. Efes seemed to be the only lager brewed in Turkey, and as such had a special position above the rest—meaning available everywhere.

One night she got back late and still wired from all the beer. Groping her way up the staircase to the third floor, she fumbled with her still new keys before finally finding the lock.

Certain there would be no one home, Lane barged in to find Reyhan sitting at the tiny kitchen table.

"Heeeeey," Lane said boozily and with a question in her voice. She noticed quickly the small glass of wine in front of Reyhan on the table, "What's up?"

Reyhan gave a simple, "Oh, you know, just drinking."

Lane, even in her state, knew this was an odd scene, mostly because she had never seen Reyhan drink at home at all, let alone by herself, "I can see that," she tried to say in a non-judgmental tone.

"Yep," was all Reyhan gave her.

Lane, unnerved, went about the business of getting some water in her system, all the while keeping an eye on the silent Reyhan, who sat, periodically taking sips from her glass.

Just about to exit the kitchen toward her room, Lane's inner voice loudly declared she should at least acknowledge what was happening, "Um, are you ok, Rey?"

The thin girl turned slightly and before even speaking, Lane knew she needed to sit down opposite her.

"It's just—" Reyhan started in as if they had been having a conversation for months and were just picked up where they had left off at breakfast, "It's just, I don't know what to do about Matt—I mean we're obviously moving toward something, but is it unfair of me to expect him to wait around for me to decide what that is? Or even if it *is* anything? I mean that seems like a lot, but on the other hand he seems completely happy to just wait with me and—"

Lane's face must have registered her complete confusion, because Reyhan stopped mid-sentence and gave her a look of horror, "Oh my god, what is it?" she inquired.

"Well first," Lane tried to order her thoughts, "I think I'm a lot more drunk than you are…"

"Oh no, it's not you, I always get this talky when I've been drinking. I mean, you wouldn't believe this but this is my *third.*"

Lane looked at the tiny chay glass and could barely contain her amusement; the whole thing could hold three ounces at best.

"Well that notwithstanding, I also have to be honest Rey. I'm not quite sure I know what you're talking about…"

Reyhan's face became sad, and without pausing she started in on another rant, "Well of course you wouldn't, how stupid am I? *I mean how dumb can I be?*"

It didn't seem to be a joke, she seemed to really want to know.

"I mean here you are, forced to hang out with god knows who while Matt and I are—well, whatever, and Colin—where is Colin? Your best friend!"

Lane was still a bit overwhelmed by Reyhan's speed, but she realized that for the first time, someone else had put into words what she was going through. Not even Marissa had offered much sympathy when it came to her absentee friends.

"You noticed that…" she inquired, sobering up.

"Well of course I did, but who was I to reach out to you? You're not the kind of girl that needs my charity!"

I'm not? she thought. *Damn, I guess I'm not…*

"And I'm embarrassed to admit how much time Matt and I have been spending together, and I always just assumed he was talking to you, but when I found out that Colin hadn't been around for a while, well I can't even talk—I'm sooooo sorry I never said anything, or took you out, not that I thought we would immediately be girl friends or anything, I get that you're not into that—just, you know, to hang out, get to know each other…"

Reyhan continued, but Lane had gone into her own thoughts. *Am I not into that? Do I seem like I don't need friends, because nothing could be further from the truth. Am I the problem…*

But before she could continue, Reyhan was saying, "I don't care how drunk you are, we need this right now," and in almost one motion she produced another tiny chay glass and filled it almost to the brim with a thick dark cherry liquid.

Lane, on the verge of a smile, spilled some of hers while clinking glasses with the obviously upset Reyhan, and then took a large gulp of the liquid, which, a second later, she barely managed to swallow.

"What the hell was that?" She said, her eyes tearing up. Squinting through the tears, the kitchen suddenly came into sharp focus: the dirty light fixture, the odd room layout that wasn't small, just awkward; the way Reyhan always kept it spotless, even when it was being used.

"Visne Sharap!" Reyhan smiled.

"Oh, I know the word for wine, but that other one is new—or, wait, I've seen in somewhere… in the grocery store maybe?"

"It's a kind of sour cherry."

"That's it! I've seen it in the juice section!" Both girls began to laugh uncontrollably.

"Whatever made you…" Lane continued

"I like sweet things, it's an embarrassing truth," Reyhan offered.

Lane took another sip, knowing now what she was getting herself into, "You know it's kind of like a grape we have back in North Carolina, it makes a great wine—as long as you don't think of it as wine."

"The muscadine!"

"How did you…" Lane was astonished.

"I don't know if you've noticed but Matt and I have been spending a lot of time together."

"Ok, we need something," Lane said and started to make her way toward the freezer, where, like in Middlesborough, she had stashed an emergency pack of cigarettes.

Reyhan, surprising her once again, grabbed one quickly out of her hands, "You know you don't have to smoke just because I'm weak," Lane said.

"Don't worry, there are a lot of things you don't know about me," she said, "I guess there are a lot of things we don't know about each other…" she corrected.

Lane smiled, "So I have to be honest, Rey, you need to boil this whole situation down for me so we don't stay up all night rehashing the details."

"Yes!" Reyhan almost screamed, "Matt said you were very good at finding a problem and dealing with it directly." It was almost unnerving how much Reyhan really did already know about her.

"Ok, here's the basics, Matt and I are—"

"I got that part—"

"Right, of course. Ok, Matt and I are, you know. And basically I don't know what I want or when I want it or why or how or, oh shit this is hard!"

Lane threw back the rest of her visne sharap and, after finishing, paused, formed her words in her mind, and spoke, "So what's the issue? You like him; he *obviously* likes you… I'm not quite sure I follow."

"Ha," Reyhan laughed to herself, "You're going to laugh, it's—it's my family."

Lane, despite trying not to, did laugh, "I'm so sorry, I didn't mean to—I just. You're living half-way across the world, and he's—and you're. I mean you're not getting married!"

Lane tried to continue laughing but noticed how serious Reyhan was and tried to control herself.

"I know! It's so stupid…" And just as Lane thought she was finished talking, "I just—UHHH, there's so no good way to explain this."

Lane made herself adopt a serious mode and asked, after a pause, "Ok, just slow down and try."

And just as suddenly, Reyhan's eyes lit up, "Oh my GOD! I know exactly what to say. Please tell me you've seen *My Big Fat Greek Wedding*."

"I was living it four months ago," Lane couldn't stop herself from saying, and then, more to the point, "Yes, I've seen it on TV."

"Oh my god, this is perfect. I'm freaking out about Matt because of *My Big Fat Greek Wedding*."

"You are?" Lane looked at her quizzically.

"Oh, shit, no, not because of the movie, because it's ME. Don't you see? My life *is My Big Fat Fucking Turkish Wedding!*"

Something finally clicked in Lane, "Ohhh… Ok, but my original point—I mean it's not like you're trying to marry Matt."

"That's just the problem, to them I'm trying to marry any boy…" Reyhan seemed inconsolable and Lane didn't know why.

"But you don't have to tell them…"

"I should tell you something," Reyhan cut her off.

"Ok, what?"

"It happened before—back home. And I *was* going to marry him—"

"You were *engaged?!*"

"—Just listen!" Reyhan swatted her arm, "I fell in love with a boy in high school. And we were together for years—I mean *years*. And it took a long time for my family to accept him, because he's not Turkish, or even Bulgarian. But they finally did, well kind of, and it was great, and then…" she trailed off but Lane was on the edge of her seat.

"And *then?*"

"And then it was over, and they all…" and Reyhan started to do something Lane never saw coming; she started to cry, "and then they all said 'I told you so, foreign boys, what do you want'," she pulled herself together.

"Oh, Rey," was all Lane could think to say.

"It's ok, but now I just…"

"Don't worry, I understand. But promise me something," Lane heard herself saying in a resolute tone.

"Yes?" said Reyhan through still brimming tears.

"Don't let what happened with that boy or what happened with your family affect what could happen with Matt; he's an amazing guy and he deserves better than that."

And much to Lane's surprise, Reyhan straightened up, looked her straight in the eyes and seemed to understand, "God, you are so right… you are *so* right," she almost said to herself.

"Tell me something," Reyhan said as the tripped off to bed not long after, "Why haven't we done this sooner?"

Lane just smiled, but she wondered the same thing herself.

—

The next day Reyhan marched directly up to Matt in the teacher's room at the Beşiktaş branch, "We need to talk," she said in her stern teacher-giving-discipline voice.

Wanda, the odd and usually oblivious German teacher, took the hint and quietly made her exit. Alone, Matt turned wide eyed and questioning to Reyhan. But before he could form a question, she answered him by throwing her arms around his neck and pulling him in for a deep kiss.

Matt was stunned, but as he pulled back to ask what it was for, he saw Reyhan's face and suddenly understood. It was the kiss he had never gotten on the Istiklal. His hands dropping to her waist, he ran through all the things he wanted to ask her about why and when she had decided to give up whatever it was that was holding her back. Finally, however, he simply said, "Ice cream or cocktails this afternoon?"

—

Colin found himself eye level with a familiar face as he exited the Dort Levent metro stop. He had been coming to tutor Metin almost daily for more than three weeks, but this was the first time he registered the small statue of Atatürk in the tiny square off the entrance to the metro. Busts and sculptures and photographs of the founder of modern Turkey dotted the city like Easter eggs but something about this one struck Colin as different. He paused for a moment to consider what it was and thought that he noticed a slight smile on the face of the worn marble. But in the next second he realized he was late, and raced off towards Trump towers.

The towers had become an oddly regular part of his day over the past weeks. Passing through the giant revolving doors into the sleek lobby the receptionist recognized him instantly and waved him through to the elevators. Once inside, he checked himself in the dim reflection of the bronze wall panels. He looked much better than he had that first day, he thought, wearing a pair of new dress pants and an expensive looking shirt he had gotten tailored near Taksim square for almost nothing. He tried to tell himself his new clothes were to present a more professional appearance in Metin's uber chic offices, but he had to admit as the elevator doors opened that he mostly just wanted to look his best for the handsome man at the end of the hall.

Metin's receptionist arched her graceful eyebrows as he approached the desk.

"Hello Colin," she stated formally, "Mr. Oldologu would like to meet with you in his residence today, if it's ok." She hadn't said it as a question.

"Oh, ah, I mean I guess that's ok, but it is very far? I have another…"

She cut him off, "It's just upstairs."

He must have looked lost, he thought, because she continued, "He lives in apartment D on the 38th floor, I have told security you are coming."

Colin had seen the giant and mesmerizing billboards outside announcing the new residences in Trump Towers with a view over the northern part of the city. But he had never imagined someone would live *and* work in the same skyscraper, like some sort of future city. He laughed to himself, as the elevator climbed to one of its top numbers, thinking about a person being able to live inside this fashionable bubble for weeks without ever leaving, while a radically different world existed just blocks away in some of the run down side streets and highway underpasses of Dort Levent.

He exited the perfumed comfort of the elevator and was about to knock on the door of 38D when Metin quickly opened it, a beaming smile on his face. Colin couldn't help but smile back even though he was telling himself silently to keep it cool in such a personal space.

"I didn't realize you lived in the same building," was all he could think to say as he readjusted his bag in the entryway of the apartment.

"Oh yes yes, it's really much easier that way," Metin said, and before Colin could determine if it was a joke, he let out a warm laugh as he motioned him towards the living room.

Rounding the corner Colin immediately took a giant step back, almost losing his balance.

"Oh, yes, it's a lot the first time—kind of like being on stage!" Metin said as Colin did a double take around the large open space. Floor to ceiling glass formed the far wall of the apartment. As Colin's eyes adjusted to the light, he realized the reason he had stepped back, the view was the same as Metin's office, except 30 floors higher; it instantly made you feel as if your were about to fall off the side of the building. Instead of the comfortable wood paneling of Metin's small workspace, these glass walls spilled light into a cavernous loft awash in shinny white surfaces. Colin took in the view of the city and realized he could see all the way south east to the Bosphorus. Transfixed, he finally moved his eyes to the interior of the apartment, where he saw long, low, white sofas; chrome accents; tasteful throw pillows. Towards the back of the giant room he caught sight of a sleek kitchen that reminded him of something he had seen in Architectural Digest one time. It was unlike any kitchen he had ever seen in person, in Turkey or America, and he immediately had the urge to start banging away on some sort of lavish meal. But before he could finish planning his imaginary gourmet dinner his eyes traveled up above the kitchen to where he saw what was certainly a lofted bedroom. He tried to bring himself back to reality, but kept thinking there was no other way to describe it. The whole thing was—sexy.

Finally, he managed to meet Metin's smiling face and was unnerved again to realize he had forgotten how attractive he was. His slightly unshaven face underlined a strong jaw and white teeth. His usual work shirt was missing a tie and slightly unbuttoned to reveal a small bit of dark chest hair.

Colin quickly mentally slapped himself as he had done every time they had met for the past few weeks. As much as he enjoyed coming up here to see Metin, Colin was equally ashamed that he basically had the hots for a man that was probably straight, and even more embarrassingly his student.

"I know it seems nice, but believe me in the mornings I sometimes wish I could put up curtains," said Metin.

"Oh boo hoo for you," Colin said, laughing. Over the past couple weeks, Metin's casual nature had put him completely at ease. As embarrassed as he was to be attracted to this man, at least there was no visible awkwardness anymore.

"You are right!" said Metin laughing with him, "I'm 'being a douche' aren't I?" Colin had taught him the phrase just a couple days ago. After the first couple of meetings, Colin realized Metin's technically correct English was more than suitable for his needs. But it quickly became clear Metin was after a deeper grasp of the language. Lessons moved from business terms to slang and contemporary idioms. Colin thought it might be unprofessional, but after all Metin was the customer, and the lessons were the most fun he had ever had with a student. Every day Metin would bring in a notebook in which he had written down things he heard on American TV shows or read in Esquire and Colin would try his best to explain the subtle meanings or cultural references.

"I'm sorry to have you to my apartment," Metin was saying as he indicated Colin sit on one of the white sofas, "My office is being steam cleaned and I'm working from here for today."

"Oh, it's fine," Colin offered, "Just don't tell EnglishSpace," he said, and they both laughed.

Over the next hour, the two men covered everything from President Obama's first few months in office to the exact meaning of the phrase 'get the lead out'. Near the end of their time together Metin opened an issue of Vanity Fair to a marked page and started rattling off phrasal verbs he had underlined. He got to one and then heisted slightly.

"Ok," he said, a bit quieter, "what does this one mean… 'come out'?"

Colin thought he must have read it wrong, so he motioned for Metin to hand him the magazine. To his surprise, Metin moved to the sofa he was sitting on bringing the article with him. His pointed to the sentence in question, "Meredith Baxter comes out…"

Colin immediately went red. Metin had asked him tons of questions in their time together about adult subjects. He had learned quickly that Metin was no prude and definitely not worried about local ideas of what was and wasn't acceptable. But this was the first time anything about being gay had come up. Colin shifted in his seat, and suddenly realized how close Metin was sitting.

"Um, oh, ahh…" he struggled. "Well it means that you have 'come out' of the dark—in a way."

Metin looked confused and pressed him, "what do you mean 'the dark'?"

"Oh, right! Ha," Colin laughed nervously. "I mean the dark in your life, so for example you can 'come out' as a movie lover, or a chocolate lover… or anything else that you kept secret before."

"Oh," said Metin, "So it means to reveal a secret?"

Colin was relieved he had found a simple way of putting it, "Yes, exactly!"

"Oh, ok…" Metin still looked confused, and then he said, "Every time I read it I feel like it has to do with being gay."

Colin's heart began to race, "OH, ha! Well, ok, yes, that's a way you can use it—I mean that's a way that a lot of people use it…" He was flustered and not even sure why.

"Is that how you use it?" Metin asked, and it was suddenly clear that he was avoiding Colin's eyes.

Colin wasn't sure how to respond so he just said, "Yes, I've used it that way sometimes."

And then Metin rose abruptly, taking the magazine with him.

"I'm so sorry, Colin, I've kept you much longer than I was supposed to."

"Oh, right, of course," said Colin, still unsure of which one of them was acting more awkwardly. "I'll be on my way," and in one motion he gathered all his papers and threw his messenger bag over his shoulder.

Making a quick break for the entry way he turned around to catch one last glimpse of the skyline and found Metin standing directly in front of him.

"Thanks for another great class," said Metin, who had regained his usual excited tone. He extended his hand to shake Colin's, something he did at the end of every meeting. Colin reached out absentmindedly and was surprised when Metin held on to his hand for a bit longer than usual. Bringing his eyes up to meet the other man's, he was surprised and unnerved to see them happy and almost questioning. Metin continued to hold his grip in a light, double handed embrace, and Colin couldn't find a reason to pull away. He searched his eyes and then suddenly realized they had been standing like that for a very long interval.

Colin swallowed and noticed his breathing had deepened. Finally, just before he was about to explode with questions and excuses, Metin leaned in slightly; that subtle move of the head and relaxing of the eyes that is unmistakable. And for the first time in recent memory, Colin let go, pulled Metin in by their still-shaking hands and kissed him.

"**T**o boldly go——it's on TV!" Metin was saying over the rattling of the two boiling pots on the stove. Colin, deep inside the hall closet that also served as Metin's wine cellar, yelled back through the jumble of winter coats, "Yeah, I know, but it's still wrong!"

"English is so weird," Metin was still yelling as Colin re-entered the steaming kitchen with a bottle in each hand. Metin grinned, "You can split phrasal verbs, but not infinitives…" he trailed off seemingly perplexed by his odd, adopted language, but quickly more engaged in the more complex matter at hand—dinner.

"I know, I know. It definitely doesn't make sense. But think of it this way—if you never split your infinitives you'll be better at using English than ninety percent of native speakers."

"Well… I do like being better than people," Metin retorted from his crouching position beside the oven and then flashed a wide smile up at Colin. "Are you sure I can't pay you for this? This kind of English tutoring is worth a lot of money in this city."

"NO!" Colin laughed, "I told you, I'm not going to mix business with pleasure. It's completely unprofessional."

"Oh I am sincerely sorry. I didn't realize you American part time English teachers had so many rules about ethics… Maybe I could just make you my male escort, then you'd take my money," he said with a wide smile and pulled Colin in for the beginning of a passionate kiss.

Colin pushed him off and hit him playfully on the shoulder but couldn't help from swooning inside a little bit.

The past three weeks had been absolute magic. After their intense first kiss, Colin was sure he had completely messed up. But he was surprised and amazed when Metin called the following day to apologize and profess his deep interest.

"I understand if you don't want to see me again, but I couldn't help myself…" Metin said over the poor phone connection and Colin could almost hear the smile in his voice.

"Of course I want to see you again," Colin replied a smile spreading across his own face, "but only socially. We can't be teacher and student anymore."

And for the past two weeks they had done just that, spending almost every afternoon together and the past three nights at Metin's ridiculously upscale apartment. Even though Colin refused to take his money for the informal English lessons, he had a suspicion Metin was attempting to pay him in kind; lavishing gourmet dinners on him and taking him out for cocktails in Bebek or in the rooftop bar of the Ottoman Palace hotel.

It was almost too much, and under normal circumstances Colin would have thought this man was trying too hard. But with Metin he just felt like he was having the time of his life.

When he finally admitted he'd been dying to cook in Metin's kitchen he was shocked the next day to find huge paper bags full of all sorts of gourmet fare from the fancy grocery store in the basement of Trump Towers. Imported cheeses, truffle oil, and expensive wine that, because of Turkey's alcohol laws, Colin knew cost three times as much as it would have in the States.

And as if all that wasn't enough, Metin then threw on an apron himself and dazzled Colin with a stellar batch of stuffed grape leaves. Colin still couldn't help thinking it was all too good to be true as he gave into Metin's outstretched arm in front of the rattling stove.

Just then he realized his tiny blue fisher price phone was buzzing on the glass coffee table across the great room. Sprinting to pick it up, he saw Lane's name scroll across the screen and suddenly stopped himself from pressing accept.

He'd been doing that to all three of his close friends lately. In and out of his apartment at odd times, he had managed to avoid all of them except Reyhan, who caught him one morning returning form Dort Levent to shower before class. She questioned him expertly, and was about to get a full confession too, if they hadn't both been late for school.

As he stared down at the missed call on his phone, he tried to think of what was keeping him from coming clean to them—especially Lane. *They just wouldn't understand.* He thought with finality. The student thing was bad enough, but then he looked around and tried to picture himself describing the scene to Lane after all the times they had made fun of kept women and cracked jokes about sugar daddies. *She definitely wouldn't understand...* he told himself again forcefully, and then looked up to see Metin holding out a glass of deep purple wine and an irresistible smile.

—

Lane realized she must have slammed her phone on the restaurant table because Matt and Reyhan's faces showed mild concern. She moved her phone to the side which revealed a cheesy placemat sporting the Turkish flag blowing in the wind and the stern glare of a slightly callous Atatürk. She rolled her eyes.

"He's still not answering?" asked Reyhan.

"No, but it's cool," Lane could hear the ridiculousness of her tone as the words left her mouth.

"You know I have a theory he's got a secret man," Said Matt, returning to his intense study of the menu for the tiny eatery Reyhan had brought them to in a slightly shabby part of Şişli. The dark wood walls and tiny tables reminded Lane of most of the tourist places near Taksim, but the smell was intoxicating and more complex than what she was used to.

"It's just this one woman who makes food like you'll find in Turkish homes," Reyhan commented as plates began to arrive bearing creamy sauces, roasted eggplants, olives, and delicate grilled fish.

So that's where they've been keeping all the truly great food, thought Lane as she dug in with her utensil of flat bread. And then out loud, "But he's never been secretive about his dating life before—why now? Colin's a lot of things, but he's not ashamed."

"You know better than us he's a private person," offered Matt, as he poured fresh lemon juice and dried mint over a lentil sausage wrapped in lettuce.

"I guess you're right," Conceded Lane, "It's just…"

"He's not going to forget your birthday. I definitely told him last week." Matt finished her thought.

"I know. You're right. I'm just being ridiculous." Lane shook off the bad thought and started to layer eggplant puree over a crisp and delicate spinach pastry, "I do know one thing—he's going to regret missing this meal."

After dinner the three of them took a chilly stroll through the northern reaches of their section of the City. Spring had finally arrived in full force, but the fickle nature of the weather in Istanbul meant that a sudden blast of Russian air could sweep in from the Black Sea at any moment and leave a person shivering.

Lane wrapped herself tightly in the cheap but thick pashmina she had bought at the covered bazar in her neighborhood as they descended a steep hill towards the Bosphorus and Beşiktaş. Matt and Reyhan fell into a comfortable silence in front of her and linked hands, probably unconsciously, she thought. She had noticed a slight but important change in them since her talk with Reyhan a month ago. There was no more asterisk on their relationship, no more holding back, they were just happy.

"I'm going to head on home you guys," Lane spoke up before they reached the shore line.

"Oh no, Lane!" said Reyhan with genuine concern, "We're going to get ice cream and beer and watch the crazy fishermen down at the dock."

They had both been so great to her over the past month, but she told herself she knew when to make an exit, and her time had definitely come, "No, no! I'm exhausted and freezing," she lied slightly, "you two have fun!"

"Alright, alright," said Matt, "but we'll see you right after work tomorrow?"

"You've got it! Twenty-four here I come!" she said with slightly fake enthusiasm as they disappeared around a corner and she turned to trudge back up the hill towards Teşvikiya alone.

—

Lane finally admitted to herself how excited she was as she dashed down the front stairs of EnglishSpace after class the next day. An orange blur of new, brightly lighted signs almost disoriented her before she could reach the street.

Once free of the building she remembered she had let class go a little too early that day, and quickly retreated down the maze of circuitous backstreets to avoid any chance of running into a branch manager.

She splurged on a taxi back to the apartment and spent a luxurious 45 minutes blaring her new guilty pleasure Beyonce song and drinking a rare and expensive bourbon cocktail while picking out her birthday outfit.

Another cab ride later and she was standing in front of the ridiculous restaurant Marissa had talked her into in Sultanahmet. It was huge, expensive, and touristy. But Lane didn't care, it was right on the Marmara Sea and there was about to be a fantastic sunset.

"The birthday girl!" squealed Marissa with unusual enthusiasm as Lane saw her standing below a large black and white photograph of a tweed wearing Atatürk wielding a fishing rod. She rushed her inside and out onto the restaurant's balcony. More people had shown up than she expected. Noah was conversing in animated Turkish with an uninterested waitress. Thom had come straight from work it seemed, and a whole gaggle of Beşiktaş teachers were laughing at some joke that had just been told. She didn't have a lot in common with these people, Lane thought, but at least they liked to party.

Marissa handed her a drink and her co-workers started to wish her a happy birthday as she settled into a sea side table. The sunset blazed into the wide sea before her, dipping near a small, clear island on the horizon. It was perfect, but as she looked around, she realized none of her actual friends were anywhere to be found.

She checked her phone, something she had gotten out of the habit of doing in Turkey, since her cheap pre-paid device was both unreliable and often lost in her deep teacher bag. No messages.

Marissa was making great conversation, but it was well past the time she and Matt had talked about and she couldn't help herself from falling into a bit of a funk. Just then she noticed that horrible guy from the Beşiktaş branch... *what was his name? Mitchell! Right.*

"Hiiiiiii Mitchell," she offered as she approached the red face boy who was holding two beers and had some other kind of drink on the table, ready to go at any moment.

"Oh, heeeeey," Mitchell obviously didn't remember her name, but it didn't matter.

"So, I was just wondering, have you seen Reyhan and Matt?"

"OH, those two!" Was Mitchell's slurred response, and Lane thought that would be it until he finally continued, "Those guys are getting pretty heavy, am I right?!"

"Yep, I guess they are Mitchell," was all Lane could think to say, "So I guess you haven't seen them?"

"Oh Yeah, I definitely saw them—probably around lunch? And then who knows—you know I'm guessing they cut out of work early for a little afternoon delight! That's the life isn't it!"

Lane bypassed the man's crude familiarity, "Ok, well thanks for the help."

"Oh shit!" Mitchell yelled, "Aren't you like friends with them or something?"

"It doesn't matter," Lane said as she finally managed to escape, but she knew it did.

Two hours into her own birthday party and Lane had worked herself in such a state that even Marissa was avoiding her. Drunk on raki and making stilted conversation with mousy Claire from her branch, she knew it was probably time to call it a night.

Just then she heard her name over the din of the entire restaurant, "Lane!" it was Reyhan's unmistakably shrill panic tone.

The thin girl deftly made her way through the crowded dining room and to Lane's spot on the patio, weaving effortlessly through the crows with Matt's hand in hers, "OH MY GOD LANE."

Lane instantly knew she was going to regret her anger towards this sweet person.

"We've been trying to call and text you for hours! We got caught behind a bus accident and you wouldn't even believe the things we've seen—I mean there was a man with part of his face falling off! And of course all of Beshiktas was fucking shut down because the bus hit a light pole and—oh my god listen to me, it doesn't matter—we're here! And it's your birthday."

Lane had been right, she almost began to cry, "you were calling? These shitty phones! I've got to get an actual cell phone."

"Let me see yours," said Matt. And after he had taken it from her he commented, with a slight smile, "Lane you're completely out of credit."

"Ugh, I am such an idiot," Lane said with a happy drunken smile and hugged both of them. But suddenly she jerked back and continued, "To think I was so angry, and of course Colin has probably been trying to call... did either of you hear from him?"

But both of their faces answered her question before they could.

"Ummm... no, but you know he's got the same shitty phone" Matt tried pleadingly. But Lane knew Colin would never let his phone run out of credit like she would—he was always thinking ahead about things like that when they had lived together in Middlesborough.

"You're right," she lied to them and herself, and then wiped away her one visible tear and turned the rest of her night into the birthday she had been so excited about.

The next morning however, hung over and slightly nauseated, she felt something even worse inside of her—sadness. Colin had never shown up the night before. She put extra credit on her phone but it didn't make a difference; no call, no text, no nothing.

She felt like she was losing her best friend to something he wouldn't even tell her about. She was on the verge of tears and at the same time wondering if it was just Colin that was causing it.

Finally, she had to admit it—despite Marissa's quirky company, Thom's occasional outings, and the tea dates with her class, she felt something that she realized she had never experienced before—true loneliness.

—

A day later, back at the apartment cooking an early dinner for herself and still working through her post-party depression, Lane heard a slight knock at the door before it opened and a person entered. She knew instantly it wasn't Reyhan or Matt, who would have simply come in unannounced.

She turned quickly to find Colin standing as close to the far wall as possible.

"Oh, hey," Lane tried to check her anger and give him a chance to wow her with a perfect explanation.

"Hey," Colin's voice was pleading as he searched frantically for the words he had rehearsed on the way to the girls' apartment from Metin's comfortable living room that afternoon. For the past twenty-four hours he had been on an emotional roller coaster. He had woken up the day before to a barrage of missed calls and texts on his forgotten phone in the coat closet. Out of instinct he immediately dialed Lane, but then hit the end button. What was he going to say?

All throughout class and back at Metin's apartment he agonized over how to explain—all the while letting the hours slip by without picking up the phone. *I thought the party was this weekend,* he tried to justify to himself. But even in his head the explanation sounded hollow. The fact of the matter was he was having too good of a time and had just forgotten.

"Lane, I know nothing I can say can really make up for…" all his rehearsed words went out the window as he looked into his friend's face.

Lane raised an impatient hand, "It's really fine—don't make it into more of a thing," she almost begged.

"I know, but—well you see I wrote it down wrong. And that's no excuse I know. I should have known…"

"Colin!" Lane pleaded for him to stop. She was on the verge of letting something out and was sure that if he kept talking she wouldn't be able to stop it.

"I know, but please just listen—"

"Listen?!" That was it, she thought. And she saw herself from outside herself, not being able to control what came next. "Like you've been fucking listening to me for the past few months?!"

Colin expression shifted to amazement, "What…?"

"You don't give a shit—do you?"

"Lane… I… I'm trying to say I'm sor—"

"I never thought you would do this to me," Lane heard herself saying, "I never thought you were this type of person."

"Lane, is this more than…"

"You're damn right it's more than this. Where have you BEEN? Who are you WITH?" Even in her rage, Lane heard the words and couldn't believe they came from her mouth. They weren't the right questions at all, but for some reason she had still asked them.

Colin was shocked into silence, and Lane heard herself continue, "You have no fucking clue what it's been like for me. You haven't called, you haven't let me know what's up—it's like we didn't even come here together! And the thing that fucking pisses me off the most is that you know I wouldn't judge you for anything—but all I get is silence and you disappearing."

"Lane, I didn't know you felt—"

"That's right, you didn't know, because you didn't bother to pick up the fucking phone or show up once in a while." It had all come out of her—the months of being alone, the constant question in her mind of why he had been so distant; the worry that it was somehow about her. It was all out, and there was no way of taking it back. She knew she had cut deeply. She could almost feel herself twist the knife. And as she was frantically searching for a way to stop herself, she saw Colin's face turn from shock to anger.

"You've got to be fucking kidding me," Colin lashed back in an uncharacteristic tone. Now it was Lane's turn to be shocked, "Are you really going to blame me for all of your problems?!"

Colin knew he was in the wrong, but the thought that he didn't understand having a rough time in this country was too much for him to listen to, "It's not my fault you've chosen to be alone here," he said and continued before he could think of how it sounded, "I'm not you're fucking keeper and if you're feeling sorry for yourself there's only one person you can blame. You know what, Lane, I'm sorry I missed your party, but you'll get over it." It was a statement with finality, and Colin knew the only thing he could do was turn and leave, even though everything in him was telling him to take it all back.

As the door slammed shut Lane slumped down into a rickety kitchen chair and stared at the wall. She knew that crying would only make things worse, but the tears were coming fast.

She did the only thing she could do to stop them—she made a plan. *If that's how things are going to be*, she thought with resolution, *then I need to be honest with myself—it's time to go.*

Still fighting tears, but focused on her goal, she pulled out her laptop and a half drunk Efes from the fridge. She spent the next three hours searching flights and re-reading her EnglishSpace contract before finally falling into a fitful and weary sleep.

Colin spent that night in his own room—knowing he couldn't see Metin the way he was. He went over the fight in his head well into the night; rehashing every detail, revising his statements, telling himself he had won, and then realizing that winning wasn't the point. He knew he was wrong, and more than that he was angry at himself for not realizing it sooner. But as much as he wanted to run downstairs and take it all back and figure out a way through it Lane's words burned in his ears about not understanding. He started for the door only once, but half way through got a text from Metin. He took off his shoes, sat down on the couch, and told himself it could wait until tomorrow.

—

The next day Colin was catatonic in class. He had managed to avoid Matt at the apartment by leaving super early. He thanked his luck that he didn't work with any of his three friends and decided his best bet was to hide out at Metin's house for a few days while the whole thing died down and he had a chance to think of what to say to Lane.

That evening Metin was waiting for him as usual with a bag full of fancy ingredients and sweet words. Colin gave him the reader's digest version of what had happened and Metin listened intensely.

"Well, it sounds like you're right," he said finally.

"Ha! You would say that," joked Colin.

"No, no! I am sad you missed your friend's birthday, but it sounds like she has more problems than just you not contacting her. Plus it meant I got you all to myself." Colin laughed but something about Metin's take on the situation seemed almost too simple. He told himself that he had done a bad job of explaining just how important Lane was.

"I know, I've thought about it and thought about it and I really can't imagine where all her anger came from—it can't be all about me…" He drifted off, and even thought Metin was still listening he snapped himself out of it, "Anyway! It'll all blow over soon and I'll apologize for missing her party and things will be back to normal. Sorry, I know this is probably boring for you."

But Metin answered him with a tight hug and a soft kiss and a short statement, "I'm interested in almost anything you have to say," he whispered softly—and Colin couldn't help but close his eyes and smile.

—

Lane told Reyhan about her fight with Colin the next day over lunch time chay on the docks. Reyhan listened wide-eyed and never offered any unwanted advice.

"This'll all blow over," offered Lane's new friend, "You two have too much history."

"I know, I know," said Lane, unsure if it was true, "I just think this one is going to take a lot of time…" she trailed off.

Reyhan seemed to sense something and continued, "So what's your plan?"

Lane immediately tensed up—had she said anything about leaving Turkey? She wasn't even ready to tell herself it was for sure. Then she realized Rey was talking about Colin.

"Oh, I'll give it a few days and then throw him an apology dinner—it's what always worked back in college"

Reyhan seemed like she had gotten the answer she had been looking for. But even still, Lane knew she would have to think of a way to tell her she was leaving. *I'll figure it out soon,* she thought.

Nine
Interjections

The Palazzo Corpi was built by master Italian architect Giacomo Leoni. When it was finished in late 1870s, it represented the height of European architectural splendor in the Pera district of Istanbul. Very soon after that, the Americans moved in. The Palazzo became the first diplomatic foreign property purchased by the United States in the world. (Although members of congress were forced into the deal by the then Ambassador General after a pivotal game of poker.)

For over one hundred and twenty years the building represented an American presence in Europe, the Middle East, The Ottoman Empire, and the Turkish Republic; first as a residence, then as an embassy, and finally as the consulate general.

The Palazzo Corpri now sat dormant, a casualty of September 11th and a push for greater American security abroad.

Lane thought, as she now stood looking at the high mortar walls of the new consulate building, how different the two buildings were. She passed the Palazzo almost everyday downtown. Its blackened neoclassical stone work and sharply carved American eagle roundel were imposing, but at least they were visible; part of a bygone era when Turks and visitors alike could catch a little piece of America on their way to dinner.

A few years ago all that changed. What Lane now found herself in front of was not a Consulate, it was a fortress. Twelve miles, sparse public transportation, and a daunting security process now separated downtown from the official American presence in the city. The only thing Lane could find written about it was an article that described it as a place "they don't even let birds fly."

The author had not exaggerated.

The new Consulate was located in far flung Istinye Park, a neighborhood like many of the upscale districts of Istanbul.

Besides Tesvikya, most of the money in Constantinople seemed to be concentrated in American style 'edge cities'. Places far out from the center, were SUVs are king, the mall is the shopping center of choice, and the landscape is characterized by spacious low rise apartments and expensive restaurants for the rich, and cinderblock housing and cafeterias for the poor that serve them.

Levent, Bebek, Fenerbaçe on the Asian side; they were all the same. Virtually inaccessible by bus, they were dotted with tiny gourmet food shops, exotic one name restaurants and punctuated with yacht-filled marinas.

Lane was now in the middle of one of these exurbs, and getting there had been half the battle.

Like so many times in the past few months, Lane had found herself aimlessly wandering around Taksim square looking for a dolmuş stop that didn't exist. After twenty minutes she finally found a grouchy younger driver who grunted a yes when she, in her firmly enunciated Turkish, asked if his vehicle went to the consulate.

Skipping along the Bosphrous, she had tried hard to pay attention to the crisp, printed, mapquest directions in her binder, but found her eyes drifting to the sparkling water that raced alongside the van, creating a watery disco ball effect on the inside roof. After a good deal of time, she realized she must have gone too far and quickly yelled the only words she could think of: "STOP, PLEASE!"

Luckily for her, the man on the stool seat had a horribly unclear accent, because she was sure his string of strongly thrown syllables as she exited the side door were not meant as compliments.

Stranded on the side of a road between a sheer rock face and the choppy water of the Bosphorus, Lane tried to take stock of her situation. She was at least twenty five minutes from downtown and had passed both the major bridges ages ago. After a period of uncertainty, she took the only option available and started walking North.

Twenty minutes, and over two hundred stairs later, Lane put her hands on her knees to catch her breath at the final landing. She could see nothing but the same standard cinderblock buildings that made up most of the outlying neighborhoods. No cars, or shops, or even people came into view. She checked the map once again and was bewildered to find that the spot she was standing in had to be yards from her final destination. But she couldn't see anything that indicated a major consulate nearby.

Giving up her plans for lunch, she finally found a small corner store, or bakal, and timidly opened the greasy glass door.

"I'm sorry sir, but where is the American Consulate?" or at least that's what she had meant to say in that tricky language.

The man behind the counter didn't even look up, engrossed in some sort of history magazine with Atatürk emblazoned on the cover amid large block letters. He must not have heard, she thought, or understood. But just as she opened her mouth to repeat her question, a door opened in the back and a young man entered. The old man pointed to her, still without looking up, and said something to him about her being American. The young man approached her eagerly.

"You are American?" his bright eyes could barely contain his excitement.

Taking his cue, Lane continued in English, "Yes, I just need to know where the consulate is—" she asked.

"Yes, yes!" he continued before she had even finished, "Please, follow me!" He almost picked her off her feet as he grabbed her elbow and led her out into the street where she now stood.

"Over there, just over there," he said quickly. But Lane could see nothing but more apartments and shops. Soon, however, she realized his outstretched arm was pointing up instead of straight ahead, and her eyes followed his index finger to above the roofline of the buildings.

Lane was amazed, "Are you sure?" she said. But the kind man had anticipated her question. "Yes, yes, American consulate." He gestured even more emphatically than before.

Up above the tallest of the apartments rose a large hill, brilliant in the hot mid-day sun, and covered with mall trees and bushes. On top of the hill, like a dream, sat a large, boxy structure, half way between the scary austerity of a prison, and the bright modern look of a newly built high school.

With the man's gentle head nod for reassurance, she crossed the street, looking back to make sure she was headed in the right direction.

Walking through the tightly packed buildings, she came to an opening bordered by a thick wall on the other side of the street. Behind the wall the grassy hill rose even higher than before.

She saw a small vestibule guarded by four Turkish policemen and an impossibly small entrance for cars. She took a breath. This was much more than she had expected.

She had seen the barbwire of the American Embassy in Berlin and noticed increased guards near the UN in New York; but this was a different kind of response to that horrible day almost a decade ago. Here, between two continents, in the only country in the world that bordered the European Union and Iran, the new world of American diplomacy looked like something out of a futuristic action movie, as if the grass itself would swallow you whole if you happened to misstep on the smooth concrete driveway that snaked up to and behind the building.

Lane decided that to get through such intense security, she would need a coffee, and turned back toward the bakal. But just as she reached the main street something happened—she heard shouting of some kind, a man—two men. Then silence, but for some reason she stood perfectly still.

Then the whole world went white.

—

When Lane opened her eyes she was face down on the side walk. She quickly checked to make sure she wasn't hurt. She felt fine, but knew that something could still be wrong. And then she noticed she couldn't hear anything.

Silence.

She knew enough to be afraid to move, but was otherwise strangely calm. *What if this is it?* She thought, oddly removed from what she was sure was a very serious situation.

She started to feel her hands.

The pavement scraped against the heel of her palm. She could move her arms. And then, faintly, a noise. Like a siren approaching from a distance, it started softly and grew in intensity as it pulsated towards her. All of her emotion seemed to rush back—she was terrified. It screamed louder and louder until, yes, it *was* a siren, and it was almost on top of her.

A hand touched her back lightly and she jerked to the side, involuntarily, out of fear. She was on her back now, her pointless navy cardigan wrapped tightly around her upper body. A man was standing over her. It was the young man from the bakal. He held out his hand.

"Are you ok?" he managed, the brightness gone from his eyes.

Lane shook her head and sat up, the pavement still grinding into her hands and legs.

"Um, yeah," she said, checking herself slowly for injuries, "I'm fine, I think." She hadn't even tried to speak the man's language.

"What…" she began, but then looked up and noticed the scene in front of her. Police cars everywhere, the entrance to the Consulate barricaded, ambulances perched on curbs. There was debris, but as far as she could see the wall was still intact. She noticed most of the people gathered around an area across the street.

Just then another man approached. He was red haired and older, with a grave expression on his face. His uniform told Lane he wasn't Turkish.

"Ma'am, are you alright?" he said in thick New York accent.

"Um, yeah, I think so, what…" but he was already putting his arm around her shoulder and leading her towards the consulate.

"Are you an American?" he said in a business like tone.

"Yes," Lane managed, "Um, where are you—"

"You should come inside and sit down while we sort things out," he responded quickly.

"Of course, just let me thank…" But by the time she had turned around the young man from the bakal was gone.

———

The bomb had been more "flash than bang" she overheard from the staff inside the lavish reception building just inside the walls of the Consulate. Intended to cause more of a disruption than actual casualties, it had claimed as it's only victim a trash can and a stray cat, but none of that seemed to make Lane feel any better.

She sipped the bitter coffee they had given her and surveyed the lobby.

It was like a newly built regional airport, except for the fact that there were no planes. Neat rows of connected black leather waiting chairs filled the fluorescently lighted room. Gray/beige polished stone covered almost every floor, wall, and counter top, reflecting what little sunlight was able to make it through the oddly small windows. It was spotless, more inviting than she had expected, but still intensely cold.

Lane was almost catatonic. She didn't even want to think of how her father would take things, having sent her to the consulate for her safety in the first place. She put her head in her hands and massaged her eyes and then, pulling them back, realized they were covered in hot tears. She was crying and hadn't even noticed. She tried to stop, sniffed her nose, and wiped her stinging lids, but soon she was doubled over again, heaving with quiet sobs.

So it's come to this, she thought, a crying heap in a fake leather waiting chair, in a strange building, in a foreign country. And through the tears the strangest thing—a small roll of laugher welled up from deep inside her stomach and shot out of her nose in quiet puffs.

For what seemed like hours she sat that way unable to open her eyes but listening to everything going on around her. The consulate was a mad house for the first twenty minutes; people running back and forth; phones ringing off hooks; door opening and slamming. And then, as things started to die down she heard loud conversations pop up. She could hear Turkish, American, and a few other accents but had no way of knowing who or where they came from.

A woman's voice said something about the PKK, the Kurdish Workers' Party and then disappeared into a back room. Two men with official sounding voices mentioned al-qaeda and then one quickly silenced the other. She heard the receptionist loudly state something about teenagers doing the same thing near the airport.

Despite it all Lane couldn't seem to care. She knew in the back of her mind that it would probably matter to her in the future. But as she sat there, continuing to move between deep breaths and quiet crying, she realized that the only thing she felt was fear and a lack of safety; there was no room for blame.

"Are you alright?" The question was in English, but Lane was too tired to care who it had come from. Without raising her head she gave a simple nod, hoping that would be the end of it.

"Ok, well I…" the voice continued. Lane raised her head sharply, and found herself staring into the eyes of a young man two seats over. He had a medium frame and dark hair, but his skin, even though olive, was bright pink, the way hers got when she was nervous. She noticed his simple blue button-down and messenger bag. Something about him seemed kind, his dark brown eyes searching hers. Before she knew it she had launched into a complete dissertation about how it was she came to be crying into a paper coffee cup with an American flag on it.

"It's not—" fighting back tears, she had started to form the words in Turkish, but quickly gave up and began talking at a clipped pace in her native tongue, "It's not even this. It's everything. I was done with this place. I was gonna move on and be able to look back on it as an 'experience', and…" The words were coming faster than she could manage, in sentences that were jumbled and incomplete.

"Oh my god." She stopped herself and took in a deep breath, "I'm sorry, I'm probably speaking too fast for you. And I don't even know what I'm saying."

"Don't worry, I understand you." The young man spoke in a low baritone that soothed Lane. She realized his pronunciation was perfect, which made her feel even more embarrassed about her feeble language skills.

"Listen," she said, not wanting to add yet another blunder to an already unsalvageable day, "I'm sure your country is very nice, but right now I think it kind of sucks, and you seem like a nice guy, so I'm not going to insult you anymore." She made a move to gather her things, but the stranger rose quickly to grab them for her.

"Please," he said, "We don't have to talk about Turkey. I'll carry your things for you."

They walked quietly towards reception, where things still seemed to be in chaos, but just as Lane was about to give up and sit down again, the man started speaking to the girl behind the desk in deliberately slow and perfectly worded sentences.

"I'm sorry Miss, but this woman has had a bad day and would like to get home, is there any way that can happen sooner rather than later?"

The girl looked overwhelmed, but soon seemed to remember Lane.

"Yes, of course," she said in an American drawl, "I'm supposed to put her in a cab as soon as she's ready."

"Thank you very much." said the man, and then, to Lane, "Do you need a minute?"

"Um, no, no," Lane stammered, "You can call the cab as soon as you get a chance… and, uh, thank you." She turned toward her helper with astonishment; she had had help from strangers many times in this country, but this was the first time someone had helped her communicate with another American.

"Thanks again… uh, I don't even know your name." The man took her hand in his, and she noticed his flushed lips turn up into a smile.

"I'm Ibrahim," he said.

"Well, Ibrahim, I'm Lane," she looked up into his brown eyes, he was a good six inches taller than she was. "What were you even doing here today?"

He laughed in a comforting way, "I came for an American visa, but from the looks of things, I don't think either of us will be able to do what we came here to do. Why were you here?"

Lane couldn't help but laugh herself, "I came to register, in case something like this happened…"

He smiled and inadvertently put his hand on her arm. For some reason it didn't scare her. After a second however, he must have noticed and quickly removed it.

"So, Lane, I take it you're leaving."

"That's my plan, and I don't think this will change things." The receptionist motioned to her that the car would be outside soon.

"Well, before you go, take this," Ibrahim handed her a small card with a number and email address on it, "I know this can be a fucked up place sometimes, but before you leave, I'd love to take you for coffee. Maybe end things on a good note?"

Lane almost laughed, but the seriousness in his voice was an odd tonic. She took his card and nodded, unsure of how to even respond. She got in the cab outside with the card still in her hand, sure that she wouldn't call him, but happy she had met him just the same.

—

Reyhan knocked over a small glass that shattered on the floor in the kitchen as she ran to meet Lane at the front door.

"Oh my God, are you ok?!"

"Yes," Lane had heard the same question far too many times that day, "seriously, I'm fine."

"We've been calling your cell all day, and all of us were freaked out, and—oh shit, I'm so sorry, you're mother called, and I didn't know what to say."

"Fuck." Lane knew she had to get on skype and tell everyone she was alright, but she wished she could wait at least a day.

"I know, I'm so sorry," Reyhan continued, "Were you near it, what happened?"

"Slow down, slow down." she knew Rey was only concerned, but she couldn't think.

"You're right—shit, I'm sorry, I just thought you were dead, and…" Rey's excitement was probably justified, but it was still overwhelming. "Ok, how 'bout this, can I get you anything?"

It didn't take Lane very long to think about the question, "A drink."

Reyhan ran into the kitchen and started rummaging. Lane, more tired than freaked out, turn on her laptop and tried to steel herself for a conversation with her parents.

Half an hour later, she was finally able to convince Jim and Myra she had been nowhere near the blast (a lie she thought would be best for everyone). Her dad, however, was still convinced of his guilt, and though he couldn't directly order her back home, he made her promise she wouldn't go near any other official buildings while abroad. It was the first time in Lane's life she could remember her father telling her to *avoid* authority figures. She managed to get off the phone only after reminding them both how she was with two good friends and a Turkish speaker. Something in her, though, made her stop just before she told her Dad that she *was* planning on coming home. She told herself it was only because she would never get them off the phone if they started that conversation.

Exhausted and oddly wired, she re-entered the kitchen to find Reyhan with a concerned look on her face.

"What's wrong?"

Reyhan made an exaggerated face and then produced a dark bottle from behind her back, "This is all I could find, but we have three bottles of it."

Lane took the bottle and examined the label. *Vishne Sharap*. "I think it'll work just fine."

She settled into a glass and decided to tell Reyhan everything. Not just about the bombing, but her entire time in Turkey to that point; the loneliness, her co-workers, her students, even not being able to ask for potatoes. She cried, she laughed at herself, she drank, and Reyhan listened—just as she had listened to Rey a month ago.

Their conversation moved on past the bomb and Turkey. Reyhan, through cherry colored lips, and slurred speech talked angrily about her parents and their expectations. Lane talked about her life in Middlesborough and Colin and how things had changed.

The boys returned to find them both, in only bras and jeans, crowding in front of the tiny bathroom mirror armed with mascara wands.

"Fucking hell I'm so happy you're alright," Colin was ashen-faced.

"Oh my god, I completely forgot to call you, fuck *fuck*," Lane slurred a bit.

"Don't worry," Said Reyhan, not much more sober herself, "I texted to let them know you were ok."

"We've been all over Istanbul, we even tried to get back to the consulate to bring you back home," Matt's large blue eyes were near tears, which sent Lane off again on a crying binge, this time out of joy.

"You two, I just—" and she dissolved.

The four sat and continued the sad party, talking over each other, gossiping, making plans. By the time Lane went to bed her story had become more adventure than horror. She dropped off quickly and with a smile, but awoke the next morning in a cold sweat, the blast still ringing in her ears.

She was happy she had her friends back, but she was still certain that her days in Istanbul were numbered.

—

Lane took the next day off work. Her *I was involved in a terrorist bombing* excuse seemed to do the trick with the usually hardnosed Mehmet.

She thought she would sleep off her shock, but mid-morning found her wide awake and restless. So she donned her favorite jeans, and headed out on a walking tour.

Uncertain of where she was going, but in a hurry to get there, she cut a quick path through Teşvikiya, past the Posh Mosque, past Armani and Gucci. She didn't even look up at the blackened façade of the technical college, with its dark windows perfect for a horror movie.

Down the hill she flew in her inadequate ballet flats, not pausing to admire any of the upscale shop windows. She didn't even glance up at the international patrons gathered for cigarettes on the pressure washed cobblestones of the city's most fashionable district.

Maçka blurred past and soon she was on the banks of Bosphorus, skipping up towards Beşiktaş as if she were late for an appointment.

All the trappings of upscale Istanbul fell away. The high priced fish restaurants, the Four Seasons hotel, even the taxis and the expensively dressed pedestrians.

She moved faster and faster towards an indefinable goal, almost in a full sprint, not even feeling her feet anymore. Soon she stopped, winded, but still feeling like she had to continue moving.

She looked around. All she could see were trees. She realized she must have strayed into Yildiz Park a while back. She finally slowed her pace, surveying as she went. The largest public park in Istanbul, Lane thought how it was odd that you could be standing in the middle of a place like this and almost forget for a second that around you seethed a city of millions.

She reached the top of a ridge and looked down towards the point at which the European side of the city spilled into the Bosphorus. She strolled along the winding asphalt, watching dogs and children on shiny new play equipment.

It was almost like the bomb at the consulate had happened in a different city, in a country far away from this place. How was it these children were playing and laughing unattended, these teenagers were kissing next to giant oaks, these elderly people were walking as if they didn't have a care in the world? Everyone was carrying on as if nothing had happened the day before.

It was an odd emotion, the desire that perfect strangers pack up their belongings and picnics and run home out of respect for what had happened to her.

She thought how it must be like this other places not very far from the city she was standing in; where bombs weren't just 'flash and bang'. Places where land minds killed people instead of just scaring them. Where every time you left your house, there was a good chance something would happen to you. And where, after it happened, you got up the next day and went to the park, because that was all you could do.

—

When Lane got back to the apartment that afternoon she found Colin sitting alone in the kitchen over a small cup of coffee. It was a rare sight, and her face must have shown her surprise, because he quickly called her on it.

"I know, I can't believe I'm here either, I wasn't even sure it was the right building at first."

Lane laughed awkwardly. It was the first time they had been alone together since the fight. She put her things down and began unpacking the small trinkets she had bought in Beşiktaş.

"What are those for?" Colin said, indicating the tiny objects wrapped in predictably flashy paper.

Lane froze, she had bought the small presents as souvenirs for her parents in light of her fast approaching return. She said the first thing that came to mind that didn't indicate her leaving.

"Small gifts for my students, they gave me a birthday present."

Colin looked crest fallen, "That's part of what I want to talk to you about, I guess… have coffee with me." He casually kicked a chair out from under the worn table.

"Ok…" Lane didn't know what to think, things had been fun last night, but the way they left things a week ago still stung. She studied his face and as she poured lukewarm coffee from the ancient pot.

"What did you do today?" His eyes were bright but almost pleading.

"Took a walk to the park. Bought those things. Just went exploring."

"Are you ok?"

Lane laughed, she was tired of everyone asking her the same question, but happy to hear it from him, "*Yes!* Please don't worry, I'm gonna be alright. Honestly, the whole thing was more of an annoyance than anything. It's over."

Colin looked pleased, but still pensive, "Good." And then again more softly, "Good."

Lane sipped her coffee in silence as she tried to figure out what was bothering her friend, "Is that all you wanted to ask me?" she asked directly.

"Yes—well. No, I mean, that was my only question. But—but I also wanted to say, I can't believe I reacted like that to you last week. I missed your birthday—that was ridiculous of me. I'm sorry, I didn't—"

"Oh, please! You don't have to apologize, Colin. I was in a bad place, and I thought I was hurt. That's not your fault. Yes, I was sad about my birthday—who wouldn't be? But it wasn't just that. I was mad in general. I was mad at everyone, including myself. But you were right—my life here is my own doing. It's crazy of me to be sad that you and Matt and Rey have made a life here. Please, we don't have to talk about it."

Colin's brow twisted into a look of mild surprise, "Made a life here?" He repeated as if the sentence was in Turkish and he couldn't figure it out. "What do you mean, I've made a life here?" He was smiling but obviously perplexed.

Lane didn't know what to say, had she *imagined* his complete absence over the past months? "Well, you know, you've found a circle of some kind, you have friends, you're dating someone. You seem happy... *you* know, you've 'made a life'. And I realize now that just because you were able to do that here and I wasn't doesn't mean I should be angry at you. It just means we've had different experiences. Really I think I was mad at myself for not getting out there more." She thought she had finally put her feelings into the proper words, which was why she was surprised to see Colin almost laughing.

"Is that what you think I've done?" He was smiling broadly now, only increasing her confusion.

"Well, yes—isn't it?" Lane eyes narrowed.

Colin rolled his eyes, "Did you know I kicked a boy out of my room during the call to prayer?"

Lane laughed before she could stop herself. "You what?!"

"Yeah, do you remember Can?" Colin was on the verge of laughing also. Lane nodded.

"He shushed me during the call to prayer. I threw a fit. And long story short we haven't talked since."

"Colin that's terrible!" Lane said through wails of laugher.

"I know, right? It was such a no-win situation."

"The poor boy just wanted a moment of peace and you insulted his religion and turned him out on the street."

"Oh I'm definitely going straight to hell if there is one."

They laughed in a way they hadn't in months.

"But is that all?" asked Lane shyly after a minute.

Colin eyed her before asking, "Do you know what the gay clubs are like in this city?"

Lane was lost, "Ha, should I? I imagine they're like the ones in Raleigh."

Colin smiled but wasn't laughing, "Not at all. They're terrible. All the gay men in a city this size and only two or three places they really feel they can be themselves? It's depressing, and definitely not the sort of place I could meet anyone."

Lane looked at the floor, "I guess I never thought too much about how you'd…"

"It's fine," he said, "What I'm trying to say is: I'm a gay man in a Muslim country, and I look very different than the average Turk. Every time I leave this apartment I feel like I'm stepping foot on a different planet. Ok—so the other day I was in Sultanahmet, and this Turkish guy started trying to sell me something, and I did that thing, you know, where I pretend to only understand French until they go away?"

Lane laughed, some of the best moments in Athens had been Colin's feeble attempts at confusion in French, "Yes, sometimes it actually works."

Colin didn't look amused, "Well this time it didn't, the guy started screaming at me. Told me how he knew I was English, and then said 'fuck you, go back to England'."

Lane studied her friend's freckled face. "Oh god, really? I mean I'd give you Irish, but British is just going too far."

He laughed, "Do you understand what I'm trying to say? Turkey isn't a cake walk for me either. No one takes me seriously unless they think I have money to spend, and even then…"

Lane could finally see full picture. She was even angrier at herself than before. How could she not have realized? She was a woman in this strange place, which was hard enough. But she started to remember all the thinly veiled remarks her upper level students had made about gay people. She knew the word in Turkish, and she also knew she had heard it used as an insult more times than she could count.

But Colin's secrets still puzzled her. Slowly she started to question him, "So, if it's that hard for you, how do you manage? I'd be on the first plane back," *hell I am getting on the first plane back,* she thought.

Colin looked down at the table and took a deep breath, "I guess that's where Metin came in."

"Is that his name? Finally! Honestly the only thing I was mad about was you keeping him from me. I thought it might be getting serious," she said as casually as possible, "This is great, Colin. Seriously."

"So, that's not all."

"It's not? I'm confused again, what else is there?"

"About three months ago EnglishSpace made me a deal."

"Made you a deal?"

"Well, they gave me an opportunity. They would pay me double the normal rate to take on a private student."

"But why would you take one through EnglishSpace? We all have privates we could have given you…"

Colin shrugged, "It was easy I guess? He's only one metro stop from here."

Lane tried to choose her words carefully, "Colin, are you trying to tell me you're seeing this student?"

"Yes," he seemed relieved, "I don't know exactly how it happened, but he was so nice, and then one afternoon…"

It was a lot to take in. Lane had to be honest with herself, of all of them, she had thought Colin would be the last to start dating a student. But life works out strangely sometimes, she thought, and here he was, silently pleading for her approval.

"So, that's great," Lane tried as hard as she could not to start cracking sexy teacher jokes.

"I think what happened was, I didn't want you to think I was with someone just because he paid me a lot of money, or he lived in a nice place, or—god, I don't know, something about it just felt like people would raise an eyebrow, you know?"

Lane understood, "Colin, do you like him?"

"He's wonderful," Colin had paused a split second before saying the words, but Lane hadn't noticed.

"Then that's what matters, isn't it?"

"You really think that?"

Lane had to check herself, even in her relief her instincts told her the whole situation was a bit off, especially with Colin's secretiveness. But she knew him, he wouldn't have just fallen into a relationship with someone that bought him a fancy drink.

"Just promise me one thing."

"What's that?" he asked.

"He's not still paying you is he?"

Colin laughed, his cream colored cheeks becoming bright pink, "No, I told him to stop as soon as we kissed."

"I'm happy for you, boo." Lane felt a sense of peace, she finally understood what had been weighing on her for so many months. As odd as it was, in five minutes, the months of strain and awkwardness had melted away. She had her best friend back.

There was only one thing left to ask, "So where *is* this condo of his… and what's his full name? Just to check up on you, of course."

Colin looked happier than Lane could remember him looking in the past year, "His name is Metin Bayazkan. And he lives in Dort Levent."

Lane smiled. She still wasn't an expert on Istanbul's geography, but she knew enough to be intrigued at the location. There were very few residential buildings in Dort Levent, and she only knew the name of one. She decided to joke around.

"Does he live in Trump Tower?"

Colin could no longer contain his excitement and burst out laughing, "YES! And it's wonderful. Lane, I want you to come as soon as possible, the view isn't like anything you've ever seen before!"

Lane squealed with surprise and excitement. Something still struck her as slightly strange about the whole thing, but she decided to chalk it up to miscommunication.

"I'm so happy for you," she said, and as far as she could tell, she meant it.

"We don't have to talk about it anymore, I know it's been a long day for you, and I'm more concerned about how you're doing."

For the first time that evening Lane actually thought about how she was doing. And then she lied, "I'm fine."

Colin studied her. They had been through a rough moment, but he was still the person that meant the most to her in that country, he was still the person that had followed her, unquestioning into the jungle of post-collegiate life.

"You're not fine," was all he had to say.

Lane sighed deeply and faced him, "You're right, I'm not fine. But it's not because of what you think… Colin, I have something to tell you, and I don't want you to freak out—and I definitely don't want you to tell *anyone*."

She stared him down until he relented, "Ok, fine, what's *so* important that I can't even tell Matt?"

Unable to ever sustain a moment of suspense, Lane continued without hesitation, "I'm leaving."

Colin didn't seem to need any clarification, "And you haven't told Matt and Reyhan yet?"

"No, I just told you you're the first to know. I don't even know what they would say—"

But like always, he knew where she was headed, "You don't want us to think you're leaving because of the bomb."

Her eyes must have been confirmation enough. He continued, "Lane, I love you. And of all people, I know why you're leaving—bombing or not. Don't worry about Matt and Reyhan, I'll tell them if you want… just—just tell me this is what you want, even now."

She didn't even have to think, "Colin, I made this decision even before that stupid bomb. And yes, this what I want—even now."

He nodded, "I love you, I'm sorry for—for all of this."

She couldn't help the smile that crept over her lips, "Why?" She said, mocking him with her eyes, "I have some of the best stories of my life."

They both laughed and Colin pulled out the expensive bourbon, calling it the perfect time. As they were about to go to bed, Lane grabbed her bag but quickly lost her grip and most of the contents fell out. Colin reached for a pile of papers on the tile floor.

"What's this?" He questioned absently as he held out a small business card in his left hand.

Lane was too tired to try and cover for herself anymore, "Oh, just a guy I met at the consulate."

Colin seemed amused but disinterested. Turkish business men hitting on attractive foreign girls wasn't exactly headline news, "Was he at least good looking?"

Lane laughed, "Yeah, he was alright I guess... honestly he really helped me out—I was kind of a mess after the whole thing."

Colin raised his eyebrows and said flippantly, "Maybe you should go out with him... I mean, you are leaving soon, it might be fun to get in one, good, no-strings hook up before you bounce, right?"

Lane playfully hit his shoulder and he responded with mock pain. They said goodnight and both fell fast asleep on their tiny single beds. But a few days later, Lane thought about what Colin had said. Not his words, exactly, but more the idea of it. What did she have to lose if she was leaving so soon? Ibrahim *had* seemed like a nice enough guy.

On a whim she picked up her phone and dialed the number printed neatly on his business card. At the very least, she thought, Turkey owes me a free coffee before I leave.

—

Normally, Lane wasn't one for chain stores or franchises. Turkey, however, had planted a seed in her that she feared she wouldn't be able to root out.

In the dark days of winter, cold, seemingly friendless, emotionally lost in a foreign city, she had given into a forbidden desire she didn't even know she had—the mall.

Cevahir wasn't just any mall—it was the largest in Europe; occupying an entire metro stop in Şişli.

Neatly lighted signs and bright, colored arrows all but physically carried Lane toward the underground entrance as she exited the train. Soon she was standing next to a multilayered water feature, transfixed. To her left, the Turkish version of crate and barrel—large, black leather couches and chenille throws framed coffee tables strewn with useless glassware. To her right, Koc, an eerie imitation of Home Depot, right down to the burnt Orange theme color.

In the middle of the miniature city she strained her neck up towards the ceiling. She had been here before, staring into a dark expanse of navy mosaics and gold leaf stars, but instead of byzantine tiles there was a dome of glass that opened up into the blue and white of the real sky. A giant clock face emanated from the apex of the ceiling. People moved everywhere; a thousand conversations surrounded her.

Where was she? She couldn't be in Turkey anymore. All the signs were in Turkish and she could hear the people around her speaking in a different tongue, but she could have been anywhere.

She was in Middlesborough at University Mall, passing the Chick-fil-a on her way to the bookstore. She was in London, window shopping at Zara and Marks & Spencer. She took the elevator and found herself in Tokyo. She rode the escalator down to Santiago. She ate lunch in a food court in Toronto.

The soft conveyor belt of easy listening jazz carried her to a thousand different places. And by the time she left, passed through security, and descended the stairs to the metro and back into Turkey, she was hooked.

Since that day she had been back more times that she could count. And not just Cevahir, but the other malls, too. There were more than she had ever seen in a major city—all of them a different escape; a chance to, for an hour or so, leave Istanbul and find herself in Rome, or Hong Kong, or even Phoenix.

The mall wasn't like the country just outside its walls. In the mall nothing was required of her; she was never expected to speak Turkish, dress in a certain way, or even talk to other people. All the mall cared about was her money.

For hours she would wander the—literally—miles of corridors, drinking the Starbucks latte she had always made fun of Colin for, happy as a clam.

So it was with mild amusement that she accepted Ibrahim's suggestion they meet for the first time at Cevahir. It was more than just a suitably public place—it was her home turf.

She found him in a large brown club chair in one of the top floor coffee shops, bent forward with an odd expression on his face, reams of paper blanketing the table in front of him.

He looked different than she remembered; but then again, they hadn't met under the most normal of circumstances. His dark hair seemed longer, his olive skin more glossy, and he was definitely wearing thick black glasses where he hadn't been before. But as he stood to shake her hand, his familiar kindness came back to her.

"I just hate the mall, don't you?" His eyes widened in a smile. He had obviously been working on his opening line.

"Yes, isn't it just horrible?" Lane surprised herself with how quickly she had turned her back on such a trusted friend. It was something in his eyes, she guessed.

"I wasn't sure you would come. Well, ok, I didn't think you would come at all."

"Well, you were so helpful at the Consulate that day. I wanted to thank you." She displayed her usual southern graciousness, but the truth was, she hadn't expected herself to come either.

He laughed softly, "Yeah. Well I couldn't exactly leave you to fend for yourself. You looked a little the worse for wear."

She paused and he dropped his smile.

"Oh, I'm sorry, it's probably—too soon for me to talk about it. I'm so sorry."

"No, no!" She assured him, "I'm fine, seriously. I was just…"

"Yes?"

"Well I don't want to offend you, but your English is wonderful… perfect, actually."

He smiled broadly, "Why would that offend me?"

"Oh, well I guess what I mean is—how?"

"Ah, I understand." He was still smiling. "You must not run into many Turks with a firm grasp on the language."

Lane was embarrassed, she hadn't meant to put down Ibrahim's country. But he quickly continued, "I'm not making fun of you, I was being serious. Istanbul isn't exactly Berlin or Amsterdam."

Lane felt more comfortable, "Good point."

"I went to a private school north of the city." Ibrahim said.

Lane had heard of the area; very expensive she noted to herself. So he might be a rich kid, she thought, and couldn't decide if it was a black mark or a gold star.

"Oh," was all she could think to say.

"Well," he continued as if he didn't want to, "and I have been living in Canada for the past six years."

Lane was caught off guard, and immediately tried to stop herself from seeing him any differently. Soon though, she had to admit to herself all the embarrassing things she had assumed about Ibrahim when she thought he had spent his whole life in Turkey. She tried quickly to move on, but found herself walking straight into another blunder.

"So your parents must be… doctors? Lawyers?"

Ibrahim laughed loudly now, and Lane instantly knew she should have kept quiet.

"Funny, my uncle is a lawyer, and I know he'd love to hear you think he has money."

"I'm so sorry, I just thought, well, anyway, I'm sorry."

Ibrahim continued, "No, please, everywhere else in the world you can actually make a decent living with a profession like that. It's not your fault, it's—well its Turkey's I guess."

Lane felt better but was still intrigued.

"My father's in the military, to answer your question."

Lane couldn't hide her confusion any longer, "How in the world did you go to private school and live in Canada on a military father's pay check?" She felt horrible for saying it but Ibrahim didn't seem fazed.

"You really haven't been here long, have you?"

He explained before Lane could decide how to answer, "In Turkey—how can I put this—the military is special."

He paused to consider his next statement, "They're kind of like, well, they're like the educated class."

Lane's brow was beginning to furrow as he continued, "I know it's not the same in America and Canada. But our system is completely different. First, every man has to serve between six months and a year."

"And second?" Lane questioned.

Ibrahim laughed, "Well, and second, if you make it a career, you can do pretty well for yourself, like my father… I think that's maybe the same in The States."

Lane thought about the higher-ups in the American military. She was sure a US General wasn't hurting for money, but she also couldn't picture a career soldier being seen as an academic.

Just then a waiter arrived with two mugs.

"I hope you don't mind," Ibrahim said, "I ordered you an Americano. I've never liked Turkish coffee."

"That's perfect." Normally a man ordering for her would have been a death knell. But for some reason she couldn't help a slight smile.

Ibrahim began clearing papers out of the way.

"So, what is all this?" Lane asked, blowing on her steaming cup.

"Ah." He looked tired of whatever it was, "All this is the reason I was at the consulate to help you the other day."

"You're trying to move to America?"

He seemed happy for the validation, "Well 'move' is a strong word. Right now I'm just trying to *go* there."

"And it requires all this?"

"Well not all of this is my visa application, but yes, it's kind of crazy isn't it? We're maybe a hundred kilometers from 'Europe', but we might as well be in Saudi Arabia when it comes to travel."

Lane thought about the twenty dollars it had cost her to come into Turkey, and how, at Athens' Airport, they had barely given her passport a second look.

"So what are the other papers?"

He smiled again and drew in a deep breath, "Remember the mandatory military service I mentioned?"

Lane inadvertently made a grimace and Ibrahim laughed in agreement.

"Wait," she said, "I thought you said the military was a good thing."

"You're right, I did. But still, would you want to go?"

"Not at all!" Her eyes sparkled as she laughed.

"I know. But for a college graduate, it's only six months, and who knows, I could get lucky and end up stationed on the Mediterranean."

Lane's curiosity got the better of her, "So what would have happened if you had stayed in Canada, and just not come back?"

He looked as if she had guessed his deepest secret and then leaned in mischievously, "I can't tell you the number of times I've thought about it. Honestly I don't know," and then he leaned back, "But I do know that if you want to work at a Turkish Embassy in a western country, they don't like it if you have a criminal record."

Lane's eyes widened, "Ah, I think it's all coming together, now."

"You know, it's true what they say, Americans are really much smarter than they look."

Without thinking Lane slapped his shoulder in mock offence, and then quickly apologized.

"Don't worry" he said, "I deserved it."

He shifted in his seat, "So what about you? I know you're from America, I know you were involved in a bombing, and I know you live in a nice neighborhood."

"How do you know that?" Lane was intrigued.

"Well, I haven't lived in Istanbul for a long time, but I do remember that Osmanbey is the Metro stop for Nişantişi, so I'm guessing…" He took a minute to size her up, "You found a nice place near Gucci that you're paying too much for."

Lane felt suddenly like she had a giant neon sign above her head reading 'foreigner', "Is it that obvious?"

"Wow, I got all that right?"

"To be fair, we got a great deal on the apartment."

Ibrahim just raised his eyebrows.

"Ok," Lane rolled her eyes, "I'm sure it would have been better if we were Turkish. My roommate even speaks the damn language, and they still treat her like an outsider."

He laughed, "You know, you might know more about Turkey than I thought."

They talked and drank coffee for hours. Before too long, the afternoon sun over Şişli had faded into the bright blue of evening. From their perch high above the tightly packed clusters of building they watched the patchwork of faded colors shift and merge into the monochrome of night. Soon, the cityscape in front of them shown yellow and red with the twinkling accents of kitchen lamps and dirty buffet signs.

"I should really get back to my apartment," Lane said unconvincingly.

"Big teaching day tomorrow?"

"Ha! That'll be the day. No, I've got to…" She wasn't sure why, but she suddenly felt weird about her leaving Turkey.

"You've got to, how did my friends call it—'get your shit together'?" Ibrahim seemed to know how to express her thoughts better than she did.

"Exactly."

Five floors down, in front of the metro, Lane turned to her new friend, unsure of what to say. Would they even see each other again?

"How long until you leave?"

"A little over three weeks," she said.

"Will you do me a favor?" She was surprised to hear him say.

"Ah, sure…"

"Well, the thing is, I've got all this time when I'm not being nearly blown up at consulates, and I'd love to take a few day trips, but traveling alone was never my style…. So, would you, possibly, think about coming with me sometime? You know, if you're not busy with everything else."

Lane didn't see it coming, but was even more shocked by her quick response, "That sounds great." She blurted out. And then, as if to explain, "Well, I mean, I've really been trying to experience as much as I can in Turkey before I leave, but you're right, traveling alone is so hard, and me not knowing the language and all…" she realized she was babbling, but Ibrahim seemed delighted to listen.

"Um, great," he managed, through a smile, "Yeah— awesome, ok." It was the first time all evening he had seemed uncertain of his words.

Riding the metro back, Lane didn't notice how slow the people moved on the escalator, or even the off-key singer on the platform.

But she did notice a girl a few seats down from her on the train. Her dark hair was pulled back in a loose ponytail and her legs were crossed. Lane watched for a few minutes. Her clothes were fashionable but simple. She carried a large black leather bag. And then Lane noticed the book she was reading was in German.

She thought about her as the girl got off at the next stop. She wasn't sure why she was so interested, but then realized it was because she couldn't label her, couldn't put her in a neat box. The girl could have been German, living the same life as Lane, teaching her native language in a foreign country. She could have been Turkish, reading a book to brush up on her business language skills. She could have been an American.

She thought about how so much of the past month had been her noticing the things about Istanbul she wouldn't miss. Making an unconscious list of the things that separated her.

But there was that girl, her age, just reading a book on the train like Lane always did.

Just then herstop came up, and she thought, with a laugh, how she had agreed to take a trip with Ibrahim and didn't even know where they were going.

"I always almost go to see my grandmother."

"Um, no," said Lane, "I *almost always* go."

"No, no," Asli shook her head and squinted her eyes—she was certain, "I always almost go to see her."

"Asli, that means you *never* go see her."

Asli nodded vigorously, "Yes, I think I will go, but I never go."

Lane looked at the rest of the class, all of whom nodded in agreement. It was going to be a long three weeks.

—

Sweat began to form on Lane's neck as she hunched over a pile of clothes beside her bed. It was hard to imagine that in less than six months she had amassed so many pointless objects. Papers poured out of shoe boxes, unworn blazers littered the bottom of her closet; candles, books, handbags filled with knick-knacks—it would all have to go.

She picked up an empty matchbook with a stylized Atatürk on the cover and shook her head at herself.

"Do you ever throw anything away?" Lane jumped up to find Colin leaning against the door jamb, smirking.

"Apparently not."

"Can I help with anything?"

"You're kind," she said, "but this whole thing is my burden."

"You know, I'd like it if you didn't have to leave at all."

Lane looked up. Colin looked more amused than questioning.

"You know, I thought I would feel weird about this whole thing. But I've gotta say, now that I'm really doing it, it just seems right, you know?"

Colin smiled, "Ok, just promise me this isn't because of the bomb."

Lane rolled her eyes, "Ah!" she screamed in mock anger, "I told you, I made the decision before all that. I promise, it's not a factor." But just as soon as she said it, she wondered if it was really true.

"So what else do you have to do?"

"Don't even ask. Find someone to sublet, make arrangements for my big bags, finalize things with EnglishSpace, contact my host family... the list goes on."

"Host family?"

"I didn't tell you?" She said mischievously, "I'm going to WWOOF in Spain for a month."

"You mean, you're going to go, all by yourself and work on an organic farm for a month?"

"You didn't think I was just going to run home with my tail between my legs, did you?"

Colin studied his friend, "No, I guess I didn't."

"It's awesome Colin, I really feel like I'm doing something on my own for the first time."

He smiled, and after a few minutes posed a seemingly innocuous question, "So when is the plane ticket for?"

Lane answered quickly, "Three weeks from today."

"Well we'll just have to make the most of the time we have you here for." He said and slipped off into the kitchen.

Lane was happy about the upcoming weeks with her friends, but realized she had broken her promise to Colin about not keeping secrets. She didn't have a plane ticket, and had no idea why she said she did.

—

Over the next few days, an odd thing happened. Lane started to think of teaching as almost enjoyable. She would engage the students in lively debate for hours, no longer just sitting on the sidelines.

As so often happens, leaving had had the effect of making her time in Turkey more precious.

Everything looked new. She took an interest in the history of the country, reading about the Byzantine Empire, and the beginning of the republic. She visited out of the way monasteries and Ottoman fortresses. She threw a party and invited everyone she could think of.

But it was more than that. Over the next week, she never sat still; every moment awake became a moment to experience something new or different. Matt, Colin, and even Reyhan were dragged everywhere from three hundred year old mosques to trendy uptown nightclubs.

It was almost as if she was trying to wipe the memory of the bomb from her mind—from everyone's mind. She refused for her time there to be defined by something out of her control. She couldn't explain it. She just knew that if, for any reason, she left Turkey because of what had happened to her, they had won.

Who 'they' were, she didn't know: the PKK, EnglishSpace, the man who screamed at Colin. Regardless, she had made up her mind; she was leaving on her own terms, whatever that took.

—

Somehow over the next week, she forgot again to buy her plane ticket. Then one day, she was in the last five minutes of a class she was sure hated her when a student caught her of guard.

"Teacher, will you stay in Turkey?" The boy was about twenty and very good with English, which is why the question sounded so odd.

"How do you mean Yakob?"

"For a while…" he responded, using the term they had learned the day before.

Lane was caught off guard, but before she knew why, she was answering honestly, "No, I'm actually leaving soon."

Yakob looked as if he had been hit, "Leaving soon?" he repeated, "but why? don't you like Turkey?"

Lane smiled, but continued to answer, "Yes, I do like Turkey," It was the first time she had heard herself say it, "But I've done all I can do here, it's time for me to go." She felt like Mary Poppins giving her 'piecrust promise' speech.

Yacob seemed to understand, but the rest of the class was in a state of shock. Three of the boys and two girls came by on the way out to beg her to stay. It was ridiculous, she thought. These were the same students that had complained about her accent en masse just a month ago, how could they possibly care whether she stayed or went? But there they were the next day with a card and a cake, both of which said, in perfect English, "To the best Teacher, Don't forget us!"

—

Ibrahim reeled from the slap of a large salt water spray as Lane laughed uncontrollably.

"I told you we shouldn't stand at the front of the ship!" She yelled over the roar of the smoke belching engines.

An hour earlier, Ibrahim had arrived at the thick metal door of her apartment, out of breath from the four story climb.

"I'm not letting you in until you tell me where we're going."

Ibrahim sized her up, and then replied, "Fine, then I'll just take my coffee out here."

Certain that she would get nowhere with him, she stepped aside and gestured him in. Without even asking if it was required, he began unlacing his tall boots to leave in the hallway.

"How did you even know I would have coffee for you," Lane inquired.

With a half-cocked smile, he replied, "What kind of woman would you be if you didn't?"

In mock horror, Lane retreated to the kitchen and lamented over her shoulder, "I guess you can take the Turk out of Turkey!"

Ibrahim sat in the creaky kitchen chair and observed, "You know, I'm surprised you let me in at all."

"You are?" Lane offered him a small but strong cup.

"Well, yeah—I mean I figured sooner or later you'd tell me you couldn't just go away with a stranger. Honestly, I can't believe I asked you—it was so forward. I mean, you don't even know me." He looked surprised with himself but unapologetic.

"I'm three steps ahead of you," Lane smiled, "My friends already have all your info, and my roommate helped me translate your Dad's profile on the government's website."

Ibrahim laughed loudly as he placed a piece of computer paper on her table. Lane opened it to find several contact numbers, a photo copy of Ibrahim's ID and a personal note written to Reyhan promising to get her back safely. It was the most adorable thing she had ever seen.

"So I guess your roommate won't be needing this. I'll just take it back." Lane snatched the paper from his hands with a wide smile and threw it onto the couch on their way out the door.

Ibrahim put them into a cab and rolled down the back windows. As they flew down the cobbled streets of Maçka, Lane's hair whipped him in the face; worked in a Medusa-like frenzy by the fresh, spring air.

Even in Beşiktaş he wouldn't allow her to look at the final destination on her ticket, and refused to let her pay him for it.

And now here they were, mastheads on a giant, dirty, blue and white municipal ferry; cresting every wave as the vessel plowed its way southwest, through the sparkling expanse of the Marmara sea.

Lane laughed as Ibrahim tried and failed to light a cigarette. In the cab he had pulled out the slim pack of Winton's, obviously embarrassed.

"I never smoked in Canada," he had said, "Well almost never—but here…"

"Everyone smokes," she observed, "Must be something in the air," And she casually slipped the lighter and tiny white cylinder from his hands and succeeded where he had not by shielding herself under the rusty metal lip of the bow. Ibrahim smiled, and they traded forbidden drags in wild defiance of the wind.

Between puffs, Lane watched most of the other front-of-boat passengers fight the losing battle against the wind armed only with day-glo lighters.

The air was cleaner out here. She had only been on the Marmara once before, but the experience stuck with her. Just the boat, the sea, and the clean air. Not so much as a single building on the horizon. After months of living in a crowded city-scape, it was almost surprising to remember such a place could exist.

But just as she was entering a kind of trance, her eyes came to rest on a slight haze in the distance. It was just a few minutes before the anomaly had manifested its full silhouette. In front of her, growing larger by the second, were the sheer cliffs of a different world; the grassy outcroppings of a place she rarely thought about. This wasn't the mirror Asian side of Istanbul. This was a continent unto itself: Anatolia.

—

They arrived in Bandirma, a coastal town with a surprising 100,000 people.

Bandirma's main attraction was its extensive bus terminal, and Lane had a guess this was not their last stop.

Ibrahim handled everything.

Occasionally, Lane's dormant feminist would emerge and she would insist on completing a small task, such as buying acma, her favorite croissant like baked good, or securing the luggage tickets. But for the most part, she simply let things progress as they would.

She thought back to when, a couple weeks ago, she and Reyhan had gone for beers in a divey little place north of their apartment. Reyhan ordered first, and the bar tender started to say one price, but when Lane added a second order of chips, the price suddenly jumped. It was a lesson learned, and she justified her silence with the knowledge that she would only hinder transactions by speaking up in her ever growing, but still perfectly childish Turkish.

It was a harsh but true revelation; that the bulk of any country—the real slimy, gutsy heart of anyplace, was out of reach without a fluent knowledge of the language that was the key to it.

She did, however, insist on paying for half of everything. A move that visibly unnerved Ibrahim, but satisfied her desire to contribute.

—

Four hours in a twelve person bus across the Anatolian hinterland proved more daunting than either of them had imagined.

A pregnant woman had become ill within the first twenty minutes.

A baby cried; a headscarf-clad grandmother tried in vain to quiet him. For two hours, the pair listened to the harsh melancholy of a child's tears interspersed with the pleading whispers of his keeper.

"Canim, Canim," she said again and again, "My heart, My soul."

The baby was callous and unmoved.

As they disembarked, Lane grabbed Ibrahim's waiting hand and stated, casually, "There's no way this can be a one night trip; you did know that that, right?"

Caught in the act, Ibrahim refused to look her in the face, "What ever could you mean?" he said.

"Well, we've been traveling for almost six hours. So I'm pretty sure we aren't going to make it back to Istanbul tomorrow."

In answer to her question, Ibrahim simply took her bag. And just as simply, she followed.

—

"I will not do it," Lane said, planting her feet firmly on the slippery rock beneath her.

"Then I completely support you," Ibrahim said. And just as quickly he had disappeared from beside her and was plummeting downward towards the water below. With a white-foamed splash, he hit the placid surface at full speed, obscuring as he descended Lane's view of the pond's sandy floor, strewn as it was with Roman columns, resting in the same place they had been for centuries, possibly since the day they had first fallen. This was Pamukale.

A Corinthian capitol caught her eye as she stood meters above the serene pool, on the fence about whether or not to jump.

She was suddenly very conscious of being in her bathing suit with a man she barely knew.

"Just do it, the water's really very warm."

Ibrahim had found a perch on top of a marble plinth and was goading her while knee deep in the tourmaline water.

Lane looked up. Around the water's edge a thick border of trees cocooned the natural pool. Their leaves were thicker than she was used to in May. Below her, Ibrahim, and less than a half dozen other bathers, floated listlessly between fluted columns and chipped sections of egg-and-dart molding.

It was an Eden, and just as quickly as she had refused to ever come down, Lane was airborne, caught in a serene space between potential and kinetic energy—alive.

The water was warmer even than Ibrahim had said— perfect, like an effervescent blanket, she thought, if such a thing could exist.

Slight wisps of stream rose above her sightline as she tried to level her eyes with the undulating water. Beneath her feet the two thousand year old wing of a Nike statue tickled her toes.

"Was it worth the trip?" Ibrahim asked, almost sarcastically.

But all she provided in the way of an answer was a splash of hot water in his face.

—

Lane acted pleased when Ibrahim handed her the key to her separate room at the pension; a tiny, clean, cinderblock structure run by a magenta haired woman.

"You know," she paused, "We could stay in the same room—I just mean there's no reason for you to pay for two rooms. There are two beds after all." She had tried to frame it as an economic argument, but it had come out just as suggestive as she had feared. Ibrahim countered her logic, "I know we're both adults, and believe me, this isn't because you're a woman. I dragged you on this trip, so the least I can do is get you your own room."

She was powerless in the face of his generosity, but walking up the stairway to her floor, she couldn't shake a slight feeling of disappointment.

—

In her tiny, now well-worn Turkish dictionary, Lane found Pamukkale to mean: Cotton Castle. It was an odd, candy land inspired term that, at first, Lane thought must just be a language oddity along the lines of White Cross or Springfield.

But the next morning, as she got out of yet another van-like vehicle, she stopped dead in her tracks and instantly realized the very literal implications of the translation.

Rising, fairy tale like, above her, was a small mountain of terraced cylinders—bone white and billowing large volcanoes of steam.

"Geothermal hot springs," Ibrahim narrated behind her, "The white is from mineral deposits in the water. What do you think?"

"It's magnificent," was all she could think to say.

They stripped to their bathing suits once again and frolicked among the multilayered structures, jumping from one steaming turret to the next.

Ibrahim darted ahead of her and into a dense cloud. She leaped after him, the bright rays of the sun streaming through fog and bouncing off the splashing water at her feet. She caught a glimpse of his lean shoulder out of the corner of her eye and skimmed across the bubbling surface of a shallow pond.

In and out of the clouds they weaved, separated, and rejoined—nearly knocking down elderly Germans who were clad in pornographically small bathing suits.

They were cherubim in a giant cumulonimbus, playing a celestial game of hide-n-seek. Lane found herself hydroplaning somewhere between myth and reality.

Ibrahim's bright, brown eyes flashed as he ceremonially conquered the summit of the other worldly palace. Lane laughed and collapsed onto a naturally formed rock throne to admire the view out over the city.

She thought about all the people who had crowned themselves ruler where she now sat. All of the names that place must have had over the centuries. She decided, without ever hearing any of the others, that she like Pamukkale the best.

———

Late that evening, Lane fought to keep her eyes open in her plush bucket seat near the back of the ferry. She must have drifted off, because the next thing she knew, she awoke in her own bed—a torrent of harsh sunlight streaming in through the window.

Had it all been a dream?

A castle in the clouds did sound fairly fantastic, but she was sure she couldn't have dreamed something in so much detail.

"He left a note," Matt's kindly, commanding voice boomed from the hallway outside her half open door.

"Oh... what?"

"Your new friend," he yelled back, from inside the hall closet. She could hear the knowing smile in his voice, "when he brought you home last night."

"Ah. Thanks," Lane rubbed her eyes and groped for her bathrobe. It was starting to come back to her, the boat docking, the cab home, climbing the stairs to the apartment.

"He was so kind! He apologized for your coming home so late." Reyhan pushed the ajar door fully open and was a vision in cooking apron and flour.

"Oh, shit! I'm so sorry, I didn't even think... I mean—I should have known you would be worried. Y'all are just gone so much, I—"

"Please, please," Reyhan was almost laughing, "It's about time you had a little fun. And for what it's worth, he seems like a nice guy."

"You checked him out in Turkish?"

Reyhan smiled, "Well, I was about to, but he insisted we speak English in front of Matt and Colin. He said it was just respectful... I was impressed."

Lane's gaze wandered as she lost herself temporarily in her memories, "Yeah, he's not that bad is he?"

"Well come have the pancakes I'm making and tell us all about it," Reyhan beamed as she moved away from the door.

"You're all here?" Lane called after her.

"I know. How odd?" She yelled back from the kitchen.

Lane quickly replayed the past two days as she threw on a summer dress (summer had come, full force into their tiny apartment). She reminded herself that it was just a trip, and Ibrahim was just a nice person she had met under extreme circumstances. Still, all throughout pancakes, she couldn't stop smiling.

—

Matt and Reyhan sat in nestled solitude at the back of Patisserie Markiz, an art nouveau relic from Tünel's European hay-day at the turn of the century. Dark wood paneling framed Mucha-like mosaics of ethereal women wearing laurel crowns and lounging deliberately. The Parisian atmosphere was only augmented by the subtle border of Ottoman tiles below the crown molding.

Matt had just told a ridiculous tale involving a student he shared with Reyhan, removing his thick glasses and pushing back his curls for effect at the punchline.

Reyhan almost knocked over her Turkish coffee in a fit of laughter and splashed the dark liquid all over the arm of her conservative work blouse. She smiled as Matt furiously moistened it with his water glass. Her bright skin turning a bit flush as she slipped her hand into his.

Just then Lane entered, and Matt was surprised to feel Reyhan's soft fingers quickly untwine themselves from his.

"Have I had a day." Lane gratefully took the chair Matt pushed out for her.

"Problems at EnglishSpace H.Q.?" Reyhan asked quickly.

"Jesus, you can't make this stuff up. Mehmet wants us all to come on the EnglishSpace field trip, but Catherine says it's not required, and Mehmet says it is, and on and on…"

Lane noticed a distracted look in Reyhan's face, "I know, it's horribly boring, isn't it?"

"No, no," Matt interjected, "I was just thinking," he chuckled, "I guess you don't have to care much longer; and here we are, stuck with the whole mess—right?" He turned toward Reyhan, who gave an unconvincing laugh in the affirmative.

"Are you ok?" Lane asked Reyhan casually.

"Me?" She seemed to emerge from a stupor, "Of course. I'm fine," and just as quickly, she was back, "So what's happening with Ibrahim? You two have been together a lot this past week. Any plans coming up?"

Lane smiled, and then caught herself, "Yeah, we're gonna see each other, but nothing big—just around the city."

"You two have really hit it off," Matt said.

"Yeah, they have," Reyhan almost said to herself.

Matt narrowed his eyes across the table, but continued to Lane, "Just make sure and leave enough time for all of us; after all, we are the ones who dragged you to Turkey in the first place."

Lane smiled in answer. But when she turned to Reyhan, her gaze had drifted even further past her, into the crowded Istiklal just outside the window.

—

Matt caught Reyhan by the arm. They had been sitting in the teacher's room in silence for the past twenty minutes, both silently waiting for the other to speak. A rare color photograph of Atatürk rolled his eyes at both of them. As she rose to leave, Matt finally couldn't take it anymore.

"Rey, I…"

"Yes?" Reyhan's eyes widened as if she knew what was coming, but moments passed and it was soon clear Matt wasn't going to continue, "I've got to get to class," she said with disappointment in her voice.

As the door closed loudly, Matt rolled his eyes at himself. For weeks he had thought things were perfect between the two of them. After her silent but clear kiss that day in the teachers' room things had turned a corner. There was no more weirdness between them; no more barrier.

They were having the time of their lives. Reyhan had showed him almost everything he could ever want to see in this strange and wonderful place. They talked deeply into the night about everything under the sun. Sometimes he let class out far too early just to be waiting for her when she got down the stairs from her top floor classroom.

But for days now she had fallen back into the same pattern. Long silent stares past him; refusing his hand in public, breaking off a kiss because she "had to get to class".

He knew he had to say something. *But what?* He thought. He'd never been one for grand gestures or bold statements. Was it just another phase? Would she even know what he was talking about?

So he started to talk to her and stopped. He let her walk out. He told himself it just needed some time and at the same time he knew he was probably wrong.

—

"How is your friend?" It was the first thing Metin asked as Colin entered his apartment one evening to the warm smell of baked stuffed eggplant and freshly chopped mint.

"Ha, she's surprisingly well," Colin said almost surprised as he slipped into Metin's waiting arms. He made a mental note of the man's constant interest in his life and his friends' lives.

They spent the evening in their usual way, cooking and telling stories and laughing. But later that evening, lying on Metin's stiffly padded modern sofa and talking over a movie, Colin suddenly sat up.

"They should be eradicated," Metin said without emotion in his voice, "The PKK that set that bomb that hurt your friend should be eradicated. Don't you agree?" The conversation had circled back to Lane and bomb and the people who caused it.

Colin sat wide eyed, trying to make sense of what Metin had just said, "Um, do you mean to use the word *eradicated*?" He finally managed.

"Well yes, why not?" Metin again displayed no emotion.

"It's just…" Colin didn't know how to continue. He knew that the word wasn't right, but he couldn't put into words how.

"The fucking Kurdish scum. They did this and many other things. They need to be dealt with. What if your friend had been killed?" This time his anger was undeniable.

Colin was still at a loss, "I mean, I don't think the PKK represent all of the Kurdish people, and 'scum' is a tricky word also…" he trailed off, realizing he sounded odd, but also knowing that the things Metin had said didn't sound right either.

"OK, ok," Metin slipped his hand under Colin's thigh, "maybe you are right, the PKK is not the same as the Kurdish people. But you don't know how it is here—we just want the Kurds to be a part of our country and sometimes it feels like they are spitting us in the face. I just think the people who did this to your friend should be brought to justice."

Colin searched Metin's face for a hint of the anger he had heard a minute ago—it was gone. He was hard pressed to think of a way to argue with Metin's concern for Lane's safety. He told himself Metin was right, he didn't understand. He wasn't Turkish. He had no clue of the intricacies and politics of this country. He told himself Metin hadn't understood the severity of the words he had used.

He slowly slipped back into Metin's warm embrace on the couch and fell asleep, but days later he still heard the words 'Kurdish scum' in his mind.

—

Lane's next encounter with Ibrahim began very much like the previous one. He appeared at her door, out of breath like before, smiling, and refusing to divulge where he was taking her.

They boarded the dolmuş this time next to the Max Mara store in Lane's neighborhood, and before she knew it, they were skimming down Abdi Ipekci past Burberry and then Louis Vuitton. They descended rapidly past the expensive grocery stores, and then into a clearing above a ravine. In the fold of the earth, Lane recognized the familiar circle of Beşiktaş's soccer stadium, a perfect turn of the century replica of Rome's coliseum.

They continued down until the familiar turrets of Beşiktaş Mosque rose above her view of the Bosphorus. Cutting quickly left, Lane barely had time to register Dolmabaçe Palace as they made a path directly towards the harbor.

Once inside the log cabin like structure that served as the boarding platform, Lane turned to Ibrahim and eyed him for a second before stating, "We're going to Asia, aren't we?"

"I don't know what you're talking about." He was doing a good job of looking serious.

"Ok, fine," Lane smirked.

On the ride over, Ibrahim tried to pacify her with cay and simit, but she continued to torment him with her knowing stare.

They arrived, as she had several times before, beneath the shadow of Kadirköy train station. For a hundred years, if you had been heading East from Europe, you would have passed through this station—the last in the West, the first in the East.

Lane watched as the multistory behemoth moved past them as if on a slow conveyor belt. They weren't even going inside. It, one of the most important transportation conduits of the 19th century, sat dormant now, a shell holding a couple unimportant offices and nothing else.

Lane had quickly realized that 'Asian side' was a bit of a misnomer. This part of the city may have technically been on the Asian continent, but it was definitely still Istanbul—simit shops, cheap shoes, doner kepab. A continent away, and still in same the place.

She turned to Ibrahim, who smiled and ushered her into a waiting cab.

They flew past the same cinderblock buildings Lane was used to, poorly manicured public gardens punctuated by soviet inspired fountains. Discount suits, discount dresses, discount anything you could want. The backstreets were the same as on her side of the Bosphorus except for the fact that they were completely flat—bargains and worthless crap stretching into the vanishing point.

Even in the fish market, the same runoff water stagnated; grudgingly making its way toward the Marmara.

They arrived, finally, at their destination, the last stop on the dolmuş route.

It was an odd place—the suburbs compared to Taksim, but still dotted with out of place skyscrapers. It was a Martian landscape, the opposite of Pera's tightly packed buildings. Air permeated the spaces between buildings here, people walked the streets slowly. If the European side was New York, this was Los Angeles—casual, car based, sunny.

Lane breathed deeply as she walked alongside Ibrahim near the coast—the air over here was a definite improvement.

They finally came to a small square and Lane was surprised to see Ibrahim turn and head straight towards a medium sized mosque that faced the sea.

Reaching the uncommonly grand entrance he turned to her with a serious smile.

"What is this…" she began, but quickly decided to follow his lead.

"It's one of the oldest mosques in the city." Ibrahim beamed with an unusual pride.

They had briefly talked about religion, and while Ibrahim had never said it explicitly, Lane had gotten the impression he wasn't a practicing muslim. So it was with some surprise that she complied when he indicated she use her light summer scarf as a head covering.

They entered the hazy space with slow reverence at first. Ibrahim said a few more words to her about the mosque's construction right before the fall of the Byzantine Empire on the opposite shore. Then he slowly broke off from her and wandered to a far wall.

Walking through the quiet, cavernous inner sanctuary, Lane traced the large carpeted flowers on the floor with her eyes to the glassy marble columns and up to the intricate frieze of geometric shapes and Arabic lettering.

And then it struck her—this was the first time she had been in a real mosque in this country. Of course she had toured the blue mosque with Marissa, but that was more tourist attraction than place of worship. Here she was now standing silently in a space not designed for outsiders but for regular, everyday prayer and reflection.

She thought about how, on some level, these mosques that punctuated every street and square had always felt off limits to her; the way she felt like an intruder in Tarlabaşi. She stood quietly in the corner and watched a small clutch of men kneeling face first in worship, quiet certainty guiding their graceful bows. She might not ever feel completely comfortable in these spaces, but it was a moment she didn't want to forget.

Just then Ibrahim rejoined her and they silently made their exit.

Walking along the shore line in continued reverence, Ibrahim stared for a long time out towards the small islands that hugged the coast.

Finally Lane asked, "So why do you like it there?"

He started to speak and then seemed to pull back the words. Then he said with a small grin, "It's quiet."

———

Lane made herself as invisible as possible the rest of the evening, in the hopes that Ibrahim would reveal himself without even realizing it.

But he never tipped his hand, ushering her from sight to interesting sight without a second's pause or hesitation.

Whatever it was that had stopped him was gone now.

Tired from a long day of sightseeing, they walked out to the Marina and watched as the sun sank beneath the distant outline of the Galata Tower that capped their side of the city.

Clad in the blue of the evening and soft voiced, Ibrahim suggested they catch a cab home across the Bosphorus Bridge.

At the door to her building, Lane was barely surprised to see Ibrahim leap from his seat and open her door for her.

"Thanks for showing me the real Asian Side," she said with a laugh, but he only smiled in response.

He caught her eye and his smile broadened, "You haven't seen anything yet," he said in his usual tone.

They stood, silent for a moment, and Lane was unsure of what was going to happen. She knew she should go inside, but at the same time, she couldn't turn around. Against her will, she slowly started to lean in toward Ibrahim. His eyes widened and he quickly caught her in an embrace.

There has never been a more awkward hug in the history of the world, Lane thought. She released herself feeling more alone that she had going in.

"Well, thanks again," she managed.

"You, too; can't wait to do it again," Ibrahim projected too loudly towards her as she raced inside the tiny entrance way and up the unforgivably twisted stairway.

—

Catherine, Lane's perpetually tired looking American boss stood a bit too far from her in the teacher's room a few days later. Her face was more sour than usual. She was not a particularly happy woman, but still, the sight of her truly grave expression troubled Lane.

"So you're leaving us," she said, and just as quickly, her sour expression changed to one of bemused acceptance.

"Oh, ah, what?"

"It's ok, well it's not *ok*. But I guess it'll be fine," she confirmed, "I already know, one of the teachers told me… I should have guessed, what with the bombing and all."

"Ahhh…" Lane was stunned, she hadn't expected it to go this smoothly.

"Well, we'll have everything settled for you as quickly as possible." She smiled awkwardly, her odd, Oregonian accent drawing out the last word in a way Lane had never heard before. It was the same way in which she managed to mangle the Turkish language on daily basis.

Lane drew in a breath, it was exactly as she had wanted it to go, but for some reason she felt lost, out of control, "Well, the thing is, Catherine," she began.

"Yes..?" The elder woman looked as if she was about to walk out of the room without another word.

"I'm not leaving," Lane stately quickly. As soon as she said it, she knew it was true, it had been true for almost three weeks.

"You're—you're staying?"

"Yes, I'm staying," Lane beamed, and Catherine shot her an undeniable look of disapproval. Even ten years in Turkey had not softened her attitude towards uncertainty. She visibly tried to adjust her face, but failed.

"Well, we're certainly happy to keep you," she stammered.

Lane continued to smile her down.

"Don't scare us like that again," she laughed uncomfortably and, for added affect, swatted Lane on the forearm.

Lane walked down the flashing central staircase of EnglishSpace Taksim, bewildered. She had meant everything she said—but where had it come from?

No time to think about that now; she had to tell her roommates before the EnglishSpace grapevine got to them—and Ibrahim; what was she going to say? She was in a daze the whole way home, but still, somewhere near the metro turnstile, she broke into a low laugh that emanated from her stomach and didn't let up until she got home.

—

Matt and Reyhan acted unsurprised. Perhaps they had always knew, or at least suspected. Or even more distressingly, thought Lane, perhaps they were too caught up in whatever was happening between them to pay much attention. Nevertheless, they were congratulatory, and expressed their excitement between furtive glances towards one another.

As soon as she had pulled herself away from the two of them, Lane raced to find Colin at their new usual lunch spot—a relatively expensive, but fabulously chic burrito restaurant. The tortilla chips were always a little soggy, and the "sour cream" was more yogurt than anything else—but in Istanbul, tex-mex was as rare and gourmet as haut French cuisine.

"Good, because the idea of living with some random German sub-letter for the next half year was really getting me down," Colin managed between large bites of the surprisingly decent guacamole.

"So that's it? No big cry or anything?" Lane asked half-seriously.

Colin just smiled, "I know it seems like we all have our own things going on, but you know, the three of us aren't blind; we kind of saw this coming."

"Was it that obvious?" Lane inquired, staring absently at the chic passengers across the street, exiting the funicular train for which Tünel was named.

"The minute you came back from you first coffee date with—uh, what's his name?"

She squinted in casual disapproval of Colin's poorly delivered joke.

"You should bring Ibrahim around more often," his tone had turned more serious.

"Should I?"

"You know we're not completely self-centered. We'd like to hang out with him, if that would suit you."

"And what about you?" It was the first time in ages Lane could remember having something to tease him about.

"What about me?" He look genuinely confused.

"When are you going to bring your man around?"

Colin was visibly unnerved, "Well, I don't know that it's quite the same—wait," he noticed a flaw in her statement and pounced, "does that mean Ibrahim is *your man*?"

Lane hedged, stuttered, and turned red. And somehow, they were back to where they had been before the past few months, before Istanbul and Greece; before all of it.

"Um, absolutely not," she finally regained her composure, "We haven't even kissed yet—god honestly I don't even think he wants to kiss me. Which is more than I can say for your situation... How many nights did you spend at Metin's this week...?" she trailed off with a smile.

"Ok, ok," Colin couldn't handle her aggressively questioning eyes, "How about we both agree to shelve it for right now?" he tried to say it with a laugh and move on as quickly as possible. He wanted so badly to be completely honest with her. To tell her about the 'Kurdish scum' comment. To ask her opinion on Metin's privilege and his nebulous job. But somehow the words just wouldn't come. So instead he ordered more guacamole and told himself things would be clearer in a day or two.

Eleven
The Present Perfect

"That is the past!" Aslan was irate. A middle aged man with a thick mustache and kingly mane that matched his namesake, he was not one for submitting easily to Colin's status of 'native speaker'.

"I know, it *happened* in the past," Colin's cool reserve had completely left him, "but we are *speaking* about it now... understand?"

"Do *not* understand! *I have gone to Ankara,*" Aslan repeated for the fifteenth time, "IN THE PAST. PAST PERFECT."

"Ok, Aslan," Colin was slowly losing his will to live, let alone teach, "So what about 'I had gone to Ankara last year?'"

Aslan thought deeply for a moment, and then narrowed his eyes as he answered with conviction, "It can be called *the PAST past.*"

Colin started to protest, but then realized Aslan was probably right. He let class out early that day.

—

June began with a literal bang. Lane and Ibrahim stood silently among the roaring throng of water-side spectators next to Ortaköy Mosque. Sparks danced on the black waves of the Bosphorus as the red and white-hot refuse of fireworks came crashing towards the water like so many tiny meteors.

The flashing, technicolor lights of the bridge revealed in psychedelic detail the mass of large ships under it. Blue and gray and green hulls created eerie silhouettes against the lights of the Asian side. One ship, however, stood out against the rest; smaller, but brilliant white, and trimmed in gold and red that sparkled in the glow of the fireworks. Atatürk's ship; a constant, water borne reminder that the night's celebration of Atatürk's birthday were for everyone, but only *about* one person.

A week before, Lane had stood in the same spot outside the posh House Café and launched into an unprovoked self-explanatory diatribe about her decision to stay. It had become clear, half-way through, that Ibrahim, while supportive, was overwhelmed by her seriousness.

"I'm excited you'll be around," he said when she paused mid-sentence, questioning him with her eyes.

She was happy he had left it at that. Still, she felt a need to let him know that he was most definitely *not* her reason for staying. *And what did he mean "excited you'll be around"?* She thought, *It's so vague, so—casual.*

But she quickly pulled herself back to earth and in the next minute they were making travel plans.

—

The summer opened up in front of them like they were anxious elementary school kids singularly focused on those first, transcendent milliseconds of summer vacation.

Lane cut back to part time at EnglishSpace—an arrangement they grudgingly agreed to, given her 'special circumstances.'

Ibrahim never would divulge exactly how it was he had so much free time on his hands, calling it "horribly boring" and insisting that he was, "just in a transitional period."

Lane, usually inquisitive, surprised herself by not pressing the issue. Sometimes, she thought about how little she knew about his plans, how little she knew about his life really—but mostly, she was just having too much fun to care.

For a time, they were both given the rare gift that usually only comes to the leisure class. They played the part well.

Educational mornings at the Pera museum gave way to long lunches at the culinary school and would sometimes even bleed into drinks by the harbor in Bebek or on the Big Island. They were ladies who lunch, only without the gossip and fund raising.

And then Ibrahim showed Lane something she never even knew existed but was immediately certain she would never forget.

Istanbul's mammoth Archeological Museum stood tucked away on the back road up to the Ottoman Topkapi palace, on the tip of Sultanahmet peninsula. With its modest signage, patrons of the much more glitzy palace often overlooked it.

The low gates belied what Lane was sure was one of the largest museums she had ever been to.

They glided past priceless tablets of Hittite cuneiform, some of the earliest texts in the world, written mere miles from where they were. They slipped forward through time to the various relics of the Egyptians, Mycenaeans, and finally the Greeks— everything close enough to touch and without any of the thick glass so commonplace in most of the world's major collections.

They stopped by an open window to catch a breeze and realized the entire building was un-air-conditioned.

Their amazement at such an incredible ancient collection soon derailed into a game of 'worst translated plaque'.

They found the winner in Room 3. An impressive statue of Mars seated on a stump held court in a far corner. Ibrahim said the Turkish label was perfect, but the English read: genuine fake Roman copy of Greek Marsh.

Still giggling, they crossed the stature strewn square to the stately Roman collection.

After a series of increasingly impressive rooms, Lane was struck dumb when she entered the final hall. The room contained only wall hung reliefs and a 2nd century sarcophagus—but it couldn't have held anymore. The sarcophagus, in pristine condition, was large enough to function as a one room house. But more than its size, Lane was almost unable to comprehend the finite detail; every inch was covered in characters and scenes that leapt, sometimes three inches, off the sheer white surface. The 'lid' was topped by an affluent Roman couple from the Empire's eastern province in what was now Turkey. She, serene, beautiful, adorned. He, strong, yet slightly pensive, holding her in the most natural embrace as they reclined, seemingly moments from receiving guests for a celestial dinner.

There were no words, and so Lane didn't speak. After a few moments, however, she broke her gaze long enough to look down and see her hand in Ibrahim's. She was startled, but thought pulling away would only draw attention to her shock. Before she could decide on a plan of action, Ibrahim deftly used the situation to his advantage, squeezed her hand tighter, and pulled her good naturedly to the other side where he let his hand drop naturally.

Well played, she thought.

—

And then it was time for Lane to show Ibrahim something he had never seen before.

Following closely behind her one misty day, Ibrahim asked her if she knew where she was going.

"Tarlabaşi," was her only reply.

After several false turns they found the tarp covered market Lane had stumbled upon that day. Ibrahim smiled silently as she haggled with vegetable merchants and then stuffed bright carrots into her bag.

After buying far too much Turkish delight, they returned to the small restaurant with the blue sign and the two tables.

Sitting across from her, making conversation over his börek, Ibrahim finally looked up and asked, "why do you like it here?"

The crowd seethed past the window as the restaurant owner talked to two women at the counter.

Thinking for a moment, Lane finally responded with a smile, "It's quiet."

—

Their outings continued. No stone in the city was left unturned as they blazed a path from the Big Lake in the far South up through the crowded neighborhoods of Bakirköy and Axeray. They sampled every café in Nişantişi, shopped (but never bought) in every high end boutiques in the garment district, pushed as far north as possible into the Black Sea town of Kumköy. They even found time to eat lunch at IKEA; Swedish meatballs and reasonably priced German beer serving as a sort of Nordic culinary embassy.

They talked. They ate. They drank. They traveled.

Lane's work at EnglishSpace became a necessary evil, a sort of penance for the criminally good time she was having with Ibrahim every other waking minute. But she was still able to find more than enough to keep her laughing at her bright orange day job.

Sitting in the teacher's room, pretending to surf the internet, she would prick her ears to catch the latest news from the increasingly ridiculous revolving cast of characters at 'command HQ' as she had come to call her branch.

Noah had made an almost full conversion into Turkish old man. Every day at noon he would take chay with several of his students from a lower level class; often speaking only in Turkish. His pants seemed to grow shorter and shorter over the coming months, revealing something very strange. Where he had once worn standard navy or black dress socks with his scuffed second hand teacher shoes, he was now wearing bright white tube socks like the men Lane saw fishing on Sundays below the Galata Bridge.

Noah told Lane funny stories about how several of the younger teachers had taken a trip to Eastern Turkey, thinking they were going to the Black Sea. Apparently the names of the cities had been so similar no one had realized that their overnight bus ride was taking them hundreds of miles into the dusty, flat province that bordered Iraq instead of north towards the holiday villages. Noah claimed, and Lane believed, that none of the ill-fated travelers would take credit for the mistake, and so they all sat in a tiny rural village for five days, drinking chay and eating stale flat bread out of stubbornness.

One day Marissa blew into the teacher's room with unusual enthusiasm and Lane froze. Over the past month Lane had completely lost touch with her one time friend. Caught up in the aftermath of the bombing and then quickly occupied with Ibrahim she had barely even seen the maroon haired woman who had been there for her in her darkest time in that country.

"Marissa, let me just say—"

"Well I finally got laid," Marissa cut in uncharacteristically. Lane sized her up and quickly realized the thing she admired most about her; Marissa hadn't sat brooding alone over the past month that Lane hadn't called or tried to hang out, she had gone out and lived her life—and as she continued her story, it was clear they were going to pick up right where they had left off.

"And it was lovely," she said, and her Australian accent lingered over the last word in a way that made Lane giggle.

"Please tell me all the details."

"Well it was Dorokan… from your level one I believe"

Lane couldn't suppress a loud laugh, "Are you serious, but he's…"

"Yeah?" she said in her Queensland twang.

"Well, he knows like three words of English…" Lane said.

"Oh, yeah, I guess he's not really a scholar or anything…"

"So, um, how did you two…" Lane paused, she had heard Marissa order in bars and her Turkish was definitely not that advanced. She continued with wide eyes, "You know, how were you able to 'seal the deal'?"

Marissa looked at her with the most serene expression and stated completely naturally, "*You know*, darling… it's the international language."

———

Reyhan placed a soft hand on Matt's cheek and he instantly calmed down.

"I'm not sure what's gotten into me," he said blushing, "It's just my family." But he knew exactly what the issue was.

Steven, Marie, and Matt's sister Marnie had arrived in Istanbul the night before and were now downstairs waiting for him to join them for dinner—with Reyhan. She was the only other girlfriend they had ever met besides Mara—and he was terrified. Luckily Reyhan seemed completely oblivious as she bounded down the stairs in front of him and excitedly introduced herself to all the

Ortegas before Matt could even get out the apartment building door.

Four courses of Turkish mezze later, the group was singularly focused as Reyhan told an intricate and hilarious story about going to see her distant cousins in Istanbul and being asked point blank for money. As the meal was winding down Marie posed a seemingly innocuous question.

"Matthew, when *are* you going to come home?" It was more of a scheduling issue than a mother's plea. Matt knew his entire family would be delighted for him to live the rest of his life anywhere he chose.

"You know, the holidays are probably the best time, and besides that, I'm not really sure. I mean I had thought this would only be year, but who knew I'd find a stable job, an awesome apartment, and a girlfriend?"

They all laughed, but as Matt turned with expecting eyes towards Reyhan he could tell immediately that her frozen smile was masking real surprise. *Weren't they officially together?* He thought in complete surprise himself. He thought back to how strained the past weeks had been quickly tried to move on. All the same Reyhan didn't say anything else that evening except a polite good night as they left the restaurant.

"What did you do to that girl?" Marnie's viciously happy eyes were fixed on him like laser.

Matt stuttered, "Um, what could you possibly mean?" he finally managed.

"You've fucked up with her somehow, I can totally tell." Marnie's words were harsh but kind in only that way a sister can be.

"Marnie…" He started, but finally gave in, "I know something's wrong, but I can't imagine what it is—it's like there's a wall between us and nothing I can do can get through it."

Marnie studied him as she had done for years. "What *have* you tried?" she stated plainly.

"Um, what do you mean?"

"I mean what have you tried to break through?" His sister's unflinching gaze continued.

"Oh, um, well you know all kinds of stuff. We talk about everything—"

"Except what's bothering her," Marnie cut in.

"Um, well," she was completely right, "Reyhan knows she can tell me anything."

Marnie almost looked amused and Matt had to remind himself he was the older sibling. "Matthew," she said, in her best professor voice, "sometimes that's not enough—sometimes you gotta fight for what you want, even if you don't know what you're up against."

Matt wasn't sure what to say so all he said was, "Mom and Dad didn't notice anything did they?"

"Please," laughed Marnie, "They're getting blind in their old age. They fucking loved her—and so did I! Maybe you should let Reyhan know that you love her too."

Matt turned beet red as Marnie ruffled his growing curls and skipped off after their parents towards the hotel.

—

Colin had just finished racking on the dusty pool table when Matt entered at the far end of the room and headed directly for the bar.

Several weeks ago Matt had sent Colin a text with only an address and the covert instruction to "come alone." When Colin found himself in front of a dilapidated apartment building on an unassuming backstreet in Cihangir, he was sure the address was wrong. But overcome with curiosity he decided to enter anyway. He climbed an ancient set of creaking stairs up a corridor that smelled faintly of urine and freshly baked flat bread from the shop next door. At the end of a dark hallway was a swinging door like one would find in a restaurant kitchen. The only thing that indicated it was a not a private apartment was a dingy exit sign hanging above it.

More intrigued than ever Colin barged through the door, certain he would definitely regret whatever he found on the other side. What he found was Matt hunched over two large glasses of Efes reading his text messages. He looked around and saw the walls were painted with a deep hunter green that had yellowed with tobacco smoke, novelty alcohol signs, and slightly scandalous calendars. Three or four uninviting tables littered the main area, and two well-worn but operational pool tables stood in the back. A modest collection of dusty liquor bottles, two taps, and a surly but young employee—it was a dive bar. Colin couldn't believe his eyes—he hadn't seen something so familiar in months.

"This place is fantastic," he said as he slipped into the seat next to Matt at the bar.

"I know, right? I got a tip from one of my students and came to check it out for the first time this afternoon. I can't believe the other teachers don't know about this…"

"I won't tell if you won't," Colin said in a serious tone and they both laughed in agreement.

Ever since that day the two boys had met in this place for late afternoon drinks and pool once or twice a week, never explicitly keeping it from Lane and Reyhan, but never actively telling them either.

This particular afternoon, Matt approached the pool table with a look so serious Colin steadied himself for the coming conversation.

"I've got to do something about Reyhan," he started.

"God—did you want to jump right in?" Colin joked.

"Come ooooon dude, I have no idea what to do."

Colin cocked his head to one side and traded Matt a beer for a pool cue.

"OK, ok, what's the issue?"

"That's the thing—I have no fucking clue."

Matt took a large swig of Carlsburg before discarding his thick glass on an unstable bar table and steadying himself for a tricky shot. Colin pondered the situation.

"Wow, I'm kind of stumped on this one. I know she's been kind of distant lately—"

"—You noticed that, too?" Matt cut in.

"Well," Colin continued, "Not *distant*, just like she's thinking of something else all the time."

"Ugh, I know—that's exactly it." Matt had defeat in his voice.

"You know man, this seems obvious, and I don't mean it as a joke, but have you tried *talking* to her?" Colin offered.

Matt rolled his greenish eyes and shoved the rubber end of the cue between Colin's ribs, "Not you, too! My sister said the same thing."

Colin swatted back with his cue in return and the surly bartender told them unconvincingly in Turkish to keep it civil. The sounds of American indie pop roared from two small speakers attached to the bar tender's expensive looking laptop.

"It's just—well it's just I don't know how to bring it up. I don't even know what to say—or when to say it..." Matt trailed off into the set up for a corner pocket shot.

"Well you better think of something fast," Colin said, and then unsuccessfully took a shot at the eight ball.

"What do you mean?"

"Well, Lane told me yesterday she plans to ask us all to the coast for some kind of vacation—and she's bringing her new guy, or whatever he is."

"Oh shit, really?"

"Yep, she says we all need a vacation and honestly I agree," Colin said.

"Oh, fuck, vacation. What a relationship killer," Matt stared glassy eyed into the distance.

"That's right dude—you don't want the dreaded break-up vacation."

"Oh my god you are so right," Matt conceded, "I'm gonna have to figure out what the problem is soon," he said almost to himself.

"If it helps," Colin said, "Lane mentioned that Reyhan had some issues with her parents and American guys…"

"Oh, yeah," said Matt, "She mentioned it, but it never really seemed like that big a deal."

"Well maybe she didn't want you to think it was. But you can't tell her I told you, secret bar code and all."

Matt smiled in silent agreement of their pact. "Thanks for the heads up," he said and sunk the eight ball, finally feeling like he knew what he was up against.

—

"You know you want to." Lane stated plainly with a knowing stare. Her slightly wild auburn hair and excited eyes danced as she described the plan. She had just finished pitching her proposal for an Aegean vacation on Turkey's western coast and was a bit afraid her usually occupied friends would find reasons to bail.

Matt, Reyhan, and Colin looked at each other in silence, each working through their own personal reasons for saying no, but realizing their friend wouldn't be swayed. And how could they say no even if they wanted to? You can't say no to a friend who's been in a bombing.

"Let's do it," Colin was the first to chime in, "This is our lives and we'll never have this chance again."

Matt and Reyhan smiled placidly to each other. She nodded slightly indicating it was alright with her.

"Ok, we're in," Matt tried to sound as positive as possible even though he dreaded the implications.

"Ah! Y'all, we are gonna have so much fun. Ibrahim says he knows exactly where to take us and we've never even been to coast and—"

"—And we finally get to meet him!" Reyhan couldn't contain her joy.

Lane turned a slight shade of pink and said, "Well, yeah, of course," trying to minimize the statement.

"And you're sure this guy knows what's up?" said Matt, half-jokingly.

"I promise!" Reyhan noticed how Lane beamed when his name was mentioned, "And Colin, of course I want you to invite Metin."

Colin froze slightly and then recovered quickly with, "Oh, yeah, definitely, but you know how busy he is. I'll definitely give it my best shot. When do we leave?"

"Three weeks!" said lane—and they all fell into an exciting discussion about plane tickets, hotels, beaches, and a change of scenery.

Twelve
Superlatives

"*The* best restaurant," Reyhan stressed.

"No... *A* best restaurant," Aysha said convincingly.

Reyhan had finally gotten the class to speak only in English, a constant struggle after they found out she spoke their language.

"Aysha, I know," she was saying, "But it's *the* because there can only be *one* best restaurant in Istanbul."

The entire class couldn't contain their laughter anymore. Finally Mohammed, a sweet faced telephone salesman let Reyhan in on the joke.

"Teacher, there are *five* best restaurants in Beşiktaş!"

Reyhan sighed and thought about her upcoming vacation with increasing excitement.

—

Colin watched with interest as Metin fiddled with his menu. They had been to this Thai restaurant in Bebek several times, but his (non-official) boyfriend always seemed to need hours to decide on dinner. It gave Colin time to think about how odd the life he was living was; dinners in Bebek, imported wines every night in Metin's ridiculous apartment, chauffeured town cars to weekend getaways on the Black Sea. And there was more: yacht excursions with Metin's international co-workers on the Bosphorus, concerts, cocktails on Istanbul's only floating club/island. Colin refused to accept material things, but he had to admit the tally for everything Metin had paid for was beyond his calculation. It was all wonderful—and extremely strange. Colin had never experienced this amount of luxury in his life, and here he was running with the one percent—in Turkey.

Metin finally decided on a curry and flashed that smile that made Colin swoon.

"What were you saying?" Metin said.

"Well my friends…"

But just then Metin gestured animatedly towards the server who arrived with a scared look on her face. In rapid fire Turkish he began to berate her. She finally left, crestfallen. Colin's Turkish was nowhere near Lane's recently, but he still understood enough to know Metin's issue with the server was trivial.

"She's just trying to do her job…" he began slowly, but Metin was still unnerved.

"She's a fuck up—is that how you say it?"

Colin was shocked, but Metin must have noticed his face because he quickly added with, "We're paying good money for this place, she should be at the top of her game."

Colin had no idea how to proceed. Dozens of these little scenes had happened over the past months. Metin saying or doing something that caused Colin to pause, and then immediately explaining himself and saying something sweet. Alone, they were forgettable, but together…

"So I was saying my friends are headed to the coast. They want to go to Izmir and then take a bus down—"

"Izmir? It's so dead there. You really need to get to Bodrum. The clubs there are the best."

It was an answer to a question Colin hadn't even asked, "Um, ok well they're really more interested in seeing the ancient sights around there."

Metin looked unconcerned, "Ok, well why would they take a bus though? They should just get a private car to take them down the coast. Or you can easily charter a boat."

And just then something snapped in Colin and he couldn't keep it in, "Metin do you think everyone is like you?"

Metin looked stunned like he was trying to figure out the English—a problem he never had.

Colin continued, unable to stop himself, "I've heard you say fifteen elitist things just sitting here at dinner. Do you ever think about how other people live? That other people don't have as much as you do? That other people might be from different places?"

"Um, I—what does elitist mean?"

Metin tried to flash his characteristic smile but Colin was not having it. "Don't do that. Sometimes I wonder why you even keep me around. I'm obviously not from a rich family, which seems to be all you care about. Sometimes I think you like having an American boyfriend because it's fashionable."

"Baby…" Metin tried in the voice that had worked so many times before, "I care about *you*. I just like the life I've made for myself," he paused, and Colin was almost ready to listen, but then he continued, "And I'm sorry if other people aren't able to educate themselves and pull themselves up. It's not my fault and I'm not sure why I'm responsible for them."

Colin sat for a long moment searching Metin's eyes for any sign he was joking. He didn't find it. He knew this was the moment he should stand and walk out of the restaurant. He could even see it in his mind; getting up, throwing his starched white napkin on the table and then leaving without a word.

But instead, he simply sat there—invisibly glued to his oversized velvet seat.

—

The next day Matt asked Colin what was wrong over morning cereal before class.

"You slept here last night—is everything alright?" Matt said.

Colin didn't even know where to begin, "Yeah, it's fine, I just like my alone time every once in a while, you know that," he said convincingly.

"Haha, true," said Matt.

"Hey," Colin continued, "have you heard from Lane? I've been trying her cell but I can't get a text or call through."

"Oh, right, she's the worst about that. Yeah, Reyhan said she and Ibrahim are off on some adventure on the Black Sea. But you'll see her soon enough for the big trip!" He said and hurried out the door to catch the bus.

Colin couldn't help but laugh. There was only one person in the world he wanted to talk to right now, and she was as MIA as he had been for her a few months ago. He tried to text Lane one more time, but the message came back as undelivered.

—

Lane watched Ibrahim intensely as he studied the bus schedule for the tiny Black Sea town north of Istanbul they had found themselves in. A cool breeze blew in and disheveled her already unruly hair as she lay, reading Turkish Vogue on a cheap beach blanket emblazoned with a neon outline of the Turkish coast and an equally bright line drawing of the face of Atatürk.

"We might not make it back before eight," Ibrahim said absentmindedly.

"That's fine," Lane's gaze drifted out into the horizon where several large, rusting Russian tankers dotted the horizon, waiting for passage through the Bosphorus.

"Your friends are excited?" Ibrahim changed the subject.

"About our vacation? They're ecstatic."

"What does 'ecstatic' mean?" Ibrahim asked, but as he did he casually brushed a hand along Lane's outer thigh and she drew in a quick breath. He quickly withdrew his hand and started to stutter.

"Uh, I've heard it before but I've never thought to ask what it meant—that's all," he said, and returned to his intense study of the bus schedule.

Lane tried to play it cool, "It means very excited," she managed to say without too much emotion.

—

"What the matter?" Matt surprised himself with his directness, "it's just your parents."

Reyhan had been pacing for hours, and even had a shot of Matt's bourbon, a rare occurrence.

"Ok, Matt, I've got to tell you some things," she began. And then seeing his look of concern, "No, no it's fine, it's fine, it's just—well I've told you about my family before and my parents and how they can be..."

"Yeah, but it's all cool right?"

"Yeah, it'll be fine, I just—I just want you to know I need to go to dinner with them alone. You understand right?"

Reyhan was repeating herself, but Matt gave her a supporting look, "It's totally fine, you do what you have to do."

"You are the best," she said as the door buzzed indicating her parents downstairs.

Once inside, Reyhan's Mother Melis took a long, pointed look around.

"Canim," she began in Turkish, the 'c' pronounced as a smooth 'j'. Then, noticing Matt, she continued in English, "Where is your vacuum?"

"Anneeeeee" Reyhan said the Turkish word for 'mom' the same way any embarrassed teenager would.

"I have a few minutes before dinner," her mother continued as her father Ardit Bereket entered the tiny foyer.

"Rey Rey, your daddy needs some whiskey," he said in a thick Bulgarian coastal accent and moved swiftly past Matt and into the kitchen where he started rummaging through cabinets.

They were a whirlwind and Matt thought how they weren't unlike his parents in many ways.

"And who is *this*?" Reyhan's mother asked, indicating Matt, after she had finally given up her quest to find the vacuum.

"Oh, Anne," she said putting a stress on final 'a' sound, "I told you about Matt."

Matt beamed silently as he shook Melis's hand.

"Matt is one of my friends," Reyhan continued, "He and Lane and Colin have been the best thing that's happened to me here."

At first Matt didn't register what had happened, but slowly he started to replay the words in his mind.

"Well it's nice to meet you Matt," said Melis in a perfectly cordial tone.

Matt was still trying to make sense of the situation when Reyhan's father reentered the small, awkward space they were all standing in, "Rey Rey, you don't got no whiskey in this house," he huffed.

"Daddy you know I don't keep any whiskey, but I could see if Matt has any in his apartment…" she offered.

"No no canim," Melis chided, "he can drink as much as he wants at the restaurant, he's just mad the hotel bar doesn't have any."

"Nice to meet you anyway," Ardit said, roughly grabbing Matt's hand in a warm but quick handshake.

"Ok, ok," Reyhan made a knowing face in Matt's direction and quickly exited after her parents, the large metal door shutting loudly behind them.

Matt, dumbfounded, stood in the entry way for several minutes unsure of what had just happened. Finally, he said to himself, but still aloud, "That's it?"

—

Reyhan shed her light cardigan as she and her parents emerged from the noisy restaurant and onto the streets of Sultanahmet. A hot Mediterranean night had blown in from the sea and surprised them after dinner. Still uncomfortably full from their buttery iskander (her father's favorite dish of hot beef and tomatoes) they strolled along the Golden Horn back towards the Galata Bridge and on to her parent's hotel—the Atatürk guest house.

"Canim," her mother was saying as they ambled along the cobblestone streets, "you should just give it a chance," she continued half in Turkish, half in English, "His name is Emir and—"

"Annnneeee," she finally managed, "I don't need you to set me up on dates—I'm a grown woman."

"Yes, yes, grown woman," her mother said in English in a tone that made her sound as if she didn't believe it, "But even grown women need help. And it's so hard dating these days… You know your father and I met through an introduction. Isn't that right…" she nudged her fading husband, "Isn't that right? Ardit. Ardit!"

"Haaaa?" Ardit came to with a start and offered a simple but effective, "Melis you leave that girl 'lone." Years of mediating and he had his one liners down pat.

"Ugh, Anne, that was like a hundred years ago."

Melis rolled her eyes, "Ok, OK. I just think it would be so nice if you met a sweet Turkish boy—"

"—Or Bulgarian boy," Ardit chimed in a he slipped down into a large club chair in the lobby.

"—or Bulgarian boy," Melis repeated dutifully, but then mouthed the words "Turkish boy" to her daughter.

Reyhan loved her parents dearly. An only child, she was everything to them. They had been her rock after her engagement ended. They never said 'I told you so' or blamed American boys the way the rest of her family had. And she believed, deep down, that they just wanted her to be happy. But at the same time, they weren't going to be disappointed if she ended up with someone from their home countries. And after the hell she had put them through with the called off wedding—she couldn't blame them.

But then Matt's sweet face flashed in front of her and she felt a little sick. What had she done back at the apartment? She told herself he wouldn't understand. She just needed time.

"Canim, you look a little pale," her mother stroked the side of her face and she almost opened up right there and told them everything. But then Melis continued, "OK, this is the last I'm going to say about it, I know you don't need help finding dates, but just IN CASE—here is the business card for Emir. We've know his uncle in Michigan for years. They are a lovely family."

"Ok, Anne," Reyhan placated her, "I'll think about it."

"Well don't think too long. A successful man like that won't last long. He wants to meet you tomorrow night before he leaves Istanbul again."

Reyhan rolled her eyes but knew her mother wouldn't give up until she had given her all the details, "Where, Anne?"

"It's some restaurant or dance place? You know I don't know about these things. It's called Reina." Melis said is an uncertain tone.

"Oh wow," Reyhan masked her sarcasm but she definitely recognized the name. Reina was one of the gargantuan open air night clubs that dotted the banks of the Bosphorus. It was famous for all night raves, a private yacht dock, and several visits from Paris Hilton.

"Good night Rey Rey," her mother and father both kissed her as she squirmed under their embrace.

"Good night," she said and as she watched them climb the stairs of the guest house she felt worse than ever wondering when she would ever be ready to be honest with them.

—

The next day Reyhan felt worse than ever. She hadn't climbed the stairs to Matt's apartment the night before and couldn't even bring herself to respond to his simple text of "?".

She thought again about the face her parents would give her when she told them and fell in to a fresh bout of anxiety. Finally, she knew she couldn't wait any longer; she had to face Matt.

Opening the door to the boys' apartment she found him standing in the kitchen still in his boxers and holding his phone.

"What the f—" he started.

"—I know, I know, I never texted back. I'm sorry, I couldn't—"

"You couldn't what?" Matt fumed back. It was a tone Reyhan had never heard from him.

"My parents can just be a lot, and I was exhausted—I'm really sorry I didn't text."

Matt's expression changed from incredulous to complete anger, "You think this is about a text?"

Reyhan knew it wasn't, but how could she even begin to explain her situation to him. There's no way he could or would get it, "Yeah, I'm sorry, ok?" the words were biting in a way she didn't mean them to be. Her own anger at herself was bubbling up and starting to take shape in front of her.

"I can't believe you," Matt went on, "you let me stand here like a fool last night, thinking this was the big moment, and then you introduce me as a 'friend'?"

Reyhan couldn't think clearly anymore. Somewhere deep inside her she knew it was wrong but she lashed out anyway, "Are you kidding *me?*" she screamed.

Matt recoiled but quickly came back, his usual easy nature completely gone, all his frustration spilling out, "God, you have no idea what I've been through, do you? The guessing, the waiting for you to be ready. But you're never going to be ready, are you? You're never going to let me in." Matt was shocked by the things he said, but just as quickly knew he needed to say them.

"What *you've* been through?" Reyhan could feel her face growing red. It was all too much. She knew he was telling the truth, but for him to stand there and act as if he was the only one suffering, "You have no idea…" she said and then couldn't form words anymore.

"You're right, I don't have any idea—because you won't talk to me!"

Reyhan exploded for a final time, not even hearing her own words, "Well maybe I don't want to talk to you," she lied through gritted teeth.

"Fine then," Matt said, still too angry to sound sad, "maybe you should go and find someone you do want to talk to."

He said the sentence with such finality that it sounded as if a door had shut. Reyhan couldn't breathe.

All she could manage as she stumbled towards the door was a simple, "I will."

—

Seven hours later and still belligerent about what had happened, Reyhan was putting the finishing touches on her mascara. A large empty glass sat on the vanity in the bathroom next to a half drunk bottle of visne sharap and the crumpled but legible business card for Emir Erdogan. She paused briefly to look at herself in the mirror and started to think about what she was doing. But just as quickly she realized that action was her only choice if she was going to keep from breaking down.

The sequins of her shiniest dress glinted in the dingy stairwell as she raced down to catch the cab waiting outside. Fifteen minutes later she was standing on the sidewalk under an imposing neon sign that read 'REINA'.

From the street she could already feel the tremors from the club, like a rapid heartbeat. She started to pause but quickly pushed herself inside. Her name had been put on the list. Normally something like would have elicited a squeal of delight, but she didn't have time to think—she was on a mission.

She found herself standing on a platform at the top of the open air club just as the music climaxed in a cacophony of intense base and siren like sounds. The club spilled down in front of her in a set of bright terraces straight into the waiting black waters of the Bosphorus. An eerie moon hung over the horizon. It was a sea of white: couches, tables, fake palm trees, bars—all accented by multicolored neon lights.

She started to make her way down a lighted stairway just as the music resumed. An electronic pulse carried her, half conscious through a throng of people. She jostled back and forth between dancing women with bare mid-drifts and gyrating men with waxed and tanned chests. Everyone was moving in sync to the throbbing atmosphere.

The music was so loud she couldn't here herself think— exactly the way she wanted it.

She found Emir perched on a mid-level terrace near the far end of the club. He had texted her he would be wearing a blazer and near a bar tender with a Mohawk. He had not texted her he would be with two other women.

"Emir?" she almost screamed over the din.

"Yes!" he said in Turkish and quickly ushered her over to 'his' table.

Reyhan had no idea what to think of her surroundings, but for the first time since that morning she was able forget about her parents and Matt and the fight and the unhappiness with herself. Soon she had an orange drink in her hand and found herself swaying to the swirling music.

—

"I've fucked up you guys."

Matt had burst into the girls' apartment where Lane and Colin now sat, wide eyed over their drinks in the kitchen.

"What?" Lane began.

"There's no time—I need to know where she is!" Matt was almost hysterical.

"Reyhan?" Lane offered.

"Yes!" he said as if they should know what was going on. Finally he snapped back to sense and started piecing the story together in short bursts, "We—I—we had a huge fight. I seriously fucked up and now she's gone—and I don't know what she's going to do, or who she's going to do, or—"

"Ok, dude, clam down—" Colin started.

"I can't, don't you see I have to find her now? I have to make this right—she's—I love her."

Immediately some switch seemed to flip in all of them. Colin and Lane stood simultaneously, ready for action.

"OK, She must have left a couple hours ago. She left a note for me that was pretty vague," Lane said, "It said she was going to some place called 'Reina'? But is that even a place? Or a person?"

"Fuck, I don't know!" Matt was more animated than either of them had ever seen.

"Y'all, Reina is a giant night club on the Bosphorous. Do you even live in this city?" Colin started to smile but realized it was no time for being coy.

"Ok, where?" Matt had regained some composure but was still clearly upset.

"Call a cab," said Colin, "I know where it is."

—

Across town Reyhan could feel her deceptively strong drink working its way into her system. She wished she had had more to eat. The music continued to beat on, making the passage of time seem like a dream. Emir's hand was on the small of her back and she didn't have the energy or reason to move away from it. For the past two hours she'd been making screaming conversation in Turkish to the two women who hovered near Emir with impressive diligence. Emir was back from another very long phone call and asked her to dance with a strong tug on her arm. She didn't have a chance to say no.

Doing her best to move with the rhythm of the crowd she followed Emir's lead into an open area packed with jumping bodies. She knew she should probably leave soon, but Emir's hand on hers was tight and she didn't know how to say goodbye. *One dance,* she thought.

They jumped and torqued their bodies to the increasingly rapid beat, sometimes unable to move at all in the crush of the crowd. Emir moved closer to her with each passing song, smiling broadly as he grabbed her waist. She gave in, telling herself again the next song break would be her last.

But then it was too late—Emir's lips were on hers and she was cringing at the taste. Had she even spoken two sentences to this man? His hand slipped behind her back as she started to move away. He pulled her to him.

That's it, Reyhan thought. *I'm tired of people telling me what to do*—and in one swift motion she hauled back and clocked Emir right on the side of the head.

It must have been a good one, she thought later, because Emir reeled back onto the ground, almost in sync with the music as bystanders formed a small circle around the unfortunate scene.

Reyhan quickly came to and realized what she had done, but for some reason she still couldn't wipe the smile off her face. Just then, through tearstained eyes, she spotted a crop of curly hair and an outdated pair of black rimmed glasses staring at her from a clearing in the crowd. He had come.

Matt raced toward her in what seemed like slow motion as the dancing crowd enveloped Emir behind her. As he put his hands on the place where Emir's had just been he mouthed something she couldn't hear but she recognized instantly, "Seni Seviorum." It was the Turkish for "I love you."

Pulling back from Matt's sweet kiss Reyhan realized the gravity of the situation. She spotted Colin and Lane standing to one side of the clearing crowd. Emir was standing again, nose slightly bloody. Three large security guards were steadily moving towards all of them to the ominous pulse of the blaring electronica. It was time to make their escape.

Silently agreeing that they should split up all four friends made their way through the now impassable crowd. Dodging security guards and drunken dancers, each one managed to fight to the top of the terraced landscape, and, finally, out the front entrance before being detained. They ran for their lives, laughing as they did through the dark streets of Ortaköy; collapsing in howls in a tiny municipal park.

"You…" Reyhan looked at Matt in a way she never had before. And then, seeing Lane and Colin smiling at each other, "ALL of you… how did you know?"

"Well we really didn't have a choice," said Lane, "Matt insisted even though I told him I didn't have anything to wear."

They all gave in to a fresh bought of laughter as Lane tugged at ratty Middlesborough tee she had on.

Reyhan put her hand on Matt's cheek. There were no words—he had said everything by being there.

"I just have one question," Reyhan said as they walked breathlessly towards a cab stop, "How in the world did you get in? There's a list and everything."

Lane and Matt simply pointed behind them as Colin rolled his eyes, taking up the rear.

"Dating a guy that lives in Trump Towers has a few perks," he finally conceded. They all made fun of him the rest of the way home.

—

Metin's large eyes searched Colin for a hidden meaning, but didn't manage to find one. One morning in Trump Towers Colin had announced he was going on vacation with his parents, who were in Turkey for the week. It was the perfect cover, Colin thought.

"They want to go to the coast, and I would invite you but they aren't exactly cool with…"

"It's ok, I totally understand," said Metin. He stood in the doorway of his apartment, playing with the zipper on Colin's jacket. His tone was the same as the man that Colin had initially been so attracted to. Maybe his behavior the other night at the restaurant hadn't been as bad as Colin remembered?

The larger man took Colin in his arms and gave him a deep kiss that made him a bit weak. Colin knew he should say something about the other night—about everything. But, even louder in his head was a voice telling him not to mess up a good thing. This extremely successful and attractive man had chosen him. And no one was perfect...

I just need some time to think, he thought. He told Metin he'd call him when he got back to the city.

—

Lane thought she could hear a slight pause in Colin's voice. He had told them Metin was working that week and couldn't come to the Aegean. It was a perfectly logical explanation, but still, she seemed to sense something a little off about the way he had said it.

But just then, she realized Matt and Ibrahim were deep in conversation in the seats in front of her—she was terrified.

The five of them were about an hour into their flight to Izmir and the captain had just announced the final descent.

"He seems wonderful," Reyhan snapped Lane out of her intense straining to hear what the two boys were talking about.

"Ha, oh, yeah. I like him!" Lane realized she had said the whole thing with a ridiculous amount of emphasis, but Reyhan just smiled.

Three hours later they were all pressing their noses to the glass of an air conditioned holiday bus. The sun glittered on the Aegean as the bus climbed and twisted around an impossibly steep cliff face. The five of them watched with detached amazement that such a large and top heavy vehicle managed to avoid crashing into the white capped sea below.

They arrived in a small but polished looking harbor town and settled into their pension. Ibrahim handed Lane another frustratingly vague curveball. He insisted she stay with Colin, and bought his own room for the week. It was her only option, but still she wondered, if the numbers had been different...

—

The next few days were clear and electric, like when an image snaps into focus on a movie screen and hangs there in a crackling and beautiful moment. Each of them wondered separately if, years from now, they would remember this time with the same gorgeous intensity.

Deep, warm breezes blew in from the ocean and pulled them down to the rocky coast line where they read Turkish tabloids and baked their bare skin next to impossibly large families grilling on tiny aluminum foil contraptions in the heat of midday.

They stood, awe struck, in front of the library of Hadrian at Ephesus. Its multi columned, 2,000 year old façade rising to frame the setting sun. They took highly staged portraits reading newspapers while sitting on stone toilets in an ancient Roman public restroom.

They went to a camel fight, cheering on their two humped champions in the hot light of a coastal arena. The boys placed bets on which hulking beast would win. The loser was responsible for ice creams and bottles of chilled and pungent Turkish wine.

Lane accessorized every outfit with a pair of the cheap sandals she had bought from the woman in Tarlabaşi. They all bought brightly colored beach bags with Turkish flags and stylized tulips printed on them.

A rusted and groaning ferry bearing the image of a contemplative Atatürk transported them diligently to an indistinguishable string of sea side villages and then back again. They took turns laughing wildly, standing at the very tip of the ship's bow; lookouts, searching for an invisible fleet of pirates.

They dove headfirst without thinking into glassy blue waters in hidden coves.

They collapsed every night after consuming platefuls of buttery seafood washed down with biting raki and Efes beer. They slept in tiny beds with the windows open to the twinkling lights of the harbor and the ever-present sound of the churning sea.

A few days in they took a long walk in their bathing suits around a rocky outcropping that held the remains of an almost unrecognizable Roman temple. Lane and Ibrahim trudged on as Matt, Reyhan, and Colin slipped into a visitor center to learn the history of the area.

After what seemed like ages, Lane stopped to readjust her inadequate leather sandals. Ibrahim grabbed her hand as she finished re-fastening the buckle.

"Ha, what is it?" she asked, following him as quickly as her blistering feet would carry her.

"We're almost there," he laughed.

And before she could ask again they were running, dust and small stones tumbling down the path and into the lapis waves below.

"What in the world—" Lane started, still holding firm to Ibrahim's strong hand. But she stopped, cut short by a bend in the road. They crested the hill with such force Lane thought she might fall the short distance into the water, but instead Ibrahim held fast to her hand, pulling her to a final stop. It was magnificent. There on the other side of the hill the two of them stood, looking out over a vast expanse of crashing ocean. An imposing Roman column marked the spot alone, the rest of the small temple that it supported having long ago tumbled into the waiting arms of the sea.

Lane could barely catch her breath—both because of the run and the beauty of the place. It was like a special, perfect dream that only comes along once in a while, and, after waking, you try your hardest to remember as it slips away.

Just then she noticed Ibrahim's firm grip still on her hand. This time he wasn't pulling away like he had at the museum. She slowly turned to face him, expecting his hand to drop at any moment. Instead, she found him staring directly into her eyes.

"I—" he started, but Lane couldn't stand it anymore. It was her turn to communicate. Grabbing him by the back of his neck as softly as she could, she pulled him towards her—a thousand thoughts running through her head. She kissed him, and to her complete surprise—he kissed her back. It was one of those rare times that it felt exactly the way she had thought it would. Soft and intense. Passionate and questioning.

Finally, she was able to pull back for a moment, her entire body certain it wanted to continue. She opened her eyes and found him still smiling, no question in his eyes anymore.

Lane wasn't sure what to do. Do they talk? Do they kiss again? Should she tell him everything he probably already knew? And then she realized there was nothing to be said. Checking her distance to make sure it was still safe, she placed both her hands playfully on his chest, pushed him back softly, turned on her heel, and leapt laughing into the effervescent Aegean.

"The person who founded the Turkish Republic," Matt repeated.

"Who?" Ismael's bright eyes returned Matt's unasked question. On Tuesday afternoons Matt had gotten into the habit of taking a small group of his higher level students for coffee and casual Turkish/English conversation. Four interested sets of eyes sat around an impossibly small table next to the water in Ortaköy waiting for Matt to speak.

"No, no, it's a relative clause. The person 'who' founded the Turkish republic," Matt said again.

"Who?" This time Ayshagul, a serious high school senior, threw the same question back at him. Had he not explained clearly enough? These were his most dedicated students and they seemed to completely miss the grammar point.

"It's Atatürk," he finally conceded. They all seemed to nod their heads in agreement, but Matt knew he should think of a better example. He searched his brain for something more relative to a crowd of people with an average age of twenty.

"Ok, ok, how about 'the person who I'm dating'?" He congratulated himself on his example.

"Who?" Ismael shot back again.

"Um, the person 'who' I'm dating. The name isn't important." He was failing miserably.

"No, no," said Ismael, "Who *is* the person you're dating?"

Matt's cheeks began to flush as he realized his example had back fired. "Oh, uh, no one," he stammered, "It's an example."

They all cracked huge smiles as they silently traded glances.

Finally, Ayshagul said, "Would you say Reyhan is the person *who* you are dating?" she stated in perfectly enunciated words.

"Oh, ahhhh, I—" Matt started and then slowly realized what was going on, "Wait a minute, you just said that perfectly." He searched all four of them as they began to burst into stifled laughter.

"So you might say we are the students *who* discovered the person *who* you are dating…" Ismael tortured him.

Matt rolled his eyes at all of them and sighed into his coffee, a large grin on his face.

"Don't worry, teacher," Ayshagul said, "We are the people *who* will keep your secret."

—

The hot morning sun pierced a tiny slit in the covers over Lane's head and brought her quickly to consciousness. She smelled coffee brewing and instantly knew Colin must be in the kitchen prepping for an epic Turkish fusion weekend brunch. She had just started to drift back into a light sleep when a soft touch brought her back to consciousness. She shivered, but almost as quickly sighed and melted backwards into Ibrahim's waiting arms.

She thought dreamily about how easy it had all been. After getting back from the coast, there had been no discussions; no what-does-this-mean; no awkwardness. The two of them were the same as they had been before leaving, only now they were the same—together.

Lane, eyes closed, reached behind her head and groped for Ibrahim's fine hair. Mistakenly grabbing an ear they both let out a sleepy laugh. Then suddenly, there were a pair of firm lips on the nape of her neck as she sucked in a deep breath. She faintly smelled the distinct odor of forbidden bacon. Colin would be finished up brunch soon. But in answer to her unspoken thought Ibrahim's firm hand caught her hip and applied a small but unmistakable pressure. Brunch would have to wait.

—

Charlotte Cameron did not look happy.

Lane gave an audible sigh as she spotted her sister at the far end of the baggage claim. *How is it possible she looks that pulled together*, she thought, a thousand different memories flooding in from as far back as twenty years ago. Charlotte's deep auburn hair (the same color as Lane's) was almost airbrushed into place. Her clothes looked formal, but not uncomfortable, and like they had been pressed for her on the plane and just given back moments before landing. Her subtle jewelry glinted as she played with the leather tag on her luggage. But Lane couldn't help but notice her usually serene face was contorted into a look of mild contempt.

"Who died?" Lane tried to assume an air of maturity but was five years old again the minute Charlotte swung around to face her.

Charlotte quickly reapplied her signature smile and grabbed Lane into a warm hug.

"I know, I know," she said while popping the handle up on her bag, "I was just thinking about the flight... A man got on in London with what looked like a wheel barrow full of junk. At first I thought it was crazy, just rolling right onto a plane with all your stuff in a two wheeled, open topped contraption. But then when we landed he just rolled it right off the plane and straight out through customs. And here I am waiting forever to get my checked bag back." Charlotte's face changed again into a strange mixture of bewilderment and grudging respect.

Lane couldn't think of any other way to characterize what was a perfectly normal experience for her over the past months, "Welcome to Turkey," she said.

—

"You know Myra and Jim wanted to be here," Charlotte was saying as she poked at a doner kebap with a ridiculous plastic fork. The two girls were wildly different, but they were able to bond occasionally through the ironic use of their parents' first names, "but it being wool shearing season—and with the economy the way it is. You know they had to let two of the part time farm hands go."

"Please, please," Lane raised a hand, "I've had to talk mom through this like five times on skype this week. She and dad are honestly way more upset than I am. I mean my contract is up in just over two months anyway, and then I'll be home before they know it."

"Oh, yeah. That's coming pretty fast isn't it? Have you given any thought to—" but just then the door to the small doner shop swung open to reveal Ibrahim wearing a broad smile. Lane breathed a sigh of relief that Charlotte's impending interrogation was put on pause.

"Charlotte, this is Ibrahim I was telling you about," Lane had jumped from her seat with nervous excitement. She had set up the meeting days ago, but now that she was actually standing there studying her sister's face as she met this man (her man?), her heart raced.

"How do you do," was Ibrahim's odd greeting. His English was perfect. Occasionally, though, he would say something slightly quirky or old fashioned in a way that made Lane stop, try and figure out if he was joking, and then like him a little more when she realized he wasn't.

An hour into dinner and Lane was almost ready to call it a success. But suddenly Charlotte's tone changed. She had made polite but interesting conversation for a minute too long it seemed.

"But there must be good jobs here in Istanbul—or maybe in Ankara? Why the U.S?" Charlotte asked almost out of nowhere. She had casually asked Ibrahim about his plans, but this was more than an innocent question—it was pointed.

Ibrahim shifted in his creaky chair and cleared his throat, "Oh, ah, well there are jobs in both cities… but…" It was one of the few times Lane had seen him look visibly uncomfortable. She wanted to tell Charlotte to stop. But even more than that she wanted to hear his answer.

"I, mean, if it's just a job you're after…" Charlotte continued in the parental voice Lane knew all too well from childhood.

"—Actually it's not a job. It's a program." Ibrahim finally said, regaining his composure. Lane swung her head to meet his eyes—why had she never thought to ask these questions? "There's a master's program I'm trying to get into… but… it's very hard," he said more quietly, and looked away as if something else had caught his attention.

"What's it in?" Charlotte wiped her perfect bangs from her forehead and continued to stare him down. But Ibrahim seemed to instantly light up.

"It's an archeology program," he beamed, "Turkey has some of the most important archeological sites in the western world—and if I can get into this program, I could work with experts in this area. There are more than 100,000 years of human history in this place just waiting to be discovered." He finished the sentence in a way that made it seem as if he could go on for hours. But he stopped himself.

Charlotte looked genuinely stunned. Lane thought her own face must look pretty surprised, also, because Ibrahim's smile faded when he looked at her.

Finally Charlotte spoke up, "Well that's fantastic. I hope that works out for you." Lane had heard the less than kind tone but thankfully Ibrahim had not.

"Thank you!" Ibrahim smiled, "It's a bit of a long shot—but it would be wonderful."

"Well, we should really get going," Charlotte directed, "Laney's taking me to some Byzantine church tomorrow—you could probably tell us all about it!" she said in her most gracious tone.

"Oh, you will enjoy it," Ibrahim commented as they slipped out into a hot Istanbul evening, "I took Lane to the Chora Monastery myself—the mosaic walls are one of our national treasures," he said with the same excitement he had shown when talking about his master's program.

They said their good nights and Ibrahim shuffled off in the opposite direction.

"Just give me a minute," Lane said to Charlotte as she sprinted back towards him. She caught him by the arm around the corner and pulled him in for a deep kiss.

"Why did you never tell me…?" she asked. But she already knew the answer.

"Because it never came up," Ibrahim said. He pulled at the collar of his worn burgundy polo and looked towards the ground.

"You'll have to tell me more soon," Lane said and squeezed his hand as she raced back to her sister.

—

Back at Lane's apartment Reyhan was predictably upstairs for the night and the two sisters sat in the kitchen for a post-boyfriend debrief.

"I know, I know," Lane answered Charlotte's unasked question, "he's not my style at all. But isn't he just great?"

Charlotte's 'concern face' appeared and Lane dreaded what she was about to say, "He's wonderful... I just..."

Charlotte had never shied away from telling her sister what she thought so Lane pressed her, "I mean, how fantastic about that master's program? And his passion. And you don't even have to tell me how cute he is..." She was starting to ramble and noticed Charlotte was giving her 'pity' face, so she finally broke character, "Ok, Charlotte," she tried to say in her most authoritative tone, "What *is* it?"

"OK, Laney, listen, I don't want you to think I'm being overly critical," she said and Lane laughed remembering every time she had experienced her sister's harsh opinion, "*buuuuuuuut*," Charlotte continued, "I think he's keeping something from you."

Lane was completely caught off guard. Hadn't they just been at the same dinner where he had come clean about his academic plans?

"Charlotte, he *just* answered all of your really intense questions. I mean what do you want? For him to write you a thesis? He told us everything."

"OK, yeah," Charlotte continued in a convincing tone, "He told us everything I asked about—but there's something more."

"What? Come on Charlotte what are you even talking about?"

"I just think there's more he's not telling. I mean how much information has he freely given you?"

Lane started to think back to every time she had told Ibrahim something about herself, her life, her family, her wants. But then she stopped, "Charlotte, ok, fine, I get what you're saying. But you're forgetting an important thing—I haven't asked him about any of these things. I didn't need to. I mean, come on, I'm leaving Turkey in two and a half months, he's going off to his program or wherever—we're…" Lane hesitated before she said it, "We're just having fun."

Charlotte studied her sister for an impossibly long time before responding. When she did, it cut like a knife, "But you're not just having fun," she said slowly, "He means something to you."

Lane shook her head in a knee jerk reaction to her sister's maternal advice, "Alright, alright you caught me!" She tried to make a joke but Charlotte knowing gaze was unbearable, "Come on, we need to get to bed—I really am forcing you to see this monastery tomorrow!"

"Oh, you mean the one *Ibrahim* took you to?" Charlotte teased as she left the room, but all the same Lane couldn't sleep for hours that night.

—

A few days later, after Charlotte had left her in an uncharacteristically tearful goodbye, Lane boarded a dolmuş from the airport to her apartment where she found Ibrahim waiting on the street. Once inside she faced him with a seriousness that she didn't know she could have with him.

"So what else aren't you telling me?" She had tried so hard to keep it in, but there it was, just spilling out of her with no context or background.

Ibrahim put on a questioning face and said quickly, "Lane, what do you…"

"Charlotte seems to think you're keeping something from me." She tried to say it in a casual way, as if it was Charlotte's problem and not hers.

"Ah." He looked away from her and sighed. After a long interval he finally spoke, "I told you everything. I'm trying to get into this program, it's very hard—I'm not sure what will happen." He said. Lane knew she could hear more details between his words but she wasn't sure how to get at them.

And then she thought about what she was doing. This man didn't owe her anything, she thought. She tried to remind herself of what she had told Charlotte, they were just having fun...

Ibrahim squirmed in the shabby kitchen chair back in her apartment, his dark eyes looking heavy.

Lane tried to salvage the conversation, "It's ok, I'm sorry, I'm sure you're stressed out about the whole thing and I'm pressing you for details," she stammered. She raised her hands in an apology and looked to Ibrahim for confirmation. But his heavy eyes continued to search her.

"No, it's ok..." he said in a soft tone, "I like that you—" He stopped himself and then repeated, "It's ok," he said with finality.

They had sex that night in a way that Lane knew was different. It felt like they were closer even though no real information had passed between them. Lane was happy and, for the first time in their easy friendship, completely confused.

—

August flew by with hot speed. Lane went back to EnglishSpace fulltime, accepting the reality of needing money. She, Matt, Reyhan, and Colin would trade stories of the latest ridiculous happenings from their branches over sketchy stuffed mussels in shabby bars under the traffic of the Galata Bridge. Ibrahim started making regular appearances at their little members' only club, quietly speaking to Reyhan in Turkish to see if the others could pick up on his scandalous statements. Reyhan squealed with delight as the other three spent several intense minutes trying to guess what he had said.

Reyhan and Matt were effectively living together—which worked out perfectly for Lane and Ibrahim who were spending increasingly long stretches of time holed up in her room talking, learning each other's languages, laughing, sleeping, watching American TV on laptops, reading Turkish poetry, and generally not giving a damn about the outside world.

Colin was gone just as much as before. But one day Lane convinced Reyhan and Matt that they needed to have an intervention.

"Colin, this is for your own good," Lane said as the four of them sat around tiny glasses of visne sharap in the boys' kitchen; a definitely drunk Atatürk smiling at them from the bottle's label, "We need to meet Metin."

Colin froze. He knew this moment would come, but he was hoping he could hold off a little longer. He panicked. How could he bring Metin around when he wasn't even sure how he felt about him himself?

Lane noticed his uncertain face and countered, "Boo, it's not a big deal, it's just a drink with the guy! We deserve to know who you've been living it up with in Dort Levent." They all laughed and Colin tried to join in.

He felt trapped, "It's just—" he began.

"No excuses!" they all yelled at him and he knew it was impossible.

"Ok, ok," he conceded. He faked a smile, but, to his dismay, no one seemed to notice.

—

Since their coastal trip, Colin had fallen back into a similar pattern with Metin. Colin cooked, Metin ate, they went to interesting places, they had sex, they slept in the same bed most nights. Metin asked about his friends and Colin about his work. It was easy. But every so often, Metin would say something that would give Colin a sinking feeling in his stomach, and he was unsure of how to continue sitting in his apartment, let alone being with him. But he stayed. Metin had a hold on him no man ever had. Metin wanted him—truly wanted him. And for some reason Colin was unable to break free.

On a particularly good night, he finally gave Metin the story, "So… my friends want to have a drink with you if—"

"—Oh, I've been waiting for you to ask me!" Metin's reaction shocked Colin into silence.

"Oh, ah, great, so…"

"They should come up here—if it's not too much trouble. There is a roof bar in the other Trump Tower you know."

"Oh, um, yeah, sure" Colin didn't know how to react, but he tried to act pleased. Metin could be so intuitive and perfect and this was what everyone wanted, right? "Well, I'll tell them Saturday night, around 7:00?"

"Perfect!"

—

Colin had been cooking and assembling food for hours. He was three wines deep and knew he needed to slow down, but it helped the anxiety, and it was a Saturday after all.

The slick electronic doorbell to Metin's apartment rang just as Colin's dill carrots came out of the oven. Matt, Reyhan, and Lane burst into the space as if they owned it. Colin briefly forgot all his worry and patted himself on the back for having such amazing friends.

"Where's Ibrahim?" Metin asked by way of an introduction to Lane.

Lane, completely astonished but equally impressed, replied, "He's with his parents for their anniversary tonight."

"Well maybe next time!" Metin responded perfectly, and Colin wondered why he had been so nervous.

The night progressed smoothly. Hors 'doevures transitioned into drinks on the rooftop bar in the twin trump tower building next door. It was higher than any of them had ever been in the city. Lane looked out over the vast, black expanse of the illuminated landscape. To the south a clear line of lights defined the main arteries of the city straight through Şişli to their apartments in Nişantişi and in the distance the bright, electric sunrise of Taksim square. To the north, an orange ribbon of streetlamps outlined the Bosphorus in a curving arc straight up to the inky void of the Black Sea.

After many minutes admiring the view they settled into small but chic chairs around an even smaller and chicer drinks table as the plush beat of Norwegian techno pop circled around them. The five laughed about common inconveniences and talked excitedly about things they loved in Istanbul. Metin traded recommendations for manicurists with Reyhan. Lane asked Metin about the best way to get to an out of the way Roman site she had heard about. Matt and Metin talked about hair products and the best place to hear indie music in the city.

"It was just over near the bakal," Metin was saying, his large hands gesturing in a way that made Colin smile.

"But, now it's a mall," Matt laughed. They had been talking about a small simit shop that Metin said was the best in the neighborhood.

"Well thank god," Metin returned.

"Oh?" said Reyhan. They were all back in Metin's apartment, casually playing with the fruit desert Colin had made too much of.

"Well, of course," Metin continued. No one heard what was coming except for Colin, "I mean that simit shop was good, but the rest of the area was horrible."

Colin felt the dropping sensation in his stomach.

"There are more than a few of those in the city," Reyhan continued laughing, "Good thing the mall came in," she said jokingly.

"That's the damn truth," Metin's tone became more serious, "kicked out all the gypsies."

A small sentence, but it was as if an electromagnetic pulse bomb had gone off at their tiny table. Matt, Reyhan, and Lane fell silent in a way that made Colin think they would never speak again. Matt shifted in his seat. Reyhan pulled out her small phone to check her texts. Lane kept her gaze on Metin, thinking.

Finally Lane spoke and Colin braced for what she was about to say, "Well hopefully they found a good place to go," she said with a placid smile. It was an innocent comment, but Colin could hear the southern 'fuck you' in every word.

"I'm sure they found another parking lot for their cheap cars. Probably in Bulgaria," Metin said almost as an afterthought. Colin looked him up and down and realized he clearly hadn't understood what had just happened. They all looked to Reyhan who quickly saved the moment.

"Oh my god, you guuuuuuuuuys," she said with mock exasperation, "Matt and I have to get across town for that ridiculous art show tomorrow."

Everyone took the hint except Metin. "Oh, no! You can't leave!" he shot back.

"I know, I know," Reyhan said maintaining complete composure, "But this guy wants to do it—you know how that is!" She said, indicating Matt with convincing happiness.

Metin grabbed Colin's shoulder and pulled him in slightly, "I do!" Metin said, still oblivious. Colin managed to stop himself from shrugging off the embrace.

The three friends said goodbye to the two of them back in the lobby. Just as they entered the revolving door at the far end of the vast sitting area, Colin saw Lane look back and meet his eyes with a mixture of questioning and disappointment.

—

The next morning Colin left before Metin woke up. Part of him wanted to stay and end it right there, but he continued to second guess himself. Maybe it hadn't been that bad? He thought, and instantly knew he was wrong. The long metro ride back to the apartment was torture. A poster for a Republic Day festival featured an unusually kind looking Atatürk—Colin couldn't help but think he was casting a non-judgmental but questioning eye in his direction.

Back in his kitchen he found a wide eyed Matt. He instantly knew he needed to offer some sort of apology.

"Matt, hey, so about last night—"

Matt raised a hand, "—No no no! Don't worry about. Actually you have some visitors in the living room," he motioned towards the front of the house where they almost never hung out except to watch the occasional dubbed American movie.

Completely confused, Colin made his way slowly to the glass interior door and opened it. Before he could even survey the room his mother, Marla, had him in a firm embrace.

"Son..." she said in a soft tone as she squeezed him tightly. Colin was so shocked he didn't have time to register the situation and hug her back. He stepped back almost involuntarily and saw his father, Robert Yates, standing a few feet away with the same uncharacteristic grin on his face that Marla had.

"What in the world…" Colin managed.

"Your mother just had to see you," Robert said in a joking tone Colin hadn't heard him use for years.

"Oh, I'm just so happy to see your face," Marla put a hand on his cheek that made him flinch from surprise. Were these the same two people he had left with polite goodbyes ten months ago? "Oh, my word, what are we doing, Robert? He must have so many questions." Marla's blue eyes were brighter than usual and almost seemed to start filling with tears. He looked at his father, his light hair thinning much more than Colin could remember. He didn't know what to say.

The three of them were soon seated in a quiet but chic restaurant in Teşvikya, staring at each other over expensive hamburgers.

"So…" Colin began but wasn't sure how to continue.

"Well I guess we should just keep this as simple as possible," It was more words that Robert had spoken to his son at one time in the past two years, "They found a lump in your mother's breast—"

"Oh my god!" Colin almost shouted.

"—Now hold on! Robert you really are terrible at these things—"

"—Well it's the truth isn't it?" Robert shot his wife a look.

"—Well that may be but you don't just go around shouting these things out without some kind of context."

"OK, fine, I mean we flew half way around the world to see the boy and I'm just trying to get to the point."

"Please do not even get me started—I know how much you hate to fly. Everyone on the damn plane knew how much you hate to fly."

"You know it's not about the plane—"

"—Can someone please tell me what's going on?" Colin finally found a place to interject. It was so odd, his emotionally distant parents had flown thousands of miles to sit in front of him at a restaurant and have a fight. Part of him was in a rage—but another part thought how… normal the whole thing was. Like the way they had been with him as a child.

"Oh my god, of course, of course!" Marla swatted Robert on the hand to indicate she would handle the story, "They did find a lump—but I'm FINE," she said with extreme emphasis.

"But you never called—you never…" Colin knew very well that he hadn't called very much either and fell silent.

"We…" Marla started to break down but pulled herself together, "Well we just never thought something like that would—*could* happen. And don't worry, they got it very early, and no chemo or anything—but," and this time she actually began to cry, "Well, Colin it kind of changed everything."

Colin studied her slightly creased face and warm smile. Her hand moved to hold his and he held it tightly. Robert cleared his throat.

"Son, we…" Colin could see him straining for some sort of help. He stopped, composed himself and continued, "Colin, we've had some really important conversations over the past months about what really matters in life—and you're at the top of that list, even if we haven't… well what I'm trying to say is, we're sor—"

"—No, oh my god, please!" Colin had already seen the 'I'm sorry' in their tired faces. Hearing the words would be too much, "I'm…" and now he was searching for words himself, "I'm just so happy you're both here…" And without missing a beat he straightened his back and added, "I've got a million things to tell you."

—

A few days and several missed phone calls from Metin later, Colin threw his tiny phone into his bag with a bit too much force.

"Son, what's happening?" Marla inquired.

Colin and his newly international parents sat across from each other at the rooftop bar of their Sultanahmet hotel. Over the past week they had been together almost constantly. Colin led them around a city he didn't realize he knew so well. They followed with wide-eyed amazement as he showed them the tiled floors of the Byzantine imperial palace, the fresh Turkish food at his favorite vegetarian restaurant, and took them on a boat tour up the choppy Bosphorus. But mostly they had just talked. Over long dinners and sea side lunches they talked for hours about everything. They had years to make up for, and they had gotten a pretty good start.

But there was one part of Colin's life they still hadn't covered. Colin looked at both his parents and sighed. Colin's father irreverently dipped a simit into his tiny chay glass as Marla fingered the hammered copper pitcher she had forced them all to search for in a dusty antiques shop in Tarlabaşi.

"It's..." Colin started.

"Is it about a man?" Marla said with such directness that Colin dropped his tiny chay spoon with a clink.

"Oh, uh..."

"Because you can tell me—*us,*" she confirmed.

He was amazed, and looked to his Father, who, not completely overjoyed, was nevertheless looking him straight in the eyes.

"It's nothing," Colin lied, "But it means a lot that you asked."

Marla studied him for another minute. "Ok, ok. But you make sure whoever he is he's treating you right," she said with conviction.

Robert added unexpectedly, "Son, remember: you come from a good family. And you make sure whoever you spend your time with is pulling you up and not the other way around, ok?"

Colin felt a hot tear run down his cheek but managed to recover quickly, "Geez, ok fine!" He laughed, "Now finish those drinks so we can make your last day here count."

—

Later that evening Colin made the trip up to Trump Tower's by cab. Metin was clearly not as dense as he seemed, because when he opened the door he didn't make a move toward him.

"Something is wrong," Metin said quietly.

"I've had so much fun with you," Colin said, "But—"

"Ok—" Metin cut him off with a raised hand. Colin knew he could do him the favor of not explaining. Metin studied him for a long time opening his mouth to speak and no words coming out. Finally, his shoulders slumped slightly in his crisp white work shirt. "Ok," he said again, and closed the large door swiftly.

Colin stood for a moment, a fleeting doubt in his mind. Then he thought of his father's words, smiled, squared his shoulders, and walked away

Fourteen
Compound Nouns

"There must be some compound German noun to describe this," Lane observed of their current situation, "like 'the difference between the time you thought it would take you and the time it actually takes you'."

"Or just 'traffic-time'," Colin offered with a smile. They both laughed in the back of the hot cab. They had been sitting on Istanbul's main southerly highway for more than half an hour, astonished at the amount of traffic at nine o'clock in the evening. Colin had convinced Lane to accompany him to a party at his boss' house in Bakirköy. Lane readily accepted.

"...So, how are yooooooooou," Lane asked in an exaggerated manner.

Colin took her meaning immediately, "I'm fine! It's been a full week, hasn't it?" he asked with a laugh.

"Ok, ok," she was excited to see the Colin she knew in his happy smile, "But, you've got to admit... don't you miss Trump Towers just a little?"

"Haha, not at all!" He said with an eye roll, and then added causally, "except, you know, for the roof pool... and the concierge service… and the sushi restaurant… and the view—but that's IT."

Lane laughed as Colin asked the driver in grammatically perfect Turkish to take an alternate route he knew of. The driver raised a hairy palm and made a clucking noise to indicate that would not be happening.

"What about your man?" Colin shot back, "Now that you two are official."

It was an innocent statement but for some reason it put Lane on the defensive, "Oh, I don't know about official," she furrowed her brow, "But he is something special."

"He's more than that," Colin said with raised eyebrows.

"Ha! Are you and my sister on some group email I don't know about?"

"Did Charlotte say the same thing?" Colin's mouth spread into a wide grin.

"Ugh, yes! I told her we're just having fun—"

"—Which you're not," he must have been reading off the same script Lane thought.

She rolled her eyes, "Annnnnnyway, he's just fine, I'm just fine, we're just fine."

Colin paused for a minute and considered his next statement. "Ok, but there's still something off."

Lane was so happy to have someone that wasn't her sister to talk to, but for a brief moment she stopped, bit her lip, and considered how to continue. Finally she decided she couldn't hold it in, "Ok, well Charlotte thinks—and I'm not saying I agree with her!—that he's keeping something from me…"

The words sounded so odd coming out of her mouth and she immediately looked to Colin to make sense of them. He stopped to consider the situation for a minute. She notice how his hair had turned lighter in the summer sun. But despite his seasonal tan, she still thought he looked older somehow, more grown up. When had that happened?

"Well... I guess that only matters if you plan on keeping in touch with him after all this is over," he said with kind but serious eyes.

The words hit Lane like a brick; she let out a large comic groan, "Holy fuck, you're right."

"Sorry boo, I think you might have it bad for this guy."

"Oy," Lane rolled her eyes and used the Turkish word for 'life', "Hayat!"

—

Summer burned well into September like the embers of one of the open air grills that dotted the beaches south of the city. Lane, Colin, Matt, Reyhan, and Ibrahim spent gorgeous nights on the rooftops of touristy restaurants in Yeniköy on the northern Bosphorus, smoking tobacco through water pipes and exhaling the clouds of apple flavored smoke out across the Black Sea towards Russia. They danced obnoxiously to the tinny but infectious sounds of the latest Turkish pop songs.

Somewhere in the back of her mind, Lane knew she should think about her rapidly approaching exit from Turkey. But everything was finally going perfectly. So she put it off.

And then one day she got an email from Catherine at EnglishSpace that forced her to sit down. It was just one sentence, "Lane, do you know if you'll be signing on for another year with EnglishSpace?"

She needed to start making moves quickly. And as a sinking feeling grew in her stomach, she realized the first thing she had to do.

—

"You are not well," Berat said in a sentence so perfect Lane did a double take.

"No, no, I'm fine," Lane responded in Turkish.

Berat ran the bakal down the street from their apartment building and he and Lane had become fairly close for proprietor and customer. He was a jolly looking light brown skinned man in his late forties (she guessed) with salt and pepper hair, a well-kept beard, and a perpetually stained polo shirt. He had become her everything man in the time they had lived in the neighborhood. No toilet paper at 11 pm? Berat had you covered. Cold soda water on the way to class on a hot morning? He practically handed it to you as you walked in the door. Ran out of beer and all the grocery stores were closed? Berat would pull a six pack out of a slightly hidden fridge behind the counter and hand it to you without judgment. Lane often wondered if she should offer to marry him and bring him back to the U.S., but she was fairly certain his wife would not be happy about that.

At some point, Lane started speaking to him only in his native language and he began testing out his passible English with her. She had learned more from him about proper usage than Ibrahim, and no matter how much of a hurry she was in, she always took the time to correct his pronunciation if he was struggling.

It was perhaps no surprise, then, that Berat could tell something was up.

"You are nooooorvus," he attempted as he handed her her usual bottle of mineral water.

"Neeeeervous," she corrected without thinking, "And no, really I'm fine." She cracked a slight smile.

Berat gave her a completely unconvinced looked and waved her on with a happy grin, "Ok, ok, see you tomorrow neeeeervous girl."

He was right, of course, she was jittery and her palms were so slick the water bottle nearly slipped right out of them. This was it—she was finally going to tell Ibrahim how she felt.

They had both said things about how happy they were; how they were mad they'd waited so long to be together; how it all seemed so perfect. But neither of them had actually put into words what was happening between the two of them. Lane went over what she planned to say in her head. Was she even going to use the word? The big fat inconvenient "L" word hanging over her like a garish motel sign. It was way too early, she told herself again and again. *But, fuck, I'm leaving—LEAVING, so it might be now or never. And when you know, you know*, she kept hearing in her head. She couldn't think about that now. She just had to make it to the restaurant and see what happened.

Twenty minutes and an unbearable metro ride later, she stood outside of the large plate glass windows of Zetin'ya, an out of the way but refined hole in the wall in Tarlabaşi. She was wearing a dress that was so self-consciously casual she considered running back up to the Istiklal and buying something more date-worthy. But then she saw Ibrahim through the window, pouring over a stack of multi-colored papers while swilling beer intensely. She smiled to herself and realized the pit in her stomach had disappeared.

"You're going to have to explain all this to me at some point," she said in a teacher-y voice as she plopped down in the plush chair opposite him, her hair sweeping across her shoulders, and showing the last golden highlights of summer. Ibrahim's cheeks blushed in the way they did when she paid him an unexpected compliment, but he also quickly swept all of the very formal looking documents into a large brown leather bag. For a moment she thought she saw panic on his face, but he turned back to face her with a wide smile.

"Horribly disinteresting," he threw his hand casually towards his bag.

Lane would have normally poked fun a bit more, but she remembered quickly her main objective and her usual directness took over.

"Ibrahim," she began, "listen, I need to tell you some things—it's not a big deal really," she paused with an over done laugh, "so as I'm sure you've guessed, I'm leaving Turkey soon…"

"Yes, yes, I had guessed that," he smiled.

"And… well, and… I just wanted to tell you…" the pit in her stomach suddenly reappeared and she felt short of breath, "that even though I'm leaving, this time—this—you have meant so much to me and…"

Ibrahim's face had become equally nervous and he started to echo her, "You too… and…" he said in a bumbling confirmation.

"And…" *I just have to do it*, Lane thought, "and I want you to know that—well that is to say I think… I might. I mean, I love—"

"—You two!" Reyhan's familiar squeal cut the air between them like a pin in a balloon, "Are we interrupting something?" Lane looked up, dazed to see her, Matt, and Colin standing over her with rapidly fading smiles.

"Oh, ahhhhh—no, no, no" Ibrahim interjected, "Lane I'm *so* sorry," he said with pleading eyes, "I thought it would be fun to have everyone along so I texted Reyhan…" he looked completely crestfallen but tried to regain the moment, "You were saying…"

"OH, ah, haha, of course, I love… this place!" she said, and looked to her friends. They all seemed to accept the cover story and quickly crowded in around the two of them.

Ibrahim jostled to one side as Matt and Colin flanked him on the arms of the chair. His eyes never left Lane's. And as everyone was dissolving into conversation over the menu he continued to stare straight at her and said, quietly, "I love… this place, too."

—

The next few days were agony. Ibrahim and Lane continued on, trying to act as if nothing had happened. They would awkwardly start to speak at the same time and then both fall silent. Every time Ibrahim called her name Lane's heart would stop; just in case that was the moment he had finally decided to finish their conversation from the restaurant. Having sex became, oddly, their only non-awkward form of communication.

Finally Lane couldn't take it anymore. October was twenty four hours away and she had to make a move.

It was one of the last truly hot days of the year. A hazy cloud of light smog and heavy cigarette smoke hung in the air around Lane's head as she dodged pencil skirted business women and newsboy capped vegetable salesmen on the back streets of Şişli looking for the out of the way Kave Dunyasi she and Ibrahim had never told any of the others about.

She noticed the familiar sketchy liquor store and remembered it was directly across the narrow, cobblestone and asphalt street. Standing outside the windows of the tiny coffeehouse, she noticed him at one of the miniscule tables, papers spread out just like they had been the other night. Maybe, after she said what she had to say, he would finally open up about all of it.

She bounded into the tiny space, the smell of richly roasted coffee and chocolate mixing with the ringing of the tiny bells on the door, a huge smile on her face.

And then Ibrahim looked up. His face was so odd Lane stopped in her tracks. It wasn't angry, or sad, or loving, or even confused. It was placid, and for a moment Lane thought it looked like he didn't even recognize her. He didn't try to conceal the jumble of papers this time. Slowly, he placed an odd smile on his face and she moved towards him.

Lane hesitated for a second and then realized it was probably just all in her head. She moved her lips in for their customary I-haven't-seen-you-today kiss. Ibrahim kissed her back. She thought about how his kiss was technically correct, the way he sometimes used the word "fellow" instead of "guy" in casual conversation. But like that word it was still just—wrong.

"Hey…" She began, completely forgetting the script she had developed on the way over, "What's up?" she said in a casual tone but longed to ask: *what the hell is up*?

"Um…" Ibrahim's face was still cold and unfamiliar, "I have to tell you some things."

Lane let out a large comic sigh, her secret weapon against situations like these. It failed miserably. Ibrahim continued to face her with his placid smile. She was completely lost, the man she knew would have found that hilarious, or at least chuckle worthy.

"So," he continued as if they were in a business meeting that was on a schedule, "I mentioned to you and Charlotte that I was applying to a master's program at Berkeley."

Lane studied him for a moment but felt oddly pressured to speed things along, "Um, yes. I mean—you never said Berkeley. I mean you never really talked about the whole thing at all before she asked you." She was rambling.

"—Yes, well, It's not going to work out," he said bluntly.

Lane was more confused than anything. This man that she had just realized she had deep feelings for was talking to her as if she were his employer and he needed to leave for another job.

"Oh, I'm—I'm so sorry?" she offered, "You didn't get in?"

"It's just—" he stuttered a bit, "It's—well, yes," he said and then quickly moved his eyes down towards the steaming latte in front of him.

"Um, ok, well I'm sure there are other schools. I mean I don't know that much about the archeology field but I've heard of—"

"I'm going into the military." Ibrahim stated it and immediately met her eyes with the same placid stare. This was the second time she had even heard about his future plans, and now he was dropping a bomb like this?

Lane felt helpless. She felt like she should fly into a rage of some kind, or grill him on why he had never told her any of this, or possibly even flip him off and exit quickly. But the facts were clear to her: he had never told her any of this because she had never asked. She thought about how she had told Charlotte they were 'just having fun'. She regretted every syllable.

Ibrahim continued as if Lane was still taking part in the conversation, "So I'll be off in a week or so," he said casually, "and you'll be gone not long after that, I'm sure. What are you going to do once you leave?" He had put too much emphasis into the last question, as if he were Catherine at EnglishSpace, and Lane's plans were of no real consequence to him.

Lane knitted her brow and fumbled with her mobile phone in her hand, picking at the edges where the bright blue plastic was chipping.

"I…" she started, "I'm not sure, I just thought that you might…"

"Yes?" Ibrahim continued his steady but detached stare.

Lane's characteristic directness melted as she grasped for the only thing she could think of, "I just—I just thought that the other night at the restaurant—"

"Yes?" Ibrahim repeated in the same robotic tone, "That was fun wasn't it? I really think your friends are great."

There was a long pause between the two of them. The light music from the coffee shop speakers died down and for an eternally long minute they sat there, looking at each other as the sound of clinking metal espresso spoons and steaming milk punctuated their silence.

Lane could feel a growing weight on her chest. She was drowning and Ibrahim stood there with a rope in his hand and casually watched. In those moments she asked him a thousand questions with her eyes and the answer to all of them was the same—this is over. She couldn't breathe.

The whole thing took less than five minutes.

She finally gripped the side of her chair with a sweaty hand. She surprised herself by almost pleading, "Well, did you want to grab dinner this evening?" She immediately regretted it, everything in her was telling her to run out and never look back.

"Oh, you know I wish I could, but these papers for the military are really complicated, and I need to be ready to go in under a week, so…"

"Sure." Lane managed to regain a small bit of herself.

And then Ibrahim surprised her with a sentence that sounded like his old self, "I'll still see you tomorrow, for drinks, won't I?"

Lane immediately looked up at him, but by the time her eyes reached his, he had regained his vacant stare.

"Um, of course," Was all she could say. It was odd confirming something that just a day ago would have gone without saying.

"Well, tomorrow then," he said with finality. Lane knew it was time for her to leave. She could barely stand.

"Tomorrow then," she said absent mindedly as she gathered her things and headed for the door. Just before she left, she looked back for some hint the whole thing had been some sort of dark joke. She saw him again looking at her with a cold smile and a causal wave. It was all she could do to get out the door, but just as she did, she noticed the large envelope on the table in front of him. A large, navy blue "Berkeley" was printed on the front. She recognized the size of the envelope and what it meant to everyone waiting on an admissions decision—it was an acceptance letter.

—

The next evening at a ridiculous bar called 360, Lane sipped her astronomically priced cocktail as she continued to search Ibrahim for answers. It was all she could do to make it there that evening. She hadn't told anyone about the coffee shop yesterday—she wasn't even sure what to think herself. And that afternoon, as she was considering whether or not to text him she wasn't coming and then flush her phone down the toilet, one thought stopped her— maybe she had misread the whole thing.

She looked past him now and out into the twinkling post-sunset blanket of the city below. Outside on the roof top patio, they were sitting on uncomfortable but striking white lacquered muffin shaped chairs. Scantily clad but still intimidating cocktail waitresses moved seamlessly around wealthy patrons, providing cigars, champagne, and packs of cigarettes from impossibly tiny trays. They had had this plan to splurge on this bar for weeks; a sort of bon voyage.

All of Istanbul seemed to lay before them; 3,000 years of history contained in a single, multi-layered, breathtaking, navy and maroon and white expanse. This should be their moment, Lane thought. This should be the moment she would look back on as the beginning of something important.

Instead, she was straining for conversation with this person who had surprised her with her own feelings. This person who had shown her how to love the city that dangled at her feet. This person… And before she knew it, her drink was almost done and Ibrahim was raising his glass to finish the last of his.

"So, I can't wait to email you everything about military training," he was saying with odd excitement, "I know it will be a real bore, but I'm sure there'll be tons of hilarious stories from my fellow soldiers." He continued to smile the placid smile.

Lane was at a complete loss, and so she played along, "Right?" she said, feeling a knot well up in her chest, "You should see a ton of funny things." What was she saying? That didn't even sound like her!

"Well," Ibrahim paused and looked out over the navy Marmara. His face grew darker with the fading light. A slightly chilly wind made them both instinctively grab their exposed arms.

"I..." he said, "My parents want to have... what did you call it?—'brunch' tomorrow morning. So I should probably get going." He gave what Lane thought was his most genuine smile of the evening as he got up from his chair.

"Oh, right, right, of course." She got up also, "It's important not to disappoint them..." she trailed off. She screamed at herself without speaking. *Say it! Say it now! Say anything!* She mentally slapped herself across the face, but it was no good, the words wouldn't come.

"So, can I take you back in a cab?" Ibrahim offered coolly.

"Um, what? Oh, ahh, no, no, I'm fine. I'm going to meet the gang out somewhere..." *The gang'?* Was she even speaking English?

"Oh, ok," Ibrahim's face finally broke, but he continued to move towards the door. And just as Lane thought he was going to slip out of her life forever without so much as a 'cheers', she felt his strong arms enfold her the way they had done just days before. She turned and buried her head in his starched shirt and thought she might suffocate for a minute—but she didn't care.

Finally she pulled her face back and saw that he had two glistening streaks coming from the corners of his eyes, "Lane... I have... you... I have had such an incredible time with you," he said.

"Ibrahim!" She spat out, but noticed his eyes looked scared, as if she held his entire future in his hands, and the next word from her mouth could destroy it all. Even in her haze she knew what he wanted, and she cared about him enough to do it.

"Don't..." She could barely control her own voice, "Don't eat any food you're not sure about—diarrhea is NOT something you want in some rural military base!" She had done it. She had finished strong—and with a joke even. Ibrahim seemed to thank her with his eyes as he laughed and finally let her hand drop. And then, so quickly Lane didn't even have time to think, he kissed her directly on the mouth in the way she was completely familiar with.

By the time she opened her eyes he was gone.

—

The next morning, Lane called in sick to EnglishSpace. She almost said "heartbreak" when Catherine asked what was wrong. She made one more call to the only person she wanted to see and threw her dying phone under a pillow before falling asleep for another three hours.

She woke up to Colin's summer-freckled face looking down at her. He smiled slightly and placed a large wooden tray on the worn but expensive looking chair they had found on the street in their neighborhood. It contained: a large piping cup of black coffee, a plate of their emergency frozen country ham, a cigarette, a seltzer water, and a shot of bourbon.

Lane immediately started to cry.

"Hey, man, it's not that special. I just threw some things on a tray!" Colin joked in a soothing tone.

"It's just... I..." But Colin already knew what she wanted to say, so he simply passed her the seltzer.

After a full debriefing, a shot, and some solid laughs over their respective love lives in Turkey, Lane turned to Colin and said, "Is this how you've been feeling for the past few weeks?"

Colin, quiet as ever, took some time and then finally answered, "No... but then again, Metin wasn't the one."

"Oh," said Lane, and then quickly realized the implication, "Oh, hey now, Ibrahim wasn't... I mean we just..." But she was tired of protesting her feelings, "Who knows what he could have been..."

"And still might be," Coiln said with a directness she wasn't used to.

"Ok, ok, we can chat about this for months—right now I want to take my mind OFF of it!"

"Of course!" said Colin and almost as quickly started producing several pamphlets and printed papers.

"What *are* all these?" Lane asked beginning to rifle through them.

"Well, Reyhan and Matt and I have been doing some research and talking about our plans for when we leave—nothing in depth and it never seemed like we could catch you to bring it up. But this seems like the perfect moment."

Lane studied the material. The names of cities popped out at her: Brussels, Amsterdam, London, Madrid, Rome.

"We've been thinking—we've all got a little money saved up, and EnglishSpace is going to pay us that bonus if we manage to make it to the end of our contracts..."

"I'm in!" lane almost yelled.

"Haha, but you don't even know what we're planning."

"It doesn't matter," she said with conviction, "If it involves us in Europe I'm there."

"Ha! Ok, great! We're gonna have so much fun planning..." Colin could barely contain himself.

"Alright, but there's just one thing."

"Anything—name it," he said.

Lane pulled out her laptop and took a large swig of coffee, "All of this is a few weeks away, and I need to do something to get over my situation now."

Colin almost felt concern as he watched Lane google search with fierce intensity, "Um... ok. Well do you have any idea of what that is?"

Lane beamed, "I have more than that—I have a plan."

Fifteen
Transitional Phrases

"Isn't this great?" Lane almost screamed with delight as she tapped her foot wildly to the syncopated rhythm. Matt, Reyhan, and Colin nodded vigorously in agreement, shaking the watery martinis on their tiny table in the process. A plungered trumpet wailed and sang up to the top of the scale and back down again as Lane pointed to a large, framed picture of Atatürk, perpetually stern-faced, but somehow still in the middle of an animated dance with a regal looking 1920s Turkish flapper type in a fringe laden dress. Behind the sleek bar hung a backlighted sign that said 'The Atatürk Jazz Lounge'.

Days before, Lane had gathered them all around her paper strewn kitchen table and laid out her plan for the rest of their time in Istanbul.

"Who's the one person who has been a constant presence since we all got to this city?" She put to them.

The three looked around at each other with wrinkled noses and quizzical expressions.

"Mitchell?" Reyhan asked. They all laughed thinking of the brash Californian that continued to terrorize each one of them at teacher bar nights.

"Demet Akalin?" Colin chimed in referring to the Kyle Minogue-style Turkish pop sensation they had been playing on repeat for weeks.

"Close," Lane laughed, "Come on y'all!"

"Atatürk, duh!" Reyhan finally offered slapping her forehead with recognition.

"Exactly," Lane confirmed, and started handing out reams of information she had printed out in the EnglishSpace teacher room.

"Haha, what is all this?" Asked Matt, taking off his thick glasses and popping open an Efes.

"We're going to find him!" Lane revealed.

Colin raised his hand in mock student style, "But Teacher, Atatürk is dead."

"Yes, Colin, good point," Lane said, "But his ghost is in every square inch of this city, and I think it's time we went looking for it."

So there they were at the first upturned rock on their search, tapping their toes to glitzy jazz standards and slowly making moves towards the dance floor. Matt, still looking unkempt even in a tie and tucked in shirt, challenged Lane, in suede heels, to a Charleston dancing contest. Colin and Reyhan, who had splurged that afternoon on new clothes, spun circles around them to a soaring trombone solo. The jazz quartet, in all black outfits and red fezzes, played expertly into the night.

The bright stage lights glinted off brushed chrome fixtures and black lacquered surfaces. It was a 1920s dream—from the wall lights to the deep red, mahogany rounded bar. In a former life, the Atatürk Jazz Lounge had been a set of smartly designed government offices built on the Asian side and used sporadically by the country's first leader after the founding of the Republic. Now it was an art deco gem and the best place to hear a Louis Armstrong cover in the city. Lane, who had been doing research for days, said with authority it was exactly the type of place Atatürk would have hung out.

—

Mustafa Kemal Atatürk, it turned, out, was a real party. Hard drinking, hard smoking, possibly bisexual, and almost definitely agnostic—the man somehow still found the time to found a republic and modernize the Turkish language.

Over the next weeks there wasn't a minute wasted. Matt, Reyhan, Colin, and Lane each found something to love about Turkey's greatest hero and founding father. They quickly discovered there was a lot about the man that wasn't discussed in official Turkish sources. 'An Atatürk for All Seasons' Matt joked.

Originally from Greece, Atatürk came to Istanbul as a young man. Lane liked to think on the same train they had taken from Thessaloniki. Over the coming years he placed his mark so deeply on Constantinople that no corner of the city was left untouched. Everywhere they looked, he was there waiting to show them something new.

One by one they each high fived a small bronze statue of Mustafa Kemal as they exited the ferry to one of Istanbul's smaller neighborhoods on the northern Bosphorus, looking for a restaurant the man used to take his mother to.

A photograph of an uncharacteristically fun-looking Atatürk on a swing hung over the entrance to a small ice cream shop that used to house his regular barber.

A dashing Atatürk on the twenty Lira note got them into Dolmabaçe palace, where M.K.A. lived out the end of his life. A somber and tired face stared back at them from a picture over the small room where his medications were kept. A more idealized portrait hung near the bed where he spent his last nights. The sign to the grand room read only: the bed Atatürk died.

There he was in an out-of-the-way square in a Black Sea village north of the city—a marble relief turning a blind eye to scantily clad late season bathers.

Here he was looking slightly confused in a black and white photograph next to a colorful Tommy Hilfiger store in a Mall in Bakirköy.

There were official looking Atatürks for the upscale hotel bars of Sultanahmet and faded patriotic ones for the greasy soup shops that lined the wet allies behind the Istiklal.

They found him on placemats and ships; novelty socks and beach towels. Sometimes he wore a fez, sometimes a mustache, never any casual clothes, and very often a cigarette or a drink in his hand.

Finally one day the four stood outside of an odd, turn of the century Ottoman house, two blocks from their own apartment building. Lane remarked how it looked like a sad wedding cake. It was the house Atatürk had shared with his mother and sister before the founding of the Republic. And now, as his official museum, it looked out of place wedged in between two high rise 70s apartment buildings. Colin and Matt turned up the collars of their coats to the surprisingly bitter October wind. Lane and Reyhan adjusted their cheap and brightly colored pashminas as they headed for the door.

Inside they found a treasure trove of personal effects and artifacts. His cigarette holder; stained and loved. His stiff neck collar he was almost never photographed without. A handkerchief, a small flask, a leather portfolio.

Lane wandered off into a top floor room and found a small alcove to duck into. The wide, worn floor boards creaked under her feet as she pulled her almost defunct cell phone from her bag. She fixed her now much longer and darker locks, as if getting ready to meet someone important. She checked her phone—no messages. For the past two weeks, three times a day, this had been her ritual. She kept her phone completely charged at all times and never let it run out of credit the way she had used to. And for three agonizing moments each day, she would allow herself to pull it out and make sure that Ibrahim hadn't called. He never had.

With a deep sigh, she stuffed her phone back into her overflowing purse and was about to turn around when she noticed a forgotten framed photograph in the dark corner she was standing in.

It was Atatürk, of course, but something about this image was different. There was his trademark starched collar and black neck tie, the worn lines on his face that he had in later years, the furrowed brow and downcast eyes as if he were working out how exactly the world ticked. In one hand an almost finished cigarette dangled from his ivory holder. He held a precariously perched Turkish coffee cup and saucer in the same hand. In the other he had a small cup or lid—raki? Whiskey? But as Lane looked at his usually taut smile, she noticed how soft his jaw was in this picture, and in that small moment, she thought for a second she could see the true man. A completely unstaged and private moment where he allowed himself to be, just—himself.

Of all the Atatürks they had seen, this was the one she liked the most.

—

The next morning Lane bounded up the neon staircase to the EnglishSpace main branch. It was officially her last class, and she was convinced it would be her best yet. She had planned hours of activities around—what else—the life of Atatürk.

But as the class worn on, she noticed the glazed eyes and courtesy smiles of the 20 odd Turks sitting in the giant conversation circle she had created. She realized, with some disappointment, that even though everything about the man was new and interesting to her, this group had probably grown up hearing it all more times than they could count. Reluctantly, she opened the floor up to a general conversation.

It was slow at first, the way the end of a class usually was. But then Bahadir, a thin, pale, twenty year old with a cassette tape tattoo and a safety pin earring, made a comment about Atatürk not being a Muslim. The class erupted.

Lane was thrown for a minute but quickly tried to quiet things down—it was no use. Students shouted across the room. Some stood in anger. Desks were moved. Small groups began to form. Lane was at a loss and considered jumping up on a chair but just then everyone grew silent and turned around.

"I think," the voice had come from the only person still seated at the corner of the room, a small, quiet girl of about twenty five named Sempa. She wore the head scarf, or türban, as Lane had learned it was called, and came to class early and every day. She never spoke until spoken to, but when she did, her answers often unnerved Lane with their gentle candor. Her uncharacteristic interjection must have come as a shock to rest of the class, because they slowly began to take their seats.

"I think," Sempa said again, "that Atatürk was a Muslim…" Lane could feel the class growing restless, but Sempa continued, "I think that if you are kind, if you think about your actions, if you do things to help others—I think *you are* a Muslim."

A hush grew over the students. It was the most silence Lane had ever experienced in class. She realized Sempa was looking directly at her. She felt a small, hot tear well up in her eye. The bell rang.

"Thank you Sempa," Lane finally said and the rest of the students thanked her also.

One by one on their way out of the classroom, they all dropped small gifts in front of Lane and hugged her tightly. Sempa handed her a tiny package wrapped in silver paper and placed a light but knowing hand on her hand.

"Don't forget us," Sempa said with a smile. And Lane knew she wouldn't.

—

The next day Lane, Colin, Matt, and Reyhan took the short bus ride to the covered spice market on the northern tip of Sultanahmet. Colin was planning the mother of all farewell dinners and insisted that they make a final house trip to the touristy food mecca.

Reyhan watched Matt, pushing his glasses up his small nose and sweeping aside his now unruly hair while dog earing a copy of *The Last Days of the Byzantine Empire*. Colin watched Lane in the next seat back as she furiously scribbled in her worn moleskine—trying to record every detail of their final week, he thought.

The four of them all looked up suddenly as the bus bottomed out along the bridge across the Golden Horn—the bright mid-autumn sun assaulted their eyes as it struck the ancient waterway and turned the whole thing a shimmering orange metallic color—its namesake, Lane thought.

As they reached the southern peninsula of the city the disc of the sun danced between the arches of a Roman aqueduct as the bus raced towards its imposing façade. At the last moment the bus took a sharp left down and off the bridge. The group saw a golden-tinged, mythic city before them; gentle domes and punctuating spires capped by glittering stars and crescents. Even though they had seen it several times before—it was somehow new for each of them. Not old or antique, Turkish, Ottoman, or Byzantine, but timeless and otherworldly—as if floating tall ships could appear from the clouds at any minute.

They arrived at the spice bazaar in a comfortable silence. This was the place that Fatih Sultan Mehmet the Third, the Turkish Sultan who finally conquered this city in 1453, had placed the original market overlooking the confluence of the Marmara, the

Golden Horn, and the Bosphorus. In the square outside, leaves formed tiny tornados while laughing children in faded fleece pullovers ran with sticks and balls through the cobblestone streets. A chilly wind forced them inside past a pigeon covered bust of Atatürk.

Once inside they were in another century. Lane always forgot how this space was one of her favorites in the city. It was so easy to remember it as a jostle of pushy salesmen and cheap trinkets like the grand bazaar next door. But this place, the spice market, even though a definite tourist destination, still held a sense of mystery and a weight she couldn't quite describe.

Entering the 400 year old doors, Reyhan quickly pulled a grudging but happy Matt down the central corridor towards yet more cheap pashminas for her friends back home. Colin and Lane slowed their pace and strolled for a while together, savoring the colors, the smells, the moment.

An ambient, glowing light caught the floating particles of spices above them and formed a thin cloud where the setting sun pierced the eves of the tiled roof.

Lane reached into her bag absentmindedly and checked her dying phone for the fourth time that day.

"He still hasn't called?" Colin surprised her as she looked up.

Lane tried to give a small laugh, "No… ha, I don't know what I'm thinking! It's clearly just one of those things." She rolled her eyes and purposefully started examining a bronze platter.

"You know I'm no expert, but I *have* seen a lot of romantic movies—and sometimes these things seem hopeless until it's almost over," he smiled.

Lane now laughed for real, "Ha! Are you saying Ibrahim is going to enact some crazy scene where he comes running after me in Atatürk airport in a week?"

"You never know!"

"Alright, you're officially cut off from Katherine Heigl movies." She sighed, "This is the real world, and I think he was just a great guy that I got to know who showed me a cool place for a while."

Colin looked at his friend and noticed a change in her he couldn't quite describe. He liked it. "Ok," he said slipping his hand into hers for a small moment, "You're right. At the very least I'm thankful he convinced you to stay. Look at this place we ended up!" He motioned around him and Lane was struck by the heady surroundings.

"That's the truth," she said. "You go on ahead and get the things you need, I'm going to amble for a minute."

Colin squeezed her hand again and then wandered off, grabbing handfuls of produce and spices as he made his way down the crowded walk way.

Lane fingered small piles of roasted almonds and dry millet. The seething crowd was chaotic but not overwhelming. She studied everything with new eyes: the man loudly grinding dry peppers in an almost pre-historic looking mortar; the sound of a woman protesting that the shoes in her hand were not the ones she had intended to buy. A young bearded merchant passed her a dark, black and orange Turkish apricot and she let its fuzzy skin linger on her tongue as she moved silently around a large group of Swedish tourist.

She stopped in front of an out of the way spice stall in one of the far reaches of the market. A rainbow of powdered spices formed a sort of living pyramid up to the counter. All of them were carefully carved and shaped into perfect tetrahedrons—like little pungent sand castles.

A kind but mischievous looking man appeared behind the counter and asked her in his native language if she would like some 'saffron'. Lane looked down to the large yellow-orange pyramid in front of her labeled 'turkish saffron'. This country still held a lot of mysteries for her, but she was street wise enough to know that this large pile in front of her for the cheap price listed was probably not the spice it was advertised as. She put up a polite hand and was about to move on when the man protested.

"No, no," he said in Turkish, "I have the real thing…" and he put up a curving finger that reminded her of the chesire cat.

Something about him made her follow his finger around the side of the stall to a small opening. There, on a well-worn wooden cutting block, he placed a neatly folded piece of wax paper he had pulled from a high shelf. As he opened it his eyes gleamed and Lane peered down into a small but precious pile of deep coral strands.

"It's real?" She said in his language. He simply raised his eyebrows and smiled in response.

"Smell," he said finally.

Lane bent down so far she was afraid her nose would touch the paper, but suddenly she didn't care. She was transported. The deep and round smell of ancient wood mixed with rare flowers and curry and filled her nostrils so fully that she thought she might faint. Her eyes watered and she closed them instinctively. She took another breath.

This was more than a spice—it was a memory she didn't even know she had. And in a single moment she saw that memory stretch back to the beginning of this city with three names on two continents. It connected a girl standing in the middle of a small Greek settlement, a Roman woman dissatisfied with her home in New Rome and pining for the old one, a medieval emperor riding his horse through a gleaming Byzantine villa, a young boy carrying water up to the Sultan's palace on a hill—and straight through to Atatürk and, finally, her student Sempa, living in a concrete apartment block somewhere north of Taksim square and walking to English class every morning. It was all there in a single breath.

Lane bought the entire package and didn't even haggle with the man. Whatever he was asking she knew she had gotten the better deal.

—

Six bottles of raki, four days, and two nervous breakdowns later, Lane, Colin, Matt, and Reyhan had all fit their lives into one checked bag and one carry-on each.

Their exit was fast approaching and they surprised themselves by attending an EnglishSpace teacher party at Mitchell's new house in one of the valley neighborhoods east of Taksim Square.

As they approached the building they were shocked to see that Mitchell had found a completely renovated glass and steel high rise in the central part of Beygolu. A small Turkish girl answered the door with minimal English and ushered them out onto a shockingly stunning terrace where most of the regular characters where making loud conversation over vodka drinks.

"Of all the things good and bad that have happened to me in this country," Lane observed wryly, "It's at least nice that most of them have happened on rooftops."

They all laughed as they mixed sweet apricot juice and seltzer water into their vodka filled solo cups. The setting sun illuminated the tops of theirs drinks and they all pulled on their waiting jackets.

Bethany made a special early appearance and Colin pulled her aside.

"I just want to say how great it's been hanging out with you." He smiled, "Are you doing ok?"

"Yeah, mate," she beamed with her classic grin, "My little sis got a scholarship to a good decent school back in Sydney, and I'm thinking of going with her…"

"Oh, yeah?"

"Yeah, yeah, but I would have a hard time leaving my girl."

Colin squinted his eyes slightly, "Your... girl?"

Bethany rolled her large dark pupils in mock annoyance, "You Americans really are thick, aren't you? I'm gay, mate." She shoved his shoulder as she delivered the news matter-of-factly.

"Oh, I, uh... Oh my god I'm so dumb." Colin grinned.

"Duh," she echoed, "But don't worry, I'm sure you'll find some bloke to take care of you back home."

They clinked solo cups as the music shifted to Hande Yener's electronic dance beats.

Lane, on the other side of the patio, looked on with a laugh at Colin and Bethany and then turned back to her conversation with Marissa, who was still talking as if nothing had happened, "...So, yeah, I could go back to Queensland for a while, teach English there for a bit and then come back abroad. Or, you know, there's always some sort of arts program. But I'm never quite sure I'm done with my travel bug, y'know? I mean I'm only thirty nine." The last part made Lane do a double take.

"You..." she began and then tried to think of a polite way to confirm, "You're how—"

But Marissa was on to the next topic, "So what do you think you'll do, love?"

Lane had to think for a minute what she meant, "Oh, uh, after Turkey?"

"Yeah, yeah" she said in her Australian twang again.

"Oh, well, we're going to travel to Europe for a few weeks!"

"Yeah, yeah," Marissa repeated, "but what are you going doooo after all that?" She had asked it casually enough, but Lane was still a bit caught off guard.

"Oh, uh, I mean… there's all that stuff you said," she offered, "And, you know, maybe school and stuff," she was rambling and was delighted to see Noah approach with a wide smile on his face.

"Ladies," he said in a think Turkish accent, the food stuck in his now cartoonish beard only adding to the effect. "Do you two want to partake in something interesting?" He gave them both a knowing look, but Lane was lost.

"Oh, yeah love, if you've got it," Marissa seemed to pick up quickly.

"Um, what are y'all…"

"Hash, love," Marissa answered her unformed question.

Lane's eyes widened. She hadn't gotten high since the dead of winter when Matt had shared a rare joint with her he had gotten from one of his students.

"Uh, totally," she smirked, "But can I ask the others?"

Noah gave a fake scowl, "If you must, but not too many, this is a 'just us' party in the back bedroom."

In five minutes Lane had pulled Matt, Colin, and Reyhan away from their respective conversations and into the far rear bedroom of Mitchell's shockingly large apartment.

"Um, I don't know you guys…" Reyhan said in her Midwestern 'I want to but I'm not sure I should' voice.

"Just do it." Colin poked her in the ribs jokingly and she instantly gave in.

The six of them sat in a dense cloud of smoke for almost half an hour as Matt and Reyhan tried to quietly tell them about Mitchell's latest blunders and how he was starting an ice cream company with some of his students. They all stifled laugher and wiped their watery eyes.

Finally, Colin spoke up, "Um, you all, um… well, do y'all feel high?"

Lane descended into laugher and Matt pushed him into a pillow.

"No, no, I'm serious, do y'all feel high? I'm not sure I do," he repeated with a goofy look on his face.

"Well I definitely feel high," Lane said with another large laugh and a swig of her vodka drink.

"Yeah, love," Marissa chimed in, "It's not the best stuff ever, but it's got the job done…"

They all continued laughing and Colin had all but given up but suddenly Reyhan asked to see the small wax paper package the hash had come in.

Grudgingly Noah handed it over, telling them it was from his coolest "gangster" student.

They all watched with amazement and then outright horror as Reyhan expertly dunked a finger into her still full cup and pushed it directly into the middle of the small square of hash.

"Hey, hey!" Noah, never angry sounding, still registered extreme concern, "I just got that! I'm not sure when he's getting any more!"

They continued to watch as Reyhan, a large smile on her face, moved her finger around, pulled it out and then traced a large line along the inside of her wrist. Her wet finger left a long, red trail behind it.

"What the—" said Noah.

"I'm pretty sure your student can get it the next time he goes to the covered market," she burst out laughing, "You guuuuuuuuuuuys—we've been smoking henna!"

They laughed all the way home and still couldn't keep straight faces over breakfast the next morning.

———

And before they knew it, their time was up.

Lane watched her three friends as they sat around the kitchen table one last time on the morning of their flight; passports in hand, laughing mutedly over a final disposable cup of coffee from the shiny new Café Nero down the street. The whole thing seemed so odd; their four bags neatly by the door, keys on the table, floor spotless thanks to Reyhan—like they had just rented the place for a week and were now off to their next destination.

In the shuttle to Atatürk Airport, Reyhan, Matt, and Colin sat in the front seat, wild with excitement about the European sites they were about to see. Lane sat in the back staring blankly out of the window. For a final time, Lane watched with detachment as the Galata Tower and the hills of Beyoglu disappeared behind them. They turned the corner around the fleeting tops of the Hagia Sophia and the Blue Mosque. And then it was a straight shot towards the airport—on one side the crumbling walls of Theodosius, on the other the Marmara Sea. Lane noticed a train pass them going in the opposite direction and a bright memory flooded back of that first morning waking up on the train into the city.

"STOP—" Lane heard herself scream.

The bewildered shuttle driver understood the English command and quickly threw on his blinker and was on the patchy shoulder before they knew what had happened.

Her three friends turned slowly towards the back seat with questioning eyes.

"I… Uh—I forgot something." Lane searched herself for answers but couldn't' find any.

"What?" Matt asked with concern.

Lane felt a cold sweat break out on her forehead. She looked at her shoes and her bag. She searched her hands and even felt the top of her head, "I… uh… I don't know," she finally admitted.

The three of them continued to look at her with concern, but finally Colin spoke up, running a hand through his shaggy hair and cupping his neck, "Whatever it is, I'll buy you a new one in London," he joked.

Lane sighed with a smile, "Oh my God, you're right, sorry guys." And they were off again.

As the shuttle pulled back into the strangely heavy mid-day traffic Reyhan slipped in the back seat and eyed Lane knowingly.

"You know you can come back whenever you want," she said simply.

"Ha, what?" Lane was intrigued.

"Here—Turkey. Istanbul—whatever. You can come back whenever you want, it's just a plane ride," she sounded more authoritative than Lane could ever remember. She looked this girl up and down who had somehow worked her way into her heart over the short time they had known each other.

Lane started to protest again, but suddenly she got it, "Thank you," was all she had to say.

They got to the airport far too early thanks to Colin's intense punctuality and decided to get through security and have a final Efes on its home turf. As they walked into the main terminal, excited in the way only air travel can make you, the rest of them walked ahead towards the one bar as Lane fell behind. A small bin caught her eye with the large picture of a cell phone and the unmistakable international sign for recycling.

The bin contained what looked like thirty or forty odd cell phones; all 'fisher-price' models like hers. And she quietly understood what she needed to do. Pulling her bright blue phone from its worn pocket in her bag she looked at it one last time. Not the screen, but the phone itself; almost completely broken, but still chugging along as she put credit on it, it was hard to believe this modest little device had seen her through almost a year in this country. For a final time she checked her messages. There was one: a goodbye and bon voyage from Marissa.

She sighed, turned it off for a final time, and tossed it casually in the bin as she walked away.

—

Europe was everything the four of them could have wanted.

The first few nights they crowded silently around a smoky, wood paneled bar in an out-of-the-way pub in northern London, reverently drinking from large glasses and looking up from their plates to occasionally make hushed comments.

"So this is what beer tastes like," Colin said with a look of genuine surprise on his face.

"I never knew beef stew was one of my favorite foods," Matt observed, equally bewildered.

They toured the cool, muted alcoves of innumerable cathedrals.

They strolled down the damp streets of Edinburgh, filled with scotch and haggis and singing American pop songs.

Reyhan wrapped herself tightly in a newly purchased wool scarf, "I just loooooove the fashion here!" she said as she pressed her face up against a shop window on Princes Street.

They stood awestruck in front of Guernica in Madrid, washing down their conversation afterward with rich, blood colored Spanish wine. They ate oysters and champagne at food stalls in a chilly Parisian market. They got drunk on the heady fumes from the steaming beer vats in a Belgian Abby. They finally got properly high in a sweetly smoky Dutch coffee shop.

And the pork. Everywhere they went—the pork. Pulled barbeque and crisp cracklings in Scotland; thin, acorn flavored serrano ham in Spain; Belgian sausages and pâté sandwiches in France.

The hot smells and crisp light assaulted them on the autumnal European air like that first whiff of fried dough at a county fair; exotic and familiar at the same time. They breathed it in deeply and, in the same breath, exhaled the dry, hazy and perfumed air of Turkey.

And before they knew it they were home, reeling from an eternity spent living another life and at the same time wondering how the time had passed so quickly.

A s Lane crested the top of the bridge she stopped mid-stride, forcing a cyclist behind her to swerve and utter what she was sure was a Dutch swear word as he passed.

She had been here before. More than a year ago, she thought, she, Reyhan, Colin, and Matt had stood on this exact bridge throwing euro pennies in the murky canal below. Even so, she was still completely lost.

She had lived in Amsterdam for almost four weeks now and was still hopelessly confused by the twisting labyrinth of streets and canals every time she left her tiny flat.

Her hot breath created a dense cloud on the cold air as she searched intensely for a familiar street name. Just then her pocket began to buzz with an incoming text message.

It was Colin: he had sent a grainy picture of a legal text book next to a can of sugar free Redbull and a message that read: "am I doing this?"

"Which", she texted back, "The Redbull or law school?"

"Both," he responded.

Lane smiled to herself as another text picture came in from Reyhan. It was a Valentine's Day table in her and Matt's apartment in Ann Arbor. A bottle of visne sharap stood directly in the center.

"Wish you were here," Reyhan said.

"Binde," Lane typed in Turkish, but quickly realized she was on a schedule and pulled up the permanently open maps function. *What did I ever do without a smart phone?* she thought, dimly remembering her tiny fisher price model and the day they had left Istanbul.

The past year had not gone according to plan: Get home. Get a career. Move to a city. Find a man. Talk fondly about her time abroad at dinner parties.

Instead, Lane had landed with a thud back in her childhood bedroom in her parent's home in a country that seemed comforting and strange all at the same time. Her plan, while simple on paper, turned out to be anything but in real life.

She applied to law school with Colin, created a post-Turkey blog, decided against law school, taught ESL at the community college, forgot to write on her blog, and generally stressed out about her life direction.

She watched as her three fellow travelers found new and interesting things to move into.

Reyhan had surprised them all and herself by getting into graduate school at Michigan for policy.

"I just wanna be a decision maker!" she had laughed as she told Lane her plans.

Matt moved with her, of course, but fought hard not to follow his parents and sister into academia. He worked days at the local independent book store and said he was happy.

"But you know Ann Arbor has a pretty good English department for when he finally gives in!" Reyhan confided.

Colin, with a standing offer at his father's law practice, had moved back to Middlesborough and was in his first year of law school at their alma mater. He had already started pushing buttons at Robert's firm by doing pro bono marriage equality work on school breaks.

A year passed. January came. Lane found herself back in Middlesborough where Colin was hosting a post-Holiday Wine Monday for all the old players plus Reyhan.

Lane watched, delighted, as this circle of people moved around her: Reyhan laughing wildly at a joke John Parker Crane had told incorrectly; Mara and Colin prepping a decadent chocolate soufflé; Matt talking 1920s lit with Big D.

Lane reached for the last of the Turkish white cheese with honey as Hall and Oats faded away in the background. Leo turned to her and smiled in a way that let her know something terrible was coming.

"So Lane, why'd you back out on Law School? You know it was your best option," his drunken smile let her know he was kidding, but it still burned.

"You bastard," she affected a large grin, "it just didn't feel right."

"Ok, ok," he continued, "so what does?"

Lane paused for what was probably too long before shaking off her doubt and saying simply, "believe me, you'll be the first to know."

Leo seemed satisfied, but the off-handed question planted itself inside of her and wouldn't go away.

Then one rainy afternoon days later back in the North Carolina mountains, still thinking deeply about what Leo had said, her sister Charlotte called and demanded a current resume.

"And make sure you include about how you speak Turkish," Charlotte had said in her direct way.

"But I wouldn't say I speak—" but Charlotte had already hung up.

It was true Lane had kept up with her language skills since she had gotten back. In a way, it was her best connection to a special year of her life. And, if she were being honest, it was her last, best connection to Ibrahim.

She grudgingly put down "Turkish—proficient" on her CV and shot it off to her sister.

A week later she was looking up flights to Amsterdam and scouring Craigslist to find a last minute apartment. It turned out Charlotte had connections with an American think tank focusing on Eurasian issues. Before Lane knew it, she was headed back abroad for a yearlong internship in Turkish/European relations.

And here she was now, racing through the streets of her confusing new Dutch home, tracing the far outer rim of the city on a mostly deserted industrial looking block searching for a Turkish Consulate she was sure didn't exist. *I just can't seem to catch a break with consulates,* she thought.

She was just about to give up when a small, shiny bronze plaque glinted in a rare moment of mid-February sun. It was Atatürk, hand outstretched and the Turkish flag in the background. Of course, she thought.

Once inside and through security she tried to readjust herself before meeting with the Turkish minister she had been sent to interview. As she fumbled with her new suit jacket her bag slipped and the contents spilled all over the floor.

"Bok!" Lane screamed before she could think about it. Several Turkish employees turned and stared in her direction. It was the one place in Amsterdam everyone knew exactly what she was saying. "Shit," she said more quietly as she knelt to start collecting her things.

A pair of polished shoes appeared before her and she began to protest that she was fine.

"You know, they don't like language like that around here," a voice said.

"Oh, I'm so sorry," Lane started to raise her eyes, "It's just, I'm late and—"

And there he was, looking almost exactly as she had pictured he would.

"Ibrahim…" Lane said quietly and without any question in her voice. He placed a soft hand on the side of her face and she felt as if she might fall backwards. His bright brown eyes sparkled. His dark hair was shorter but still messy in the way it had been.

"Don't…" Lane could feel her throat contracting. She was sure that if she chose the wrong words the entire moment would pop like a soap bubble and Ibrahim would vanish into thin air, "Don't move," she said with conviction, "I'll be back in thirty minutes."

As she walked away from his smiling face, she knew it was the coolest thing she had ever, and probably would ever say in her entire life.

After an embarrassingly distracted twenty minutes with a Turkish diplomat who seemed mostly distracted himself, Lane floated back to the soviet style lobby, convinced she had had a full-on mental episode and Ibrahim would be nowhere to be found.

But just as she was convinced she should commit herself, she saw him standing there, next to an angular bronze bust of Atatürk. He was taller than she had remembered, possibly because of the euro leather jacket he was wearing? He beamed at her. And something about his face made Lane forget all the questions she knew she should be asking.

Instead, in probably her second coolest moment ever, she simply took his hand in hers and led him out of the building.

All the way back to her flat they barely said a word.

"This way," she instructed softly, and he followed. The tram quietly transported them through the streets of the darkening city. The water of the canals and the dark façades of the centuries old buildings melding into a single beautiful blur of multi-shaded blue as they simply looked at one another across the car.

She led him delicately up the creaking stairs to her attic apartment on the fourth floor of a three hundred year old house, and into her dimly lighted and all white bedroom. The lights of the city reflected off the Amstel and pulsed gently onto the pitched ceiling and weathered rafters above her bed.

Lane took Ibrahim's face in her hands and stood that way for a long while, opening her mouth once to speak, never quite finding the words, and then realizing she didn't need any.

The next morning Lane sat bolt upright in bed. The harsh morning light temporarily blinded her as she noticed she felt short of breath. Had it all been a dream? And then she looked behind her to see Ibrahim's long body on the other side of the bed. His eyes were shut tightly and his mouth was slightly open—a sight that Lane remembered instantly. She smiled and felt a wave of peace come over her. Despite the northern European early spring she impulsively threw open the large windows that acted as her headboard. A rush of beautiful, cold, Nordic air and bright morning light flooded in. She reveled in it, her skin turning to goose bumps. Turning in her seated position she lifted her wild hair into a messy bun and let the air race around the back of her neck.

"Hey! It's fucking cold," Ibrahim grabbed her from behind and pulled her backwards on to the bed with a large laugh.

Their eyes met with him over her and they fell back into the easy silence of the night before.

Finally, Lane spoke, "How…" was all she said.

Ibrahim sighed and looked away, "I didn't get my US study visa," he said firmly. Lane put the pieces together. He had gotten into Berkeley but hadn't gotten the visa.

"They never said why, but I think it was because my father is in the military," he added.

"But…" Her question hung there unanswered.

"I didn't—" he searched for the words and she placed a light hand on his, "You don't know how much I wanted to…" and finally he found a way to explain, "It was too much to ask of you."

Lane understood. It was strange to her, all the pain she had had, the blame, the self-doubt; it all seemed to float out of the open window as if it were a bad dream and she was just now waking up.

"I would have waited," was all she had to say, no blame in her voice.

"I know that now," he said back, "I knew that the minute I saw you yesterday."

The rest of the words passed between them silently, the apologies, the forgiveness, the I-love-yous. After another long while Lane spoke again.

"And here?" she said

"My parents made me a deal. A year in the military and they would pay for school here. Masters of Mediterranean Archeology at Vrije Universiteit." He had said VU's full name with a perfect Dutch accent that made Lane laugh and remember everything about him she loved in the same moment.

"Wait, how in the world did we run into each other?!" she finally blurted out.

"I was waiting for you," he said simply with a straight face.

"Haha, come on! Ibrahim, there's no way this just happened."

He just put his hand on hers and continued his stare, "Well, I like to think it was fate, but I have to admit that fate had some help from Colin."

"Colin?!" she questioned.

"Yes, yes. I was too embarrassed to contact you after my military service but I knew I had to see you. So I sent him a crazy email… He's a pretty careless guy that friend of yours. He really shouldn't just hand out your personal information to every crazy Turk that contact him. He even gave me your address!"

"I'm going to kill him!" she laughed.

"When he told me you were coming to the same city as this program, I knew it was my chance."

"But the consulate, you…"

"Just there for some immigration paperwork. That part was fate, I promise. I guess we're just the type of people who keep meeting in consulates."

She shook her head in disbelief, it was all too scripted, too planned.

"And you?" He said.

"An internship in Turkish relations," she said and rolled her eyes at the irony of it all.

"For how long?"

"A year," she sighed.

"Mükemmel" he said the Turkish word for perfect.

"It is." She gave him a final, questioning look and, banishing everything from her mind but love, she shut the window with a cold slam and dove headfirst into his arms.

It was mükemmel.

A gentle, turquoise wave lapped against the peach and gray colored pebbled beach. Colin, bored with his historic biography, raised his eyes towards the water. He exhaled a thin stream of vapor from the electronic cigarette in his mouth and watched as it dissipated in the sparkling light of the afternoon.

At the water's edge Reyhan was involved in animated conversation with Reece. To Colin's amusement, Reece was completely engaged, his short beard and graceful hands both twisting upwards as he started to respond. Colin and Reece had met in the second year of law school and been together ever since. He had met Colin's friends before, but a group vacation was a completely different beast. It was going perfectly.

"He's so awesome," Matt said casually from the beach chair next to Colin putting down his dense publishing trade journal. "I'm sure he has no idea what Rey is talking about," he laughed.

Colin smiled, "Yeah, I guess I'll keep him around."

"Where are we, anyway?" Colin continued.

"Huh? Oh, ah, the Aegean?" Matt offered.

"No, no I know that. I mean what country? I mean we're staying in Greece, and we chartered a Turkish sailboat, but I can see Turkey right there." He motioned towards the horizon over the flashing sea where a thick landmass anchored the sky. They had found a small uninhabited islet and staked claim to its rocky beach, "Are we in Greece or Turkey?"

"Well," said Matt, intensely mulling it over, "Neither... both."

"I like that answer."

A minute later Reyhan descended on them with a spray of salt water and excitement, "You guuuuuuuuuys," she said, "They must be bored silly back on the boat—and I think it's cocktail time anyway!"

Reece, who had become instant friends with Reyhan echoed her, "Well I'm sure they've found a way to entertain themselves—but it is cocktail time," Colin laughed loudly and then realized he must sound like a love struck teenager.

"Agreed!" said Matt as they began packing up their beach camp and heading for the small row boat they had taken to the deserted beach.

As they approached their rented home for a week, Reyhan marveled at the bone colored sails as they unfurled in the dry, bright Aegean breeze. Just then, Lane and Ibrahim ran to the bow of the lacquered navy ship, waving as if it were their first sighting of the four, and holding drinks in their other hands.

As they boarded the boat from the bleached rope ladder, Matt looked down towards Reyhan's bright eyes just long enough to catch a group of dolphins shoot down under the row boat and skim the stark white bottom of the lagoon.

"You all missed the popping of the cork," said Lane sternly as they hit the deck with a splash, "But I'm sure they'll taste just as good," she instructed as she handed out plastic flutes filled with Prosecco. The hammered copper of her serving tray flashed and illuminated her wide smile for a moment.

They weighed anchor and with a jolt the large ship groaned into the wind and back towards the Turkish coast. A Bruce

Hornsby riff swept them up to full speed and down the gleaming shoreline.

"But first!" Ibrahim shouted producing another small tray with six glasses of milky liquid.

"Oh, god no!" Matt said in horror.

"Oh god yes!" Ibrahim commanded.

"And it's just in time," Lane pulled them close and pointed towards the approaching coastline where the city of Ankara spilled into the ocean, "Look! There it is!"

"Haha, what are we looking at?" said Colin, excited and confused.

Lane motioned them all towards the side of the boat and pointed more directly, "See that small house on the hill with the gate?"

"Just baaaaaaaaarely," laughed Reyhan.

"That's it!" said Lane, "it's Atatürk's house."

Matt led the charge, standing precariously on the highest point of the deck, "Well then here's to him!" he shouted, raki glass raised high into the air.

They all followed suit. The six of them raising their glasses as they pressed up against the side of the boat—the salt spray mixing into their drinks and hitting their faces.

"Merhaba! And Şerefe!" They saluted the man as they sailed swiftly past. And as she threw back the liquorish flavored drink and squinted into the bright distance, Lane was sure she could hear the clink of a glass in return.

About the Author

R. W. Barwick attended the University of North Carolina at Chapel Hill. He lived and taught English in Istanbul and Budapest, Hungary before returning stateside. He currently lives, teaches, and travels from his home in Durham, North Carolina.